The Doom

Hendricks tapped the plans. 'In that case, how much waste do you reckon there is at Vulcan Hall?'

The man in the check suit hesitated. 'I've only been able to make a rough calculation based on the size of the heat cloud, but I'd say in the region of two-point-five billion curies, plus.'

'What does that mean in terms of quantity?' Hendricks demanded. 'I'm not a nuclear physicist.'

'It means the largest concentration of nuclear waste in the world,' said the man in the check suit.

No one spoke. The walls of Jericho suddenly cracked: Hendricks smiled.

'I have formed a theory, gentlemen,' he said, 'one which ties all these seemingly disjointed facts neatly together.' He turned to the man in the check suit. 'What would be the effect of releasing all that waste into the environment?'

The man in the check suit scribbled on his paper and looked up. In a tightly controlled voice he said, 'It would be another Chernobyl only worse . . . Much worse . . .'

James Follett trained to be a marine engineer, and also spent some time hunting for underwater treasure, filming sharks, designing powerboats, and writing technical material for the Ministry of Defence before becoming a full-time writer. He is the author of numerous radio plays and television dramas, as well as seventeen novels including *Savant*, *Churchill's Gold*, *Dominator*, *Swift* and *Trojan*. He lives in Surrey.

James Follett

The Doomsday Ultimatum

Mandarin

A Mandarin Paperback
THE DOOMSDAY ULTIMATUM

First published in Great Britain 1976
by Weidenfeld & Nicholson Ltd
This revised edition published 1991
Reissued 1994
by Mandarin Paperbacks
an imprint of Reed Consumer Books Ltd
Michelin House, 81 Fulham Road, London SW3 6RB
and Auckland, Melbourne, Singapore and Toronto

A CIP catalogue record for this title
is available from the British Library
ISBN 0 7493 0364 6

Printed and bound in Great Britain
by Cox & Wyman Ltd, Reading, Berks

*To JL who hid the manuscript
and lied convincingly*

Contents

Prologue

The army escort in the car park suspected nothing.

Suddenly a nerve-gas grenade exploded in their midst but they never saw the figure that fired it. Choking, they collapsed as the paralysing fumes swirled round them.

And inside the 'Westward Ho' transport café the staff and the handful of late-night customers lay unconscious.

The attack by the armed group had taken only thirty seconds.

Thirty seconds is a long time in the application of chemical weapons. The CIX nerve-gas grenades, shattering and scattering fragile capsules in all directions, completed their task within five seconds. Inside the café the Special Air Service's captain who commanded the escort had tried to stagger to the door and shout a warning to his soldiers in the car park guarding the olive drab army transporter, but he collapsed before he could croak a single word.

His NCO, a Royal Artillery sergeant, had tried to pick up a hissing capsule from the floor and throw it out of an open window, but he too had passed out.

The tray of coffee cups for the escort lay on the floor, the cups broken. All was silent.

Two men entered the café. They wore NCB protective hoods with integral breathing sets, and held smoking grenade guns. They walked through air thick with nerve-gas fumes. The hooded men glanced casually around the confusion. The taller man checked the time against the information stored on his Psion Organiser pocket computer and pressed the 'enter' key.

'We're four seconds behind. Go on Phase Two,' he ordered. His voice sounded flat and indistinct behind his faceplate.

The second man went to the mains switch. He knew exactly where it was.

The café lights flashed three times. The taller man checked his Psion again. They had to work fast; every twenty minutes the army mobile unit was required to enter a status green security code into their radio facsimile unit.

At a signal a petrol tanker drove into the car park. It stopped beside the army transporter.

'Everything okay?' asked a woman's voice from the driver's cab.

The tall man was cutting the lashings of the tarpaulins that covered the army transporter's cargo. 'Tell him to hurry up in there,' he commanded.

The woman vaulted down from the tanker's cab and ran into the café. She too was hooded, and wore a brown jumpsuit.

A mobile crane, parked under the trees, burst into life and rumbled across the moonlit car park towards the tall man, who was now standing on top of the army transporter, guiding the approaching jib with arm gestures.

'Get the tanker opened,' he yelled.

His manner was military. He was used to giving orders and the others obeyed without hesitation.

The woman and the other hooded man came running from the café.

'Help him,' ordered the tall man nodding at the crane driver. He looked at his Psion Organiser again.

'You've got five minutes.' He was wearing a headset hooked up to a portable AR1000 scanning receiver clipped to his waist. It was programmed to all Thames Valley Police C Division repeater output radio channels. Right now most of the mobile channels were taken up with a serious RTA on the nearby M4. So far everything was going according to plan.

It took longer than five minutes but finally the first tanker was loaded and the two halves of the dummy petrol container were snapped shut, The woman started the engine. The tanker moved away to block the entrance to the car park.

The tall man's scanner hung on a channel. He checked the receiver's display. It was reading 451.475 megaHertz. End stop signal strength. 'For God's sake get a move on!' He hissed. 'We've got a unit working Burnham's channel 13 and he's nearly on top of us!'

Working silently, every move planned ahead, every detail rehearsed, they loaded the second tanker.

The captain who commanded the escort was the first to regain consciousness. His head felt as if an asteroid had fallen on it. He staggered out of the café. The army transporter and escort vehicles were still there. The soldiers lay bundled inside. The canvas covers of the transporter trailed on the ground. There was no sign of the vehicle's cargo. The weapons had been old stock, on their way to a Royal Ordnance Factory for dismantling and junking. Nevertheless they were no less deadly.

The transporter had been carrying two surface-to-surface Honest John missiles.

Sunday

1

At 08:34 hours precisely General Conrad Pyne's black official Rover 800 stopped outside the ugly wrought iron barrier that guarded the entrance into Downing Street. He sat perfectly still, barely acknowledging the polite salute of the police officers who checked his driver's credentials. There was a three-minute delay as a truckle mirror and an ion discharge explosives detector was passed under the vehicle.

Even at this hour on a hot Sunday morning there was a gaggle of sightseers and tourists clustered along the pavement hoping to catch a glimpse of the famous. They ducked their heads and tried to peer through the Austin-Rover's black-tinted glass. Japanese tourists clicked Canons in polite salute as Corporal Ian Garnet drove through the gates and into Downing Street. He did something unusual; instead of first dropping his passenger, he turned the car around in the narrow cul-de-sac and eased it alongside the kerb. The wing-mounted pennants of the Royal Army Ordnance Corps furled dejectedly in the oppressive heat around their silver stems.

Pyne made no attempt to move when the officer on duty opened the rear passenger door. The policeman was about to speak when he encountered the hard grey eyes.

Pyne pressed the airmail envelope into his hand. 'See that the Prime Minister's secretary gets that,' he ordered.

Pyne jerked the door shut and tapped on Garnet's shoulder. There was a click as the automatic transmission engaged. The big car pulled briskly away and swept through the gates, much to the surprise of the police officers who had been told that Pyne's visit would last at least fifteen to twenty minutes.

It was done.

The Doomsday Ultimatum had been delivered.

Pyne felt the constriction across his chest relax. He eased himself back into the soft cushions and glanced at his watch.

08:40. So far, so good.

So far . . .

He looked back through the rear window; a police officer was staring after him and another was yacking into his two-way radio. The scene behind the black-lacquered door of 10 Downing Street ran through Pyne's mind: using his official car would ensure the letter went directly to Simpson and not down to the sorting-office. The lightweight airmail envelope, containing a single sheet of closely typewritten paper, was hardly likely to arouse suspicion as a possible letter-bomb. Simpson would be told who had delivered the letter, and was probably opening it at this moment.

Corporal Garnet looked up at the frozen hands of Big Ben as he turned on to Westminster Bridge. From where he was sitting Pyne could see in the driver's mirror the ugly scar that transversed Garnet's left cheek. It was like a ragged furrow created by a drunken ploughman. A lucky escape from an Armalite bullet when Garnet had been serving in Northern Ireland.

'Still stuck at half past three, sir.'

Pyne made no reply. A handful of striking maintenance workers had achieved more than wartime bombs: the stationary hands were a symbol of the anarchy that now gripped the country – schools working a three-day week; water and electricity supplies frequently interrupted; sewage overflowing into the streets; and a government hamstrung by the reluctance of privatised public utilities to use what powers they had against the trade unions.

13

In the 1980s the power of the trade unions had been broken by a combination of high unemployment and punitive legislation. In the zeal of social reform that had followed the repressive government of the previous decade, many of the trade unions had regained their traditional powers by shifting their headquarters to the Netherlands and Belgium where they were beyond the direct jurisdiction of British courts. The will of national governments was thwarted by fax machines and international credit transfers. Adding to the government's problems was a plethora of militant social unions: patients unions; telephone users' unions; the Green Warriors; Poll Tax protesters. Even more worrying was the wave of fundamentalist Moslem movements that wanted to establish Moslem governed enclaves throughout the United Kingdom – states within a state.

08:43. The Rover was hissing over Westminster Bridge and away from the stench of a rotting refuse mountain in Trafalgar Square guarded by thousands of strikers.

Corporal Garnet slowed to pass a ragged demonstration. The marchers were not holding their banners properly, making it impossible to read what they said. The odd word unfolded briefly as the protestors swayed and chanted.

'INFLATION . . . FOOD PRICES . . . POLL TAX . . . SAVE BILLIONS WITH THE EUROPEAN DEFENCE FORCE . . .'

The last phrase held Pyne's attention. He studied the marchers more closely as the car crept past them. They looked like respectable middle-class clerks with their wives and children – not the type who would normally take to the streets. A woman was carrying the EC flag. She waved the blue banner with its circle of stars angrily at Pyne's car.

The tightness across his chest returned. He closed his eyes on the symbol and pictured the events taking place in Downing Street. Simpson would now be rereading the letter. Perhaps he was already reaching for his telephone to ring the Prime Minister. No. Simpson was much too

14

cautious: he would call the police and make doubly certain
it was Pyne who had delivered the ultimatum:

> As from 10:30 hours today, Vulcan Hall nuclear
> power station on Canvey Island is now under the
> control of the recently formed United Kingdom
> Policy Control Group. The purpose of this group is to
> advise and co-ordinate the activities of Her Majesty's
> Government.

> How we will carry out this task and our specific long-
> term and short-term objectives will be communicated
> to you later today. For the time being, it is sufficient
> for you to know that we are in possession of two
> MGR-1B Honest John surface-to-surface ballistic
> missiles in addition to the large quantity of tactical
> hardware supplied to the Oil Platform Defence Force
> which, as from today, is also under our command.
> One of the Honest Johns is now trained on the East
> End of London and any attempt to interfere with our
> operations on Canvey Island will result in the
> immediate discharge of the missile.

> Our first directive is that our ultimatum should not be
> made public until our terms have been implemented
> by Parliament, and have received the Royal
> Assent . . .

There were certain conditions in the ultimatum that Keller
was unaware of. Pyne frowned. Keller had proved himself
during the raid on the Westward Ho transport café three
months earlier; he had obeyed orders without question, and
had always shown respect for Pyne. But there was something about him that Pyne disliked. His unsmiling politeness
at the planning meetings and insistence that only extreme
right-wing measures would cure the country's problems,
had forced Pyne to supply Keller with a phoney draft of the
ultimatum to keep him quiet. Pyne disliked having to do it —

the success of the power station takeover depended on mutual trust between the four members of the group. Had there been time, Pyne would have looked around for an alternative to Keller. But there was no-one – Keller had been responsible for the installation of the emergency radioactive waste silos at the Vulcan Hall nuclear power station – he knew exactly where to position the high-explosive and how to shutdown the power station's two gas-cooled nuclear reactors.

For the time being Keller would have to be tolerated.

Pyne was pushed gently into the cushions as the Rover accelerated through the quiet Sunday morning streets. Occasional wisps of smoke drifted across the road as householders ignored clean air regulations in their efforts to dispose of rubbish. Traffic lights obligingly winked to green at the car's approach –their solid state relays triggered by the sonic beam from a PATH (Priority Alert Traffic Hold) transmitter concealed behind the Rover's grille; a useful device fitted to all official cars used by government ministers and high-ranking service officers.

By 08:55 the car was nearing Woolwich, and at 09:00 hours precisely it was cleared by the civilian police and allowed to pass through the ornate gates of the Royal College of Artillery. The smartly turned-out sentries checked the documents Garnet handed them and accorded Pyne smart salutes before raising the steel barrier arm. Although Pyne never wore a uniform, he always received a salute.

Pyne walked across the sprawling, close-clipped lawn with Corporal Garnet one step behind carrying the briefcase. Someone had wiped the dew off his Westland Scout helicopter so that it gleamed damply in the early sun. It was the last Scout still in service with the army; Pyne had fought several battles with MoD Procurement to keep the machine in service. The faint circular scratch marks on the Perspex windows – the result of carelessness with a hard rag – annoyed him. He checked his irritation.

Did it matter any more?

'Back to Weybridge, sir?' inquired Garnet, unlocking the Scout's door.

Pyne shook his head. 'I'll fly her, corporal. I've not logged enough hours this year. I ought to keep my hand in.'

'Yes, sir.' Garnet held the door open as the general climbed into the pilot's seat. Pyne waved away the offered briefcase.

'I don't need it any more.'

The corporal looked uncertain. 'Do you want me to come with you, sir?'

'No. Take the car back to the MT depot. Tell them I've finished with it.' Pyne avoided his NCO's eyes – the savage scar seemed to glow in the harsh light.

'Garnet, would you do something for me?'

'Sir?'

'Not as an order – I can't give orders now, but as a favour.'

'I don't understand, sir.'

'There's a buff envelope in the briefcase which contains your discharge papers. You've been a civilian since midnight. That's why I can't give you orders.'

Garnet looked astounded. The briefcase nearly slipped from his grasp.

'I'm going away on an important mission – possibly for a long time. It's not fair to expect my daughter to look after the house, so I'd like you to do it.' Pyne paused and flipped the Scout's power switches. The toggle switches closed with soft clicks and the instruments came to life. 'There's a copy of a letter in the briefcase instructing the Midland Bank at Weybridge to make you monthly payments as my caretaker. You'll also find a cheque in there payable to you so you can have some plastic surgery for that scar, and there's some cash for civilian clothes. Will you do it?'

Garnet stood transfixed.

'Well?' snapped Pyne.

The corporal nodded dumbly.

'If you see Maggie at the house, tell her I'm sorry to have missed the birthday party she was planning for me.' Pyne paused to operate the Scout's controls. The rotors turned slowly. 'You can sell the boat for whatever you can get.' Pyne wondered why he was telling Garnet this. He gazed at the unreal red-brick facade of the college. It looked like a film set dropped amid the disciplined flowerbeds.

'One last thing: don't think too badly of Maggie. She's young and thoughtless,; and doesn't mean to be cruel. She still hasn't got over her mother's death,'

Corporal Garnet stared at his general.

'And you're to tell no one what has happened to me,' said Pyne. 'Absolutely no one. Understand?'

Garnet found his voice:

'How long will you be gone, sir?'

Pyne hesitated. 'Not more than twelve months if all goes according to plan. But it could be five years.'

Pyne slammed the helicopter door shut before Garnet could reply. The rotors became an iridescent disc that bit into the hot morning air until their downward thrust cancelled the Scout's weight. The machine lifted, and dwindled towards the Thames, watched by the bewildered upturned face of Corporal Garnet as he clutched the black leather briefcase with its gold E11R crest.

2

Simpson moved quickly after he had finished reading the ultimatum. He knew exactly what he had to do. He notified the valet to wake the Prime Minister immediately and then called the duty air traffic control officer at West Drayton to establish the whereabouts of General Pyne's helicopter.

Simpson was certain he knew the answer, but with so much at stake there was no room for mistakes – the call had to be made. The officer returned his call two minutes later, confirming what Simpson already knew.

Simpson opened a desk drawer and studied a computer print-out which listed data on every helicopter pilot in the armed services. He crossed the office and pulled a wall map of southern England down by its tassel. His finger traced the winding path of the Thames and stopped at Chatham. He smiled to himself and put a priority call through to the officer in charge of helicopter air-sea rescue operations at Chatham naval base. He kept his finger on the red button so that the alarm would sound continuously in the command-ing officer's office until the telephone was answered. He gave his emergency number and pressed the cradle to cut the line. He remained impassive for some seconds with his outstretched finger holding the line closed until the tele-phone warbled. He removed his finger and issued instruc-tions in his curt, matter-of-fact voice and requested them to be read back to him. He listened attentively and carefully replaced the receiver.

The conversation was safely recorded on tape in case the Prime Minister's enemies later accused the department of not trying.

The door opened Simpson looked up at the thickset figure standing in the doorway.

'Good morning, sir. I trust you slept well?'

It was a courteous greeting rather than an inquiry.

The Prime Minister always slept soundly. But the week ahead would change all that.

3

Pyne cleared his routing with West Drayton and passed over Woolwich at a thousand feet. He altered course above the Thames to follow its molten silver path towards the estuary. The free ferry was ploughing across the current on its new restricted service. Pyne felt a pang of regret at the passing of the old paddle steamers. His greatest joy as a cadet from a poor background had been the daily free trip across the river and back on the pounding old side-wheelers.

To the north towering office blocks stood like brooding memorials to the prosperity of a bygone era. Once the angular steel and concrete stakes, driven indiscriminately into the docklands clay, had pinned down fat profits for their owners; now they scarcely acted as windbreaks against the chill draught of depression that seeped and spilled across the country.

Pyne settled more comfortably into his seat.

There was so much to be done.

And undone.

He glanced at his watch. 09:15 hours,

The Thames yawned wider in its lazy, indifferent sweep to the North Sea. The helicopter's grounded shadow chased vainly after its owner – occasionally racing up the sides of slab-sided refuse barges now manned by the Royal Marines – fleeting across cargoes of rotting vegetable waste and plunging back to the gleaming, hammer-beaten water.

So much to be done.

Pyne squinted into the sun as the Thames Haven oil refinery came into view thirty kilometres ahead. Beyond the lacework of pipes and distillation columns, and ten kilometres further eastward down-river, he could just discern the salt-cellar cooling towers of the Vulcan Hall nuclear power station on Canvey Island. The pale structures shimmered in the haze that was being sucked off the water by the strengthening sun and smeared across the horizon like a ghostly shroud.

The power station could wait. First, the refinery.

09:22 hours.

Pyne took the handheld Icom transceiver from its mounting clip and pressed it to his ear. The two-way radio was already set to the correct frequency. He pressed the talk key.

'Pine Needle to Victor Hotel control. Do you copy? Over.'

The direct, line-of-sight reply from the visible power station, ten kilometres beyond the refinery, was loud and clear. 'Victor Hotel control to Pine Needle,' said a voice in the headphones. 'Go ahead.'

It was Keller. The polite nasal accent with the faint American twang he had acquired when working in Michigan for the US Atomic Energy Commission was unmistakable. At least the man was alert.

'I'm thirty kilometres west of the target,' said Pyne. 'I'll remain in this area until after 09:45 hours. I don't want to be too close. Over.'

'Correction, Pine Needle, we have you positioned at twenty-nine point two kilometres west of the target according to our radar display,' Keller answered with his customary politeness.

Pyne frowned. He was never certain with Keller whether the man was being supercilious or subordinate.

'Are you all set? Over.' asked Pyne.

'All set,' affirmed Keller. 'You should have a grandstand view. Did the delivery go as planned?'

Always so bloody polite, thought Pyne. 'Affirmative. Any messages? Over.'

'Negative, Pine Needle, but we picked up Captain Stacy trying to contact you. It looks as if the camp is ready for inspection.'

'I'll call him direct,' said Pyne. There was nothing more to be said. He cut Keller off and set the tranceiver to scanning the 451 megaHertz band. There were the usual police reports in jargon from mobiles and the occasional clear-language directive from their controls. Nothing about Pyne or the Scout helicopter. He checked the air band with the same result. It was only to be expected. He anticipated that the ultimatum would take at least an hour to sink in, especially Article Two in the covering instructions:

As a demonstration of our determination, we will destroy the Thames Haven oil refinery with one of the Honest John missiles at 09:45 hours. Be warned: Canvey Island is now equipped with the latest

21

horizon surveillance radar; the surrounding countryside is flat, giving us two minutes' warning of any missile or low-level aircraft attack, and we require only one minute to launch the second Honest John.

Any attempt to employ radar jamming or any form of ECM (Electronic Countermeasures) against us will be regarded by us as a hostile move and we will act accordingly. Should you decide to sacrifice the lives of many Londoners by forcing us to fire the missile, it would be best if you considered the implications of an explosion from the hundred tonnes of Cyclonite high explosive we have placed round Vulcan Hall's radioactive-waste storage silos.

(signed)
Conrad Pyne OBE
(Major-General)

Pyne remembered deleting his rank and the letters after his name before signing the document.

4

Lieutenant Steven Thorne, RN, had been trained to do everything with a helicopter except how to bring down another helicopter.

He debated the problem with himself as his Mark 10 Lynx, the fastest rotary-wing machine in the world, thrashed westward above the Thames from Chatham.

His one crewman was not much help either.

Marine-Sergeant Hopkins, secured to the floor of the open helicopter bay by a harness and clutching a floor-mounted machine-gun, had no experience of aerial combat.

Thorne scanned the expanse of brilliant blue sky. The sun was behind him, so this terrorist, whoever he was, flying an old Army Scout helicopter, should be easy to detect. That's all they had told him: a terrorist flying a stolen machine who was to be stopped at all costs.

'There he is sir!' Hopkins' voice suddenly shouted in Thorne's headset.

Thorne spotted the whirling splinter of sunlight immediately. It was a Scout helicopter. 'Okay Hopkins. I've got him!'

Thorne pulled his machine upwards to put himself into the sun.

It was a mistake.

In the Scout, Pyne squinted up as the shadow of the Lynx flitted across the Perspex windows. He cursed Keller for not warning him, and pushed the cyclic pitch yoke forward.

Thorne slewed his tail-boom around and aimed his machine at Pyne's Scout that was now windmilling low across the Thames leaving a wake of flattened water in the downwash from its rotors.

The distance between the two machines closed rapidly. The Lynx's airframe shook violently as the screaming rotors sliced into the haze-laden air. Even if Thorne had lost the advantage of surprise his Lynx was the fastest helicopter in the world – Pyne was finished – when he got close enough.

And then Pyne did something completely unexpected – he swung his Scout around like a cornered cat turning on a pursuing dog. Thorne was forced to bank sharply to avoid a mid-air collision. Pyne deftly leapt the Scout over Thorne's plunging Lynx, and stole the larger machine's lift. Thorne frantically increased pitch as the Lynx's rotors failed to bite on the air already being forced downward by the wash from the Scout. For a sickening moment Thorne thought his machine was going to plunge into the river. The Lynx's wheels actually dipped into the water before the flailing rotors jerked the helicopter upwards.

Pyne spun the Scout around and flew backwards away from the Lynx – a move which cost Thorne several seconds as he went plunging after Pyne in the wrong direction. Pyne continued to fly backwards, watching the spinning ellipse of Thorne's rotors harden to a fine line as the powerful Navy machine came roaring after him. Pyne glanced over his shoulder; the main building of the Ford Motor Company was racing towards him.

Pyne felt trapped. Attempting to climb out of trouble would cost too much in ground speed. The distance between the helicopters narrowed as they flew towards the giant car parks where Ford's stored their thousands of unsold cars.

Pyne reached under his seat for the Verey signal pistol, slid a fat parachute flare into the breech, and pulled back the hammer. It was the only armament the Scout carried.

By now, Thorne had a healthy respect for Pyne's flying skill and approached cautiously.

'Try now sir!' said Hopkins urgently. 'I'm in range!'

Thorne brought the open bay to bear, but Pyne thwarted the move by twisting his more manoeuvrable machine within the Lynx's turning circle.

The two helicopters were like cats circling each other as a preliminary to battle. Thorne broke the rhythm. The Scout slipped out of sight down the starboard side of the Lynx towards Hopkins' field of fire. Pyne did not hear the machine-gun, but saw darts of light flicker from the barrel and felt bullets slam into the aluminium skin behind his head.

On the ground Ford drivers pointed excitedly up at the sparring machines.

There was no second burst of fire. Hopkins swore and released his safety harness to kick the jammed gun. Pyne aimed the Verey pistol at the big Navy machine, bracing his arm against the down-wash from the Scout's rotors. His finger tensed on the trigger.

Another burst of fire as Hopkins freed the jammed ammunition belt. The flare arched gracefully towards the Lynx, but it was too high. Pyne cursed his mistake.

Thorne made another mistake: he saw the trail of the flare against the sky and, thinking that it was coming straight for him, banked sharply. It was over in a matter of seconds. The wash from the Lynx's rotors deflected the flare downward. It blasted past Hopkins and exploded like a miniature sun against the far bulkhead. Hopkins screamed to Thorne and actually tried to pick the flare up. He was too late. The fireball melted through the bulkhead and dissolved the fuel line from the armoured tank beneath the floor. Blazing fuel sprayed on Hopkins as he rolled screaming on the floor.

The Ford drivers scattered as the blazing machine came skimming towards them above the rooftops of the unwanted cars. The last thing that registered on Thorne's mind before it ceased to exist, was the kaleidoscope of brightly coloured metal boxes racing towards him.

One wheel of the Lynx struck an Escort. The impact sent the helicopter somersaulting through the air. The burning body of Marine-Sergeant Hopkins was ejected fifty-metres through the air. He landed on the roof of a white Sierra and etched his outline in the blistering acrylic paint.

The Lynx ploughed upside down through the ranks of ownerless cars, its still flailing rotors scything saloons to instant mangled convertibles.

The bewildered drivers, crouching behind tape-shrouded bumpers, cautiously emerged and surveyed the blazing wreckage. Two drivers tried to approach the helicopter but were driven back by the heat. More drivers stood up, then immediately dived for cover as heat-fired bullets from Hopkins' machine-gun whacked into unscathed cars. Windshields shattered and tyres collapsed with reproving hisses at the random onslaught from Lieutenant Steven Thorne's spiteful funeral pyre.

Pyne wasted no time on regret for the unknown crew of the Lynx. He turned the Scout back towards the Thames.

A corner of his mind noted what a beautiful day it was.

5

The shockwave from the exploding oil refinery which rocked the Scout helicopter a hundred seconds after the flash was felt as far away as Chelmsford in the north and Maidstone in the south. Holidaymakers on the Kent beaches scanned the sky for a glimpse of the aircraft that had caused the sonic boom. A ten-tonne slab of metal shaped like a segment of orange peel – part of a propane gas pressure vessel – developed sufficient lift under its curved surface to demolish a row of houses twenty kilometres away. The intense heat fused sixty caravans on a site near the refinery to neat rectangular blobs of solder. The pulverizing shockwave, destroying everything in its path, originated from a single, catastrophic explosion, but the squat containers spread out on the vast tank farm adjoining the refinery site eliminated themselves one by one with their own individual explosions.

One hundred and forty-five refinery workers were flashed to steam before the sound of the blast reached them. A colliery vessel capsized, sank, poured a thousand tonnes of coal on to the river bed and surfaced bottom-up. A two metre tidal wave raced upriver. It was destined to reach Teddington Lock after a journey of appalling destruction where it would sweep away most of the vehicles parked round the television studios, smash down the lock gates and dissipate its energy against the unleashed flood of water raging through the ruptured gates.

Pyne flew cautiously towards the devastated refinery. Apart from the blazing containers on the tank farms round the site, there was no fire amid the twisted, flattened remains of the distillation columns and hydro-cracking towers; everything inflammable had been swept away or vaporised by the blast. The giant globular LPG tanks were no more – they had been pricked out of existence like balloons. The approach roads were empty of traffic. Despite the whine of the gas turbine above Pyne's head, an atmosphere of stunned silence and stillness pervaded the site.

A flash below caught his eye. Seagulls were swooping down and settling on agitated water round the sinking colliery vessel – even the few fish in the Thames Estuary had been stunned by the blast. Pyne watched the birds screaming and fighting. Perhaps it wasn't fish they were interested in.

He switched on the radio to listen to any official announcements, turned the Scout towards the four distant cooling towers of the Vulcan Hall nuclear power station, and felt in his pocket for a cigar. His fingers encountered a piece of paper: 'St Georges Hill New Golf Club. Annual subscription. Received with thanks.'

He crumpled the link with the past and tossed it out of the window.

His watch said 10:00 hours.

The Doomsday Ultimatum was now in force.

6

There was one seat empty when the Cromwell Two Committee sat to finalize details of their plan to seize power and install a temporary military government.

'Where's Pyne?' asked the chairman, a cabinet minister.

Sir Michael Powell, head of the Civil Service, looked up from his notes. 'An apology for absence, Mr Chairman. Pyne called me yesterday and said he wasn't able to make himself available today.'

The chairman nodded and glanced round at the ten faces. 'Shall we start, gentlemen?'

There was a murmur of assent.

The first item on the agenda was the list of two hundred names prepared by the head of the Civil Service of people to fill the top administrative posts in the new government. Several of those present, such as the head of the Special Branch, and the chairman of the Governors of the BBC, General Sir Richard Markham and Sir Oswald Fox, were to retain their existing jobs.

'Supposing the Prime Minister recalls Parliament if Selkirk does call a general strike?' asked the chairman of the Independent Broadcasting Commission.

The man at the head of the table shook his head. 'He won't do anything to risk another defeat. He's playing a wait-and-see game. He daren't even declare a state of emergency for fear of the palace turning it down.'

'Surely he'll resign?' said a voice.

The chairman smiled. 'Only when he really knows he's lost. And that may take another month. By which time our gold and dollar reserves will be exhausted and it will be too late. Right now, the old bastard's praying for a fairy godmother.' The expletive did not raise an eyebrow in the select gathering.

'Very well then,' said the chairman at the close of the meeting. 'We move one week from today.'

A bottle was opened and the company of distinguished conspirators drank a toast to the Queen.

7

There were times when Howard Mitchell regretted the self-indulgent impulse which had prompted him to import a Mustang from the United States. The left-hand drive car was often at a disadvantage when he was trying to overtake on Great Britain's crazy, twisting roads that seemed to go nowhere once and everywhere twice.

Mitchell shifted to a lower gear and crawled patiently behind an electric milk float, grinding painfully up the hill leading to the golf club. At one point he was tempted to pass but was immediately deterred by an XJS which appeared from nowhere and boomed throatily past in the opposite direction.

The milk float glided past the turning to St Georges Hill New Golf Club, which belonged to one of the most exclusive housing estates in the country. There was no sign of the black Austin-Rover when Mitchell parked near the clubhouse and went in.

'Where's General Pyne, Harry?' Mitchell asked the barman.

'I've no idea, Mr Mitchell,' he replied. 'I don't understand it. Hardly anyone here. I wondered if it was Sunday when I unlocked this morning. Only three games out on the course.' The barman gloomily surveyed the deserted lounge. Sunday-morning tips were the only thing that gave him a decent standard of living.

Mitchell ordered a lager and sipped it slowly. 'Did he leave a message for me?'

The barman glanced at the shelf behind the bar. 'No. Nothing, Mr Mitchell. Had you arranged to play a round with him?'

'That's right. The loser to vacuum both swimming pools.'

The barman smiled politely. God, how he hated these bastards with money. Nothing the government did seemed to strip them of their fat. Even with the country in its present state they still had more than anyone else.

Mitchell finished his drink and left the clubhouse. He paused by his Mustang. It was a fine morning, so he decided to walk to Pyne's place.

Pyne's house was one of the older, more conservative homes on the expensive estate. It had the traditional curved drive so that the house could not be seen from the road.

He rang the doorbell and waited.

Mitchell was a shy, thirty-seven-year-old New Yorker who owned a small but thriving shipping and forwarding agency. The success of his business sprang from his knowledge of the North Sea oil-exploration programme rather than a shrewd business brain. People tended to think his easy-going nature disguised a degree of ruthlessness. They accepted his prices and delivery dates because his prices were reasonable, and his dates always met. Howard Mitchell was not ruthless – he was efficient.

Pyne's daughter, Maggie, answered the door.

Mitchell had met her on a number of occasions when Pyne used to invite him back to the house for a drink after their Sunday game of golf. The invitations had ceased with the death of Pyne's wife six months previously. The only times he had met the girl since then was in Weybridge shopping. She always seemed to have Corporal Garnet in tow carrying her purchases.

Maggie gave the American a warm smile and pulled the door open.

'Hallo, Mitch. I thought you'd forgotten me.'

Mitchell almost laughed aloud at the spectacle before him. Maggie Pyne's elfin face was streaked with flour.

'I'm sorry to disturb you, Maggie. But I'm supposed to be having a game of golf with your father.' He looked at the girl with amusement. 'You seem to have had a slight disaster.'

Maggie smiled, and held the door open. 'I've just lost an argument with the food-mixer,' she explained, leading the way to the kitchen. 'Would you like some coffee?'

'Only if you promise to make me four cups.'

The kitchen was in a mess; every available square centimetre of working space was piled high with evil-looking sandwiches, a chocolate éclair was floating in a bowl of punch and the floor was gritty with sugar.

'What happened, Maggie?' said Mitchell as the girl held the kettle under a trickle of water from a tap that was turned full on.

'It's to be a party for Daddy,' said Maggie apologetically. 'It's his birthday today – his forty-fifth I think – so I thought I'd try making some cakes.' She spooned ground coffee into an espresso machine's strainer and latched it into place. 'I did everything by the book and was getting along fine until I tried using the mixer.'

Mitchell glanced at the food-mixer, and tried not to laugh.

'You used that glass jar?'

Maggie looked at the machine in concern.

'Yes.'

Mitchell looked round the kitchen. Everything was covered with a fine film of flour. 'Without the lid?' he inquired.

Maggie frowned at the gadget. 'Is there a lid?'

30

'Honey, that's the liquidizer attachment. Anything you try mixing in that without a lid immediately gets out.'

'Maybe I should just stick to drink,' said Maggie sadly. 'I can manage a corkscrew. I wish Corporal Garnet was here – he's good at these things.'

'Isn't your father around?'

The girl shook her head, and brushed cake ingredients from her T-shirt and jeans.

'He and Corporal Garnet went off yesterday. I haven't seen them yet. I hope Daddy comes home. I want all this to be a surprise.'

She saw Mitchell hiding his face behind his hands. 'It's not funny,' she snapped. 'You try cooking in this weather.'

Mitchell nodded soberly and made a strange noise in his throat.

He watched Maggie as she operated the espresso machine's pump and wondered what she would look like in a dress. She had a figure that was made to be expensively dressed: tall, slim with long dark hair. Mitchell wondered why she didn't spend some of the money her mother had left her on clothes. Her first purchase with her newly acquired wealth had been an MG sports car. Mitchell remembered how Pyne had complained during a game of golf.

'There's too many people with too much money,' Pyne had said, 'and far too many with far too little.'

Mitchell had laughed. 'A car, general? You can't blame her. It's what every kid wants.'

'The latest thing is a house,' Pyne had grumbled.

'You can't say she's wasting it.'

'Well, perhaps not. But it's made her independent. When Helen died I thought we'd get to know each other. I've never had much time for family life – and now, when I've decided to adjust to it, I've got no family left.'

'You should make a clean break,' Mitchell had replied. 'Change your whole way of life before you discover you're too old to change.'

Pyne had nodded. 'That wouldn't be difficult. I've considered throwing up everything to do something really positive with my life.' He had dropped the ball neatly into the seventh hole.

Mitchell had looked puzzled. 'I would've thought being a major-general was pretty positive.'

Pyne had laughed. 'My entire army career has been spent in an office. I'm an admin man -" flying a desk" my RAF colleagues in Whitehall call it. I've never seen any form of active service, and I can't remember when I last wore a uniform. I'm not even certain if I've got one.'

'But you're going to command this new oil platform defence unit?'

'Oh yes,' Pyne had said lightly. 'One advantage of working in Whitehall is that you're in the best place for a spot of wheeling and dealing when a plum new job is in the offing.'

Maggie's voice suddenly intruded on Mitchell's thoughts.

'Don't you want your coffee?'

Mitchell sipped cautiously. Even with an espresso machine, Maggie managed to louse things up; it was the worst coffee he had ever tasted. He struggled to keep a straight face.

'If you laugh . . .' Maggie said warningly.

Mitchell replaced the cup on the saucer

'Believe me, Maggie – your coffee's no laughing matter.'

She stared at him for a moment and then laughed. Mitchell joined in when he felt he was on safe ground.

'If only you could've seen your face,' said Maggie.

Mitchell nodded to the plates of sandwiches. 'What will happen to those if your father doesn't show up?'

'Feed them to the birds, I suppose. It'll be a nuisance if he doesn't come home. I've spent a fortune on food and drink. And I got the corporal to clean and refill the pool.'

'I bet he loved you for that,' said Mitchell, 'with temperatures hitting eighty in the shade.'

Maggie shrugged. 'It's what he's for.'

32

The casual way in which she said it reinforced Mitchell's belief that the British class system still had a firm hold.

A dull boom rattled the windows.

'At least the RAF can still afford to make sonic booms,' commented Mitchell. 'What time are you holding this party?'

'Eight,' said Maggie.'If you can drink the rest of that coffee without pulling a face, I might add you to the twenty I've already invited.'

'Sure I'll come, sweetheart. A party in the dark sounds like fun.'

Maggie stared at the American.

'What do you mean?'

'The power cut for this area starts at nine.'

Maggie looked alarmed. 'But it's this afternoon, surely?'

Mitchell shook his head. 'The electricity rotas are one thing I make a point of knowing. Today's Sunday. The new rota started at midnight. Check it out on the radio if you don't believe me'

Maggie tuned the portable radio to a local London station. A newsreader was describing the latest government talks to avert the impending general strike.

'I'm surprised you haven't gone home, with the state the country's in,' said Maggie. 'It's just like the Seventies all over again.'

'Well North Sea oil isn't in a state,' replied Mitchell. 'The new Hebrides field means that it's the fastest growth industry in Europe. Anyway, I'm one of the few who's keeping quiet about Britain. Back home, they're all writing epitaphs. Dangerous when the corpse isn't dead. They have a habit of suddenly getting better.'

'What does your business do? You don't smell of oil.'

'An oil rig needs a piece of equipment in a hurry, and I usually know where I can lay my hands on it.'

The newsreader interrupted an interview with a trade-union leader.

'News is just coming in of a large explosion at the Thames Haven oil refinery on the Thames near London,' he said.

'Turn up the sound please, Maggie,' Mitchell requested.

The girl did so. 'What's the matter?'

Mitchell gestured her to silence.

'The explosion was heard all over the London area,' continued the newsreader. 'Eye-witness reports say the entire refinery was devastated in one catastrophic explosion. The Thames Barrage was raised for routine testing with the result that a two metre tidal wave is now racing up the Thames through London . . .'

The newsreader broke off. Mitchell's attention was riveted on the radio.

'Mike Bowden is on the phone from near the site,' said the newsreader. 'Can you hear me, Mike?'

'Hallo, Ted,' squawked a distorted voice from the speaker. 'The scene here at Thames Haven is unbelievable. The entire refinery has been flattened out of existence. There's nothing left but a great mass of smouldering wreckage. Police are just about to evacuate the area in case there are more explosions, but it's hard to believe there's anything left to explode . . . About one hundred and forty-five workers are believed to have been . . .'

Mitchell swore, and jumped to his feet.

'What's the matter?' asked Maggie.

'Oh, shit. My car's at the golf club. Maggie, will you do me a big favour and drive me to the Fairoaks Flying Club?'

Thirty minutes later they were airborne in Mitchell's pale-blue Bonanza and heading east at five thousand feet. West Drayton ATC refused Mitchell's flight plan to approach the refinery from London. He studied the charts spread out on his knee and decided to follow the M25 orbital motorway before turning north to intersect the Thames a few kilometres downstream from the refinery.

Maggie watched him covertly. He had ignored her questions during the short car ride, preferring to hunt for news reports on her car radio.

34

There was a faint smell of rotting refuse in the aircraft.

'You can even smell it up here,' said Maggie. She stretched out in the bucket seat and planted her feet on the instrument panel. 'People like you are morbid.'

'Why?' asked Mitchell, looking up from a chart.

Maggie looked at him in mock surprise. 'Good heavens, it's alive.'

'Any more of your bitchy comments and I'll push you out so you can walk home. Why am I morbid?'

'Flying off to look at a blown-up refinery.'

'It just so happens,' replied Mitchell evenly, 'that I've got a brand new drill-string at Thames Haven waiting for shipment to Nordic Queen platform tomorrow – when its UK insurance comes into force.'

'What's a drill-string?'

'The lengths of steel that fit together to make a drill.'

'Isn't that careless? Not insuring it?'

'There was a shipping delay,' said Mitchell. 'Your dockers at Southampton refused to unload it. A prefabricated import, they called it – so I had to pay to have it sent on to the unloading facilities at Thames Haven.'

'How will you know from the air if it's okay?' Maggie asked.

'I'll know sure enough. It's two hundred tonnes of steel in three stacks.'

Maggie looked down at the main roads radiating from London. The heat was tempting the unemployed to find money for petrol to drive to the beaches.

'Are you better at loading cameras than blenders?' asked Mitchell.

'Sure.'

Mitchell jerked his head at the rear seats. 'There should be a camera in that bag behind, and some rolls of film. Maybe you'd load one for me?'

'Say please.'

'Will I hell. You can earn the extra gas your weight is costing me.'

35

Maggie sighed and eased her feet off the instrument panel. Her heel knocked against the toggle switch on the radiotelephone.

London Airport tried several times to contact the light aircraft that was approaching the zone prohibited to all air traffic since 09:45 that morning. The green blip crawling across their radar screens was either ignoring their calls or did not have its radio switched on. Provided it maintained its present eastward course, it would pass through the outer periphery of the zone. A computer was set to monitor the aircraft's progress, and the Air Traffic Control officers returned to their task of diverting incoming London flights to Manchester and Luton.

Thirty minutes later the computer drew their attention to the blip, which had altered course and was now on a heading which would take it right over the Thames Haven prohibited zone.

Simpson had told London Airport that the Prime Minister was taking a personal interest in the Thames Haven disaster and wished to be kept informed of all developments – no matter how minor.

At twelve noon the ATC Officer at West Drayton telephoned Simpson on the special number and told him that an unidentified aircraft was approaching the refinery.

Simpson sat at his desk pondering this unexpected turn of events. He decided to take no chances and reached for his telephone.

At 12:10 an RAF Tornado screamed down the runway at Manston and lifted its graceful nose to the deep blue sky. At two thousand feet its attack radar locked on to the unauthorized blip, and the pilot flipped the switches that primed the ignition circuits in the twelve air-to-air missiles slung beneath the Tornado's wings.

Mitchell's navigation was better than he expected. Straight ahead were the giant cooling towers of the Vulcan Hall

36

nuclear power station standing like sole remaining rooks in a chess game of the gods. To the left, ten kilometres from the power station, were the scorched, still-smouldering remains of the Thames Haven oil refinery. As Mitchell banked to turn upstream towards the refinery Maggie grabbed his arm and pointed back at the power station.

'Look! Those two helicopters! One of them belongs to my father! The olive green one!'

Mitchell turned in his seat and looked back at the power station. On the concrete apron that separated the main building from the waterfront stood two helicopters, a Bell JetRanger and a Westland Scout. Mitchell throttled back.

'Are you certain?'

'That's his registration. And I think the other helicopter belongs to Hugh Patterson.' Mitchell swung the machine round in a wide circle. The Bonanza was about six kilometres from the power station – halfway between it and the remains of Thames Haven. He wasn't particularly interested in the machines at the power station, but they seemed to worry Maggie. A little way from the helicopters two gasoline tankers were parked. He could see figures near them. Maggie was right about the JetRanger. It was definitely the one owned by Patterson – he had often seen it dropping into the dense trees that surrounded the industrialist's house on St Georges Hill. JetRangers were common enough in the United States, but quite rare in England.

'Doesn't Patterson's company make nuclear waste containers?' asked Mitchell. 'Maybe he's showing your father his products that are used in that power station?'

It wasn't a convincing explanation, but he was anxious to fly on to the oil refinery.

He pulled the Bonanza out of the turn and flew on upstream towards Thames Haven.

'There's a holiday camp or something beyond the power station,' said Maggie, craning her neck round to look back.

'The whole of Canvey looks like a holiday camp,' commented Mitchell. 'One big shanty town of factories, beach huts and caravans.'

They flew on upstream.

When the Bonanza was two kilometres from the refinery Mitchell took his first picture and wondered why the site wasn't swarming with rescue workers.

'Can you see anything?' Maggie asked.

Mitchell took another picture. 'Not yet.'

The Bonanza swept over the devastated site. There was no sign of his drill-string amid the twisted, blackened wreckage. It was all very worrying.

He clicked the camera shutter four times and was about to take another picture when Maggie touched him on the shoulder.

'Look.' She pointed to the north.

A Tornado jet fighter was about six kilometres away. Mitchell recognised it by the wing configuration as it banked sharply, turning towards the Bonanza as if closing in to attack.

8

Fifteen minutes after the explosion Pyne flew over the Vulcan Hall power station for an aerial inspection of his new Oil Platform Defence Force camp, which had been established the day before on Canvey Island.

His hands were still trembling as they rested on the Scout's controls. Partly because of his recent encounter with the Lynx helicopter, but mostly with anger at the heavy casualties and devastation caused by the Honest John. Keller had assured him at the final planning meeting held the week before that there would be no more than five of six maintenance workers at the refinery on a Sunday morning. The first urgent police signals picked up on the radio suggested that nearer one hundred and fifty men were in the refinery at the time of the explosion and that several people whose houses were near the tank farm had been killed.

Pyne looked down at the dazzling glass facade of the power station's administrative offices, which presented a burnished face to the Thames. Keller, Patterson and Louise Campion were probably watching him through binoculars from the control room which covered the entire top floor of the main building.

The power station's fifty-acre site was now enclosed by the horns of the new camp that reached to the river on either side.

Operation Oilguard, launched the previous day to establish the camp, had been used by the Royal Engineers, at General Pyne's suggestion, as an exercise in speed. Work had begun in the early morning with the arrival of a convoy of Pickford transporters carrying six kilometres of chain-link fencing with concrete posts already attached. More trucks had arrived ten minutes later, each one laden with fifteen tonnes of barbed wire – enough to make an entanglement over ten kilometres long.

By 11:00 the fences had been complete.

The inner fence encircled the power station at a distance of a hundred yards and the outer fence had been erected two hundred yards away. Two barriers had been constructed where the access road to the power station intersected the two fences. A number of caravan owners whose trailers would have been trapped within the new camp had watched helplessly as soldiers had hitched their holiday homes to Land Rovers and towed them away. A fork-lift truck had shifted a row of beach huts.

By 11:45 bulldozers had been levelling uneven ground, followed by soldiers spraying the earth with quick-drying asphalt. One of the army's cherished machines for making white lines had marked out the positions of roads, crossings and buildings.

The real hardware which makes an army had waited for the afternoon – after Pyne's second in command, Captain Peter Stacy, had inspected the fences.

It had arrived in several trucks: Clansman communications equipment from the Signals Research and Design Establishment; one tonne of night optical and intruder surveillance equipment from the Central Inventory Control Point; armoured cars from the Fighting Vehicles Establishment; and two ex-army Hueycobra helicopter gunships, which had arrived in two huge containers together with their grenade launchers and missile armament from RAF Harrogate.

There had been a moment of confusion when two petrol tankers arrived which were not included on the duty officer's list. Fuel for the camp had already arrived. The tanker drivers had explained that their loads were for the power station, and shown the soldiers their delivery notes. The two tankers had been allowed to pass through the camp and into the power-station compound.

The work had proceeded at an urgent pace through the hot afternoon. The soldiers had been too busy to wonder why the power-station decommissioning staff showed no interest in the developments going on round them.

At 16:00 hours water purification equipment had arrived from the General Stores Depot, followed by a long convoy of trucks laden with two hundred tonnes of food and clothing – enough to last the camp five years.

Captain Stacy had walked methodically round the camp at 17:30, holding his indispensable clipboard. He had been well pleased with what he saw: the huts were in straight lines, the roads were neatly marked and the flowerbeds were being dug.

He had telephoned Pyne's quarters at the artillery school and told him everything was in order.

Pyne had thanked him and continued playing patience. The airmail envelope had stood on the mantelpiece. He could hear Garnet moving about in the next room. Pyne had moved the telephone on to the card table at 20:00 hours – thirty minutes before he expected another unscheduled call from Stacy. The telephone had rung as he was laying the cards out for the twentieth time. It was Stacy sounding slightly agitated.

'I'm sorry to trouble you, sir, but we've got a problem.'

'Nothing serious, I hope, captain?'

Stacy had paused:'Well, I'm not sure,sir. But a convoy has just turned up from the Royal Ordnance Factory with a load of Cyclonite HE which isn't on our procurement lists.'

'Tell them to take it back,' Pyne had snapped, wondering if his acting was good enough. Apparently it was, for Stacy's reply had sounded hurt: 'The drivers can't take it back, sir, because police escorts haven't been arranged with county constabularies for the return journey. They were expecting to return with empty trucks.'

'How much is there?'

Stacy had hesitated before answering. 'Twelve trucks.'

'Fully loaded?'

'Yes, sir,' Stacy had said miserably. The complex operation had gone so well until now. 'There's a hundred tonnes of the stuff and a dozen cases of detonators.'

Pyne had erupted: 'Good God, man, who the devil signed the LPOs?'

'It looks like your signature, sir.'

Pyne had thought a pause would be just right at this point. 'I see,' he had said slowly. 'So it doesn't look as if you checked them before releasing them?'

'I suppose not,' Stacy had said.

Pyne had noticed a trace of insolence in the man's voice, for which he couldn't really blame him.

'Have you signed the delivery notes?'

'No, sir. I thought I'd better contact you first.'

Another pause had been required before Pyne had said: 'Well? What do you propose doing with all this high explosive?'

41

'I don't know, sir. I don't like having the stuff on the camp.' Stacy had sounded hopeful, as if Pyne would have the answer.

Pyne had allowed himself a faint smile. The conversation was going extremely well.

'All right, Stacy,' he had said at length. 'Leave it with me. I'll call you back in ten minutes.'

'Thank you, sir,' Stacy had said with relief.

Pyne had replaced the receiver, waited seven minutes and dialled a number.

'Keller? Pyne. The explosive will be delivered in about thirty minutes. Captain Stacy will be asking you where he can store it. I suggest you get him to put it as near the access tunnels as possible . . . And Keller did anyone get a good look at you when you drove the tankers through the camp?'

Keller's answer had been satisfactory. Pyne had cut the line and called Stacy.

'I've been onto National Power and they say you can store the HE in the power station until I arrange transport to have it moved. The superintendent will show you where to put it.'

Thirty minutes after the call the army had shifted five-thousand cases of Cyclonite high explosive into the Vulcan Hall nuclear power station, and so enabled Captain Stacy to enjoy a comfortable night, secure in the knowledge that he had done his best. He hadn't even considered it odd that National Power should agree to storing a huge quantity of high explosive at a nuclear power station.

As Pyne looked down from his Scout he admitted to himself that Stacy had done an excellent job establishing the camp. The U-shaped hundred-acre site was a model of what an army camp should look like.

Pyne set the Scout down in the exact centre of the landing pad and studiously avoided the anxious face of Stacy standing back from the downwash of the slowing rotors. He held the door open as Pyne stepped on to the compressed soil bearing the marks of yesterday's assault by the bull-dozers. Pyne looked curiously about.

42

'You seem to have done extremely well, Stacy,' he said after Stacy had welcomed him.

Stacy's worried face eased slightly. 'It's been a hectic twenty-four hours, sir.'

'I can imagine,' said Pyne, climbing into the waiting Land Rover.

Stacy hesitated before starting the engine. 'You must've seen the explosion, sir?'

'Yes,' replied Pyne noncommittally.

'We had a request from the police for assistance.'

'Of course,' said Pyne coldly. He wanted to change the subject. He pointed. 'What are these men doing?'

'Testing the soil with pH meters, sir. To see what sorts of plants and shrubs will do well here.'

Christ, thought Pyne.

The tour of inspection ended at the camp's nerve centre – the operations room lined with radar screens and dominated by a floor-to-ceiling glass map of the North sea.

Stacy fingered his clipboard and nervously cleared his throat. 'Sir, you may remember I rang you last night about a quantity of HE that arrived from Blackburn?'

Pyne regarded the captain coldly. 'So?'

'I'm afraid some more supplies arrived at midnight,' Stacy confessed, as if it was all his fault. 'It was four large containers from private contractors. The drivers said it was more than their jobs were worth to take the stuff back without a senior officer's signature on the six-forty forms.'

Pyne held out his hand for the sheaf of papers Stacy had removed from his clipboard.

The first list covered a wide variety of tinned food, dried food, clothing and personal effects. The second list authorized the supply of radar equipment, intruder surveillance equipment and a quantity of small arms – all in addition to the stores already supplied from Central Inventory Control Points.

'The superintendent at the power station is a decent sort,' said Stacy, wondering if Pyne was about to explode. 'He said I could store the stuff in the power station along with the HE.'

Pyne thrust the papers in his pocket. 'Very well, Stacy. I'll sort everything out tomorrow with the procurement people. And now I'd like to address the men.'

'There's another thing you should know,' said Stacy, avoiding Pyne's eye.

Pyne sighed.

Stacy pressed on: 'None of the power station staff has come through the camp. We haven't had to issue a single pass.'

'That's right, Captain. I didn't want them coming through the camp. They were taken off by boat. They won't be coming back because there's still some construction work to be done and the engineers have gone on strike. The power station is being closed down. That's why I've decided to use the superintendent's quarters until my trailer arrives.'

Pyne addressed the soldiers for ten minutes. He stressed the secrecy concerning the camp's true function. Although their job was to go to the aid of any platform threatened by terrorists, it was anticipated that the force would eventually become the long-debated third force similar to the French CRS. For the time being the camp was under the direct control of the Cabinet Office and could act only on their orders. At a nod from Pyne, Stacy produced an example of the new uniform and outlined the pay structure; most of the men could expect a fifty percent pay increase. There were smiles all round by the time Stacy had finished speaking.

'One last thing,' said Pyne. 'In view of the civil unrest in the country, you may be called upon to act at any moment. The camp is now on a twenty-four-hour alert, so I'm afraid leave is out of the question, and you won't be able to telephone home.' Pyne smiled. 'The weather is somewhat hot at the moment. If you care to examine supply item fifty-two in Hut . . .' he broke off and glanced at Stacy's clipboard, '. . . in Hut Fifteen, you'll find it's a large portable swimming pool complete with filtration and purification equipment.'

9

Only when he had reached Waterloo Station and locked himself in a toilet cubicle did Corporal Garnet dare open General Pyne's briefcase. Inside he found, as the general had said, his discharge papers and a letter to the Midland Bank. There was also a generous cheque, a letter to the Thames Water Authority notifying them of the transfer of ownership of Pyne's seven-metre Freeman cabin cruiser to Ian Garnet, a bunch of keys and a wallet containing several credit cards, which were useless to him, and £500 in cash.

Dazed, the former corporal stuffed the papers back into the briefcase, pushed the money into his hip pocket and left the cubicle without pulling the grubby piece of string that served as a chain.

He drifted aimlessly round the station, uncertain what to do. Blackboards outside the platform barriers announced British Rail's regret at their failure to provide normal service owing to continuing industrial action. Even their electronic arrivals and departures boards weren't working.

The general had mentioned his daughter, Maggie. Even thinking about her made Garnet's toes curl in embarrassment at the way she used to treat him – always taking it for granted he was her personal servant, making him carry her shopping, clean out the swimming pool in blistering sun.

Bitch, thought Garnet savagely. Stinking, cock-teasing little bitch.

There were no trains to Weybridge until tomorrow.

Garnet decided to spend the night in London, He would find a woman – a special woman who would do all the things they usually demanded extra money for. He touched

45

the money in his pocket, savouring the characteristic banknote texture.

He could afford that special woman now.

The general's daughter would have to wait.

10

Pyne's flight from the camp to the Vulcan Hall power station was only a matter of lifting the Scout to two hundred feet, skirting the cooling towers and landing between Hugh Patterson's JetRanger and the two petrol tankers on the wide concrete apron that separated the power station from the river.

He remained in his seat as the rotors slowed, and decided on an immediate confrontation with Keller. The nuclear physicist was in charge in the control room: he should have warned Pyne about the Royal Navy helicopter. It would have to be now; there was no point in letting the man undermine his authority over a period of several days and then acting.

Louise Campion came out of the glazed front entrance to the power station and walked across to the Scout helicopter. Pyne watched her approach while he thought about what he would say to Keller.

Louise Campion was the country's top radiation biologist. She was a few years younger than Pyne. She was always immaculately dressed in well-cut clothes that disguised her slightly overweight figure. The long battle throughout her career to establish her supremacy in a man's world had left her with a brittle personality and an aloof nature. Pyne felt that even after the many meetings when the takeover was being planned he still knew very little about her.

'We were worried in case you were too near the blast,' she said as Pyne climbed out of the Scout.

'Thank you, Louise. But I was even nearer a Navy helicopter,' Pyne replied sarcastically. 'The damn thing tried to blast me out of the sky.'

'Didn't Ralph warn you?' She sounded genuinely surprised.

'I'm not prepared to discuss it now. Tell Hugh and Keller that I want to hold an immediate progress meeting.'

The floor-to ceiling glass walls of the power station's control room afforded a panoramic view of the Thames to the south, the four film cooling towers to the east and the entire power-station complex to the north with the new army camp just beyond. In the days when the power station was fully operational, every function could be controlled from the curved consoles grouped round the main console near the table where the four terrorists were sitting. A radar repeater stood on a tubular trolley beside the table. The beam of light sweeping round the screen created a glowing out line of the Thames Estuary.

Pyne looked up from his check-list and met Keller's blue-flecked eyes.

'And the closed-circuit television is working satisfactorily?'

Keller smiled. 'Perfectly, general.'

'And the radar?'

Keller nodded to the repeater. 'You can see for yourself,' he said.

'If Mr Patterson and Miss Campion can answer questions properly, there's no reason why you shouldn't.'

Keller glanced at Hugh Patterson and Louise Campion. 'The radar is working, general.'

'Then why the hell didn't you warn me about the Lynx?' Pyne demanded.

'Is that what it was? I tried to identify it from Jane's. Keller pointed to an open book on the table. He smiled at Pyne. 'We couldn't see it very well as you were too far off, but you seemed to be giving it some trouble.'

Keller's tone was infuriatingly smooth.

'You could've called me on the radio!' snapped Pyne.

Keller looked hurt. 'I'm terribly sorry for what happened, general. But how was I to know it would attack you? I thought it was a routine flight – it was so soon after your delivery, and too soon for the government to close the zone to air traffic. Which they have now done, of course.'

Keller's mannered behaviour angered Pyne. He checked an impulse to reach across the table and hit him. 'I suppose you've heard about the refinery?' he said icily.

'Only that our aim was good. You can see what's left from the fuelling machine roof.'

'One hundred and forty-five maintenance workers killed,' said Pyne icily.

Hugh Patterson looked shocked. Louise Campion's face went pale.

'It's terrible,' said Keller before anyone could speak. 'But at least they didn't die in vain. Their deaths will prove to the government that we mean business.' Keller looked down at the table, avoiding the three pairs of eyes on him. 'We agreed a gesture was essential to demonstrate our determination. We couldn't afford for the government to think we might be bluffing. And besides, if you look at the inspection tunnels, you'll see we've prepared to kill millions.'

Pyne closed his eyes.

'Are you all right, general?' asked Keller.

Pyne opened his eyes. Keller was looking at him in genuine concern. Pyne wished he could understand him. He turned his attention to Hugh Patterson, who had been waiting patiently to speak. Patterson was a large, powerfully-built man with a ready sense of humour. His small factory outside London had struggled to survive during the fifties until Patterson had decided to switch to the design and production of radioactive waste containers. Since then his business had steadily grown and now was one of the largest suppliers to the world's nuclear-energy authorities. When Keller had returned from the United States Patterson had offered him the post of technical director – a task Keller performed well, apart from his refusal to return to America.

'Hugh?' invited Pyne.

Patterson cleared his throat. 'Everything went according to plan, Conrad. The explosive is all in place and the supplies are stowed away – including all that bloody corned beef. The supplies turned up just as you said they would. Captain Stacy was anxious to get rid of them. I must congratulate you on your choice of executive officer,' Patterson grinned at Pyne.

'Where are the hostages?' asked Pyne.

Patterson hesitated and glanced at Keller.

'I let them go,' said Keller.

Stacy told me they hadn't been through the camp'.

'By boat,' Keller replied, meeting Pyne's stare.

'Louise?'

'Radiation levels throughout the station are normal,' said Louise Campion. 'I've installed the extra hazard monitors round the reactors. But I'd like to check all of us in two weeks when we've had a chance to settle down and I've ironed the bugs out of my X-ray equipment.' She smiled. 'I'll be pestering you all for urine, Blood and lung tissue samples.'

Pyne smiled, and looked down at his check-list. 'You've all covered your absence?'

Louise Campion grimaced. 'I've taken a job with CERN. I heard someone in my department say at my presentation that I was probably off to look for a husband.'

Everyone laughed.

'Mind you, I could be tempted by the man who's rented my house.'

'Ralph and I are on a round-the-world trip to seek new markets,' said Hugh Patterson. ' My ex-wife is acting chairman while I'm gone.'

Pyne nodded. He looked carefully at the three faces before speaking:

'We've discussed this several times already, but now we're actually in the power station, have any of you got any doubts about what we're doing? Now is the time to say if you have.'

No one spoke.

'And the length of time we might have to remain here?'

Again silence.

'God forbid that it should be five years,' said Pyne. 'If all goes well, we'll be out in a year, but if you're not prepared to accept five years, then say so now.'

Silence.

Pyne folded his check-list and stood up. 'Hugh, I'd like you to take me on a tour of inspection, please.'

'We found everything laid out exactly as per my plans,' said Patterson, leading Pyne down the stairs beneath the concrete apron. He set the knurled wheel combination lock on the massive door at the bottom of the rough-cast steps. Both men grasped the spoked hand-wheel and heaved backwards.

The circular, tapered door which fitted into its corresponding hole like a giant plug swung open. The opening was just large enough for one man to climb through. It reminded Pyne of a bank vault door. Patterson went through first and helped Pyne to scramble in after him.

'There's a safety interlock that prevents the door being locked on the outside if anyone is in here,' said Patterson as he pulled the heavy door shut.

They were in a concrete-lined tunnel about two-metres high. Wall-lights in wire cages extended into the distance along each side of the tunnel. Armoured power cables snaked along the walls. The footsteps of the two men sounded curiously muffled in the claustrophobic surroundings.

'How does air get down here?'

Patterson pointed up. An opening in the ceiling disappeared into the darkness. 'Ventilator shafts,' he said.

'Did you use the hostages to shift the Cyclonite as we planned?' asked Pyne.

'Yes,' Patterson's voice sounded strained. 'Over here we have the–'

'Were they co-operative?'

Patterson hesitated. 'Yes. Keller made certain they would be.'

Pyne saw the fear in Patterson's eyes. 'What did he do?'

'Conrad, I–'

'*What did he do?*'

Patterson looked down at the concrete floor. 'He shot one of them.'

'Jesus Christ,' Pyne muttered. 'Why?'

'A girl . . . Just here. Look.' Patterson pointed to the floor.

There was a large brown stain that had spread over a wide area due to the capillary action of the unsealed concrete. Footprints, the same colour were etched into the surrounding floor. They led away and disappeared where the tunnel branched to the right.

Pyne picked up some spent nine-millimetre shell cases. 'Why?' he repeated quietly.

Patterson looked away, refusing to meet Pyne's eyes. 'I came down when I heard the shooting. According to the staff, she dropped a case and caused a pile-up in the chain. Keller said she tried to rush him.'

'Who do you believe?'

'Keller. I can't imagine him hurting anyone unless he was forced to.'

Pyne took in the bloodstains splattered on the walls and ceiling. 'Can't you, Hugh? In that case you're a worse judge of character than I imagined.'

Neither man spoke for a moment.

'I'll show you the charges.' said Patterson at length, moving to a branch in the tunnel.

The radioactive waste was stored in stainless-steel flasks housed in three triple-lined containers whose total capacity was 100,000 cubic metres. Each container was encapsulated in thick biological shields of concrete and lead. A system of high-pressure water pumps removed the heat from the vicious liquid that seethed and boiled in their own primitive energies. A period ten times longer than the day since the laying of the first stone of the Great Pyramid would have to pass before the deadly plutonium and strontium isotopes could be released into the environment.

'This is far more than was shown on the plans,' said Pyne.

'I did warn you,' said Patterson. 'The Green Warriors stopped half this lot being dumped in its repositories. It was moved here for interim storage while the courts tried to sort out the mess.'

Pyne nodded. The previous month five Green Warriors had been killed in a demonstration at a repository site in the Midlands. As a result the truck drivers handling the waste flasks had refused to deliver their cargoes.

The inspection tunnel which skirted the periphery of the silos was lined with hazard monitors which maintained a continuous check on background radiation levels – a task they and their descendants would have to carry out for the next forty-five thousand years.

Pyne followed Patterson down the sloping access tunnel beneath the silos. The faint noise he had noticed when he first entered the tunnel was now much louder. He asked Patterson what it was.

'It's the cooling water passing through the outer jackets,' Patterson explained. 'Electricity for the pumps is on an uninterruptable supply line with backups. They won't risk cutting us off therefore we've tapped into them for all our other supply needs.'

'Odd that we should be occupying a power station and worried about our electricity being cut off,' Pyne observed wryly.

Patterson waved his hand round. 'So what do you think of our arrangements?'

52

Pyne was impressed. The cartons of Cyclonite high explosive were stacked in neat rows along the inspection tunnel's inner wall. The gap between each carton was bridged by a short length of wire connected to a detonator on the side of each of the cartons. Each case was marked with an ICI batch number and the chemical formula for nitrated hexamethlenetetramine: one of most powerful explosives in the world.

The line of grey cardboard cases extended to the far end of the tunnel, where it turned through ninety degrees.

Pyne noticed more of the bloodstains round a steel hatchway set into the wall. 'What's in there, Hugh?'

'It's just a thousand mill pipe we've filled with Cyclonite.'

The urgency in his voice alerted Pyne. He placed his hand on the hatch. Patterson stepped forward and grasped him by the arm.

'It would be best not to, Conrad.'

Pyne brushed Patterson's arm away, opened the hatch and peered into the dark pipe. He could see nothing.

'A torch please, Hugh.'

Patterson reluctantly passed Pyne his torch. The narrow beam of light revealed a chain of the grey cartons disappearing into the darkness. There were more of the bloodstains. They were still wet and glistened when the feeble light flashed on them. Pyne crawled a little way into the pipe and shone the light ahead. Ten yards from the hatch the cartons changed colour. Something had been placed on top of them. It was a girl, lying face down. Naked, with a line of nine-millimetre perforations across her shoulder blades. Pyne tried to turn her over but she seemed to be stuck to the cartons. He pushed hard. Her body came free with a sickly tearing sound. There was nothing left of the front of her body: the nine-millimetre shells had left a gaping hole where her rib-cage and breasts had been. She looked about Maggie's age.

Pyne felt the waves of exhaustion drain his vitality. The shattered body of the girl had, more than anything else, impressed upon him the sheer magnitude of the irrevocable step he had taken. He backed down the pipe. Patterson watched him with concern as he emerged.

'Is she there?'

'Yes – she's there all right.' Pyne handed the torch back to Patterson. 'Why is she naked?'

'One of them complained about the heat. I think Keller made them all strip.'

Pyne clenched his teeth. He had a vivid picture of the scene in the tunnel the previous night: the silent, sweating power-station decommissioning staff passing the heavy cartons from hand to hand; the girl who let one case slip from her exhausted hands and the thunderous roar of Keller's Sterling in the confined space. She weighed only about eight stone – the impact would have slammed her against the side of the tunnel.

Pyne sat on one of the cartons. 'How long have you employed Keller?'

'Five years.'

'And in that time, you never realized–'

'He's a first-class physicist,' Patterson interrupted defensively. 'We needed him.' He paused and looked at the hatch. 'Keller said the girl rushed him.'

'She was shot in the back.'

'Don't be absurd, Conrad.'

'Take a close look. Her chest is a mass of exit wounds.'

Patterson sat beside Pyne and stared at the opposite wall. He could think of nothing to say.

'He's mad,' said Pyne shortly. 'A fucking psycho.'

Patterson turned to look at Pyne. It was rare for the army officer to swear. 'Aren't we all?' he said quietly.

Pyne stood. 'Let's get the inspection over and done with,' he said brusquely.

The two men spent the next five minutes examining the IRIS (Infra-Red Intruder System) detectors that had been deactivated for the inspection tour. The sensors were positioned at regular intervals along the tunnels. It would be

54

impossible for anyone to enter the galleries without their body heat sounding the alarms in the control room.

They were about to enter the last tunnel when a nearby public address speaker clicked and hummed.

'There are two aircraft in the vicinity,' Keller's voice grated metallically. 'One is fifteen kilometres away and closing in fast, the other is much nearer. I can see it through binoculars. It's a Beechcraft Bonanza, flying straight towards us. It seems our instructions are being ignored, so I'm proposing to launch the second Honest John within five minutes.'

11

Now that sex was beyond him, one of the few pleasures Arnold Cox-Spender had left was the ritual morning in bed reading the Sunday papers, looking for his name.

He always read the colour supplements first in the way that a child will always turn to the brightest pebble. Maybe it was a blessing that the Sunday papers were getting thinner each week – there was less to search through. But once again, his name appeared nowhere.

The smell of cooking wafted up the stairs. He would get up in time for lunch and remind his housekeeper to use the extractor fan.

A sudden dull boom shook the windows.

He was mentally composing a complaining memorandum to the Marshall of the Royal Air Force when his bedside telephone rang.

It was a fast journey to London in the Downing Street car sent by the despicable Simpson; all the traffic lights on the route changed to green at their approach. Cox-Spender reflected that it must be urgent for the PM's private secretary to send a ministerial car.

He perched on the edge of his seat to prevent his suit sticking to him in the heat. He had been unable to have a bath because his housekeeper had filled both baths to the brim to provide a drinking water supply during the cuts. He opened the window, but the stench from uncollected refuse simmering in the sun was appalling. He noticed that the fool of a driver was taking him to the Trafalgar Square end of Whitehall. He tapped on the glass in annoyance several times before he noticed the microphone.

'Downing Street's the other way,' he said three times, remembering to press the button only the third time, 'opposite Richmond Terrace.' The driver was obviously a Sunday standby who didn't know his London.

'Yes, sir,' replied the driver, who knew London better than Cox-Spender. 'But I was instructed to take you to this end.'

The car stopped outside the Old Admiralty Building – a four-hundred metre walk from Downing Street. Simpson came out to meet him.

'Good morning, Spender.'

Cox-Spender bristled. He detested Simpson, if only because he never used his full name, certainly never deigned to call anyone 'sir' except the Prime Minister.

'What's all this about, dragging me up here on a Sunday?' demanded Cox-Spender, trying to shake off Simpson's grip on his arm as he was led into the building.

'I'm afraid we'll have to use the tunnel, said Simpson apologetically. 'All the corridors are locked. These new security precautions you know.'

Cox-Spender wondered if Simpson's mother had loved her son.

Halfway along the tunnel was a spur which branched under St James's Park to Buckingham Palace. Nobody could remember if it had ever been used, and in any case it was sealed by a massive iron door whose key had been lost in the days of empire.

After two hundred metres Cox-Spender's legs were aching, but he strode on grimly, determined not to show weakness in front of the disagreeable Simpson.

56

'You've heard about the Thames Haven oil refinery?' asked Simpson.

'No. What about it?'

'It was blown up about forty-five minutes ago. By terrorists.'

Simpson smiled at Cox-Spender's horror-struck expression.

Ten minutes later Cox-Spender was shown into the Prime Minister's private office. The politician was sitting at his desk. He made no attempt to rise to greet the Government's Assistant Scientific Adviser.

'I thought there was to be a meeting,' began Cox-Spender, sitting suddenly as Simpson pushed a chair into the back of his knees.

'There is,' said the Prime Minister. 'Right now. Between the three of us.' He smiled at Cox-Spender. Simpson was right, he thought. Just the manageable sort we need.

There was an opened airmail envelope on the politician's desk and a single typewritten sheet of paper. He pushed the document across the desk to Cox-Spender. 'Read. Digest,' he invited. 'And then bubble over with brilliant suggestions.'

Cox-Spender picked up the document and started to read:

POLITICAL MEASURES
1 Government to commit UK to the setting up of a
   single defence force for the European Community
   by the end of the century.
2 Capital punishment to be re-introduced for murder
   and illegal possession of hard drugs.
3 Capital punishment to be introduced for possession
   of all firearms after a one month amnesty period for
   handing over of firearms to police.
4 Trial by jury for terrorist offences to be suspended.
   Indictable terrorist offenses to be heard by tribunals
   and right of appeal to be abolished.

5 Immediate withdrawal of armed forces from
  Northern Ireland. Administration of Ulster to be
  transferred to Irish Republic.
6 Overseas aid to be suspended until further notice.
7 Public transport to be free and financed from
  central government.
8 500,000 hectares of land to be made available
  immediately and sold in quarter hectare plots to
  enable people to build their own homes.

Cox-Spender reached the foot of the page and looked up at
Simpson and the Prime Minister.

'Where've you got up to?' demanded the Prime Minister.

Cox-Spender's eyes scrabbled wildly over the sheet of
paper. 'Number Eight,' he said, barely able to choke the
words out. 'Now turn over and read the economic measures,' the Prime Minister suggested.

Cox-Spender's near lifeless fingers fumbled turning the
document over.

ECONOMIC MEASURES
  9 Government to participate in the negotiations for
    the setting up of a central European reserve bank
    and the introduction of a common EC currency
    before 31st December 1999.
10 Credit card and charge card purchases to be
   limited to £50.
11 100% luxury duty to be levied on all
   manufactured goods imported from outside EC.
12 Poll Tax and business rates to be scrapped. All
   local government funding to be from central
   government.
13 VAT to be raised to 25%.
14 Scope of VAT to be extended to include all retail
   goods including insurance, domestic energy
   supplies and agricultural supplies.
15 Draft emergency bill embracing all these
   provisions to be submitted to us for approval

within a hundred hours of the time given on the envelope.

(Signed)

Conrad Pyne, formerly of
'Sand Hills', St Georges Hill

Ralph Keller, formerly of
'High Pine', Ashley Park

Hugh Patterson, formerly of
'Brunel Hall', St Georges Hill

Louise Campion, formerly of
'Badger Place', St Georges Hill

Cox-Spender finished reading and looked up in bewilderment at the two men who were watching him carefully.

'I don't understand it,' he said. 'What is it? A list of the government's future plans?'

'It will be unless you come up with something,' replied the Prime Minister sourly. 'Read the last condition again.'

Cox-Spender's eyes skated over Article 15. It still didn't make sense.

The Prime Minister sighed. 'Those four signatories have seized the Vulcan Hall nuclear power station on Canvey Island. The power station is about to be decommissioned and by some administrative cock-up, the nuclear police unit had been withdrawn. The signatories claim to have placed a large quantity of high explosives round the radioactive-waste silos and have threatened to blow them up unless we introduce those measures. Now do you understand?'

Cox-Spender stared at the Prime Minister and Simpson in turn. His eyes dropped to the sheet of paper that had slipped from his hand and was lying on the table.

'But there's no radioactive waste stored at Vulcan Hall,' he protested. 'Only empty silos. The Cheshire repository—'

The Prime Minister sighed. 'It was agreed that the Cheshire repository wouldn't be used until the report into

59

the riots was published. The waste was moved to Vulcan Hall for temporary storage

'But . . . it's impossible to blow-up those silos!'

'Why?' demanded the Prime Minister.

'They're deep underground. The sides, if they're to specification, must be at least three-metres of stainless steel, lead and concrete. They've been designed to withstand a major earthquake.'

'They couldn't blow them up?' inquired the Prime Minister. 'You'd stake your professional reputation on that?'

Cox-Spender saw the trap. 'How much explosive have they got?'

Simpson smiled. 'A hundred tonnes of Cyclonite, whatever that is.'

Cox-Spender began to sweat and wondered why it had to be him. Why hadn't they called in the Chief Scientific Adviser? It wasn't fair.

The Prime Minister noticed the beads of perspiration with satisfaction. They had chosen well. 'I don't know what this Cyclonite is,' he said smoothly. 'But if it's placed under the silos, would I be right in assuming that a hundred tonnes is enough to blow not only them up, but most of Canvey Island as well?'

Cox-Spender could only nod. For a wild, escapist moment, he could considered resigning on the spot, but his pension . . .'

'Maybe they're bluffing,' he blurted out.

'It's possible,' agreed the Prime Minister. 'But they certainly weren't bluffing about Thames Haven.'

'How did they do it?'

'With an Honest John missile.'

There was total silence in the room apart from the refined tick of an eighteenth-century clock over the Adam fireplace.

'We'd have another Cheynobel on our hands,' the Prime Minister commented.

'It would be worse than Cheynobel,' said Cox-Spender. 'There would be the fallout from the waste and the power station's reactors.'

'If only they were asking for something sensible,' complained the Prime Minister. 'A million pounds would be much more convenient. I could call the governor of the Bank of England and get him to produce it here. That's if we've got a million pounds,' he added as an afterthought.

'Perhaps they *could* be bought,' said Cox-Spender hopefully.

'Take another look at those who signed,' invited the Prime Minister. 'Hugh Patterson's got more money in Swiss numbered accounts than we've got in gold and dollar reserves. Also, one of his companies designed and built the silos, so he probably knows the best place to position the explosive for the best, or rather worst, effect.'

'Conrad Pyne,' said Cox-Spender, looking at the ultimatum. 'I've heard of him.'

Simpson intervened: 'He's in charge of the new oil platform defence force which was set up at your suggestion, Mr Spender.'

'Oh, now look. I only suggested it. The idea was approved by the Policy Review Committee and the chiefs of staff. You can't blame me—'

'Nobody's blaming you for anything,' said the Prime Minister soothingly. 'All we want you to do is to take a look at the Thames Haven site and make plausible pronouncements on the possible cause. I've had the area sealed off. After all, we don't want DTI and health and safety inspectors tramping all over the place picking up bits of Honest Johns, do we?'

'I'll go first thing in the morning, Prime Minister,' said Cox-Spender.

'First thing now, Cox-Spender. After that, I want you to take a look at the Vulcan Hall set-up and see how strong they are.'

61

Cox-Spender was appalled. 'Go to Vulcan Hall? But . . . but how do I get in?'

The Prime Minister looked blankly at Simpson before turning to Cox-Spender. 'Try the front door,' he suggested. 'That is, if power stations have front doors.'

Cox-Spender had the feeling that powerful forces were being aligned against him. The ground was being sucked from under his feet, Simpson and the PM were smiling at him as if he could save the situation. He decided to show them the sort of person he really was. He would be like Harry Truman and rise to the task. With a firm jaw he asked: 'How do I contact them?'

'Try the telephone,' said Simpson. 'You'll probably find them listed under Power Gen, or the Central Electricity Generating Board if your phone directory's out-of-date.'

'Are they armed?' The question made him sound scared – which he was.

Simpson glanced at a paper on his desk. 'They've got command of two hundred soldiers with full combat kit, several armoured personnel carriers, God knows what in the way of small arms. Oh yes – and a couple of Apache gunships.'

Cox-Spender blinked. The Harry Truman resolve melted. 'How did they—'

'The new base depot and headquarters of the Oil Rig Defence under the command of General Pyne were established yesterday by the Royal Engineers,' said Simpson. 'They're located on Canvey Island because Pyne assured us it would be the best place for training purposes and launching offensives against oil rigs that have been taken over by terrorists.'

All the fight went out of Cox-Spender. 'Don't you think the Chief Scientific Adviser would be better able to deal with the situation, Prime Minister?'

'He's in hospital,' pointed out Simpson.

This was news to Cox-Spender. 'I didn't know. Is he . . .?'

'It was a road accident. Hit-and-run when he was crossing the Mall. Nasty business, but he's expected to be up and about next month.'

Cox-Spender felt the two pairs of speculative eyes boring into him. 'Well, I'd better be off then,' he said lamely. 'May I use the front door please? It's rather a long walk to the Admiralty—'

'I'm sorry ,' said the Prime Minister. 'But your car will be waiting for you there. So perhaps . . .'

'Yes, of course, Prime Minister.'

Simpson opened the door.

'One thing,' said the Prime Minister as Cox-Spender turned to leave. 'Don't try any heroics will you? We don't want you attempting James Bond stunts on this job?' He smiled at Cox-Spender and continued. 'I'm the only one round here who's got the sort of licence he was supposed to have, and if you mess things up, I might be tempted to use it.'

Cox-Spender had never read a James Bond book but the Prime Minister's words carried an ominous impact.

After Cox-Spender had left on his long walk back to the Old Admiralty Building the Prime Minister sat at his desk and toyed with the massive amber paperweight presented to him by Welsh miners . . . what was left of them. Simpson watched him carefully.

'Do you think we've picked the right man?' said the Prime Minister.

'Personally, I think he's ideal.' replied Simpson evenly.

The Prime Minister allowed the paperweight to slide from one hand to the other. 'Too bad if we're wrong,' he said.

'Disastrous. But I don't think we are.'

The paperweight spun on the blotter. Yellow light flashed round the walls.

'Let's hope so, Simpson.'

Pyne was the first to leave the inspection tunnel and race across the apron towards the two petrol tankers. Then he hesitated, uncertain which tanker still contained an Honest John. Patterson followed only a few paces behind.

'Which one?' yelled Pyne.

Patterson pointed to the tanker facing the Thames.

Pyne could hear the electric servo motors start as he dived into the driver's cab. 'How do I shut it off?' he shouted desperately at Patterson.

'You can't!' croaked Patterson, gesturing up at the power station. 'It's radio-controlled. Keller has the control transmitter!'

Pyne cursed and jumped down.

In a few seconds the dummy five thousand-litre tank would be separating into two halves and opening to the sky like a giant clam. Pyne experienced a wave of panic as a new sound was added to the steady whine from the servo motors – the harsh growl of powerful motors building up hydraulic pressure for the rams to thrust the Honest John to its launch elevation. The tanker had been parked with its tyres positioned on carefully drawn chalk marks so that its concealed cargo, when exposed, would be pointing at the densely populated East End of London.

'A Sterling!' Pyne yelled to Patterson. 'For Christ's sake hurry!'

Patterson disappeared into the power station.

Pyne stood staring helplessly at the tanker. He could hear the piston engine of the approaching aircraft. Then there was another sound – the metallic snap of the electric latches that held the two halves of the dummy tanker closed. The long, oval container began to shudder.

Patterson appeared carrying a Sterling submarine-gun. Pyne snatched it out of his hands and raced towards the tanker.

A widening gap had appeared along the top of the tanker as Pyne threw himself flat on the concrete and released the Sterling's safety-catch.

The tankers's only source of power when its engine wasn't running was a large lead-acid battery hanging in a cradle beneath the chassis. Pyne took careful aim and fired. The battery exploded into shards of bituminous compound that clanged against the underside of the petrol container.

Pyne held the stream of fire steady his eyes tightly shut and face turned away from the jets of acid spraying from the shattered battery. Bullets tore into the battery cradle. It fell. The unrecognizable bulk of the accumulator swayed drunkenly back and forth for a few seconds before the remains of it's black casing fell to the ground leaving only a cluster of riddled power cells hanging by the two heavy power cables.

Pyne stopped firing. His ears were ringing in the sudden silence and his hands were burning painfully from the splashes of sulphuric acid.

The tanker was now impotent, as was the missile. The second Honest John could never be launched.

The pale-blue Bonanza flashed past above the river – heading towards London.

13

Simpson read the telex from RAF Manston at 13:15 – fifteen minutes after Cox-Spender's departure to examine the devastated Thames Haven oil refinery. For the first time that Sunday, he felt slightly uneasy. He crossed the carpeted corridor and tapped on the door to the Prime Minister's office. He entered without waiting for an invitation – a system devised many years before to let the Prime Minister know he had an urgent message.

The Prime Minister looked up expectantly from the Sunday papers as Simpson entered the room.

'I'm afraid an aircraft has penetrated the prohibited zone, sir,' said Simpson, without preamble. 'A Beechcraft Bonanza.'

The Prime Minister's face showed a fleeting trace of alarm. 'When was this?'

'About forty-five minutes ago. I don't think it's anything to worry about, sir. Not now, anyway. Manston scrambled a Tornado to intercept it, but they were too late. The aircraft was too near the power station–'

'But Simpson,' interrupted the Prime Minister. 'You issued strict orders that no aircraft was to be allowed in the vicinity of the Thames Estuary – correct?'

Simpson fumed inwardly. He detested mistakes. 'There was a breakdown in communications, sir. Manston said the Bonanza wasn't interested in Vulcan Hall – it flew straight past.'

'They didn't harass it, did they?'

'No, sir. They told the Tornado to break off – on my orders.'

The Prime Minister relaxed.

'Just as well. Probably a Sunday joyrider. Chase one with a Tornado in a prohibited zone and it'll be all over the flying clubs in southern England before nightfall.' The Prime Minister looked sharply at his secretary. 'Did the RAF get its registration?'

'Yes, sir. I'll see if I can get onto someone at the Air Registration Board. I'll have the owner's name and address on your desk in sixty minutes.'

'Thirty minutes please, Simpson.'

14

Cox-Spender was hungry, thirsty, sweating profusely and feeling very much aggrieved at having to spend his Sunday afternoon stumbling round the wreckage of the Thames Haven oil refinery. The only consolation was that it took his mind off his coming visit to the Vulcan Hall nuclear power station.

He sat on a section of smashed pipe and wondered what sort of statement he could issue that would convince everyone that the area was too dangerous to allow rescue teams to start work.

As he gloomily surveyed the devastation he could hear the distant arguments between the police and families of missing refinery workers who were protesting because a search and rescue operation was not allowed to start. The strident voice of the chief constable of Essex was telling the crowd over a loudhailer that work would start as soon as the government's Assistant Scientific Adviser had declared the area safe. Fighting had broken out as the crowd tried to break through the police cordon.

On the river, what was left of the Thames Division fleet of police launches battled to head off an armada of small craft crowded with sightseers whose boats had not been swamped by the tidal wave.

Cox-Spender climbed to his feet and stood forlornly amid the nightmare of twisted pipes and flattened distillation columns. Chemical engineering had not been his subject, and he suspected that whatever he said would be torn to shreds by engineers and designers who knew the refinery.

He walked slowly along an avenue that seemed reasonably clear of debris – probably a road originally, but there was no way of being certain, so total was the appalling destruction.

There was a sickening smell hanging in the still air. Cox-Spender shivered despite the heat. Perhaps it was the smell of death. Cox-Spender did not know what death smelt like, but he was sure if it smelt of anything it would be the suffocating stench that was now clinging to the refinery.

A pale-blue Beechcraft Bonanza light aircraft circled above, drowning the notes he was dictating into a pocket tape recorder. He tried not to look at the far-off cooling towers of Vulcan Hall standing to pale attention ten kilometres away in the heat-warped distance. His scalp crawled at the prospect of the forthcoming visit and the people he would be talking to there. In his mind was a picture of ruthless terrorists with hard eyes staring through slits in black hoods.

Half an hour later he returned to what had been the refinery's main gate.

The chief constable came forward anxiously to greet him. 'We were getting worried about you, sir,' he said, relieved that Cox-Spender appeared to be intact.

'I'm, quite capable of looking after myself, thank you,' Cox-Spender replied acidly. He enjoyed exercising authority over important officials. The Prime Minister had given him sweeping powers and he intended making full use of them.

The chief constable ignored the childish jibe. 'There's a Mr Maynard wants to see you urgently,' he said. 'He's waiting in the trailer.'

Ivor Maynard was a small, dapper man who came straight to the point.

'Thank Christ you've allowed no one on to the site,' he said breathlessly to Cox-Spender.

Cox-Spender blinked.

'We'd cleared out one of those fractional distillers to process some special liquid rocket fuel, and now it's leaking out of the underground storage tank. If it combines with–'

'How do you know it's leaking?' demanded Cox-Spender, determined to remain master of the situation.

The little engineer stared at the Assistant Scientific Adviser.

'Christ man! Can't you smell it? We've got to get all these policeman and people back another hundred yards!'

Cox-Spender beamed at Maynard and wondered if his visit to the power station would be as successful.

15

'There's one thing you should know about me, Mitch,' said Maggie, setting the eight by ten prints on the general's dining-room table. 'In case you ever decide to propose to me, I'm warning you that I'm better in a darkroom that I am in a kitchen.'

'Don't worry, honey. I'm a gifted cook. It's just that I'm too modest to boast about it.'

Mitchell picked up the damp prints. There was no sign of the drill-string. Nothing had survived that terrible explosion.

'Well?' said Maggie.

Mitchell swore softly. 'Sabotage.'

'How do you know?'

Mitchell jabbed at one of the photographs. 'I can't be absolutely certain, but it looks as if that's the point where the explosion took place. Right at that hub. One explosion – not the whole series of explosions you'd expect when a place like that goes up.'

Maggie studied the photograph closely. Mitchell was right: most of the wrecked, flattened columns radiated outwards from a central focal point at one end of the refinery.

'Perhaps they had something special there which would've caused the explosion?'

Mitchell shook his head. 'I know that refinery. It looks as if the explosion took place in the employees' carpark. That can only mean sabotage.

There was silence for a few moments. 'Perhaps there's some more news on the radio,' Maggie suggested.

She went into the kitchen and returned with the portable radio. The news was still scant. The government's Assistant Scientific Adviser had just issued a statement saying there was a danger of further explosions. An interview followed with a senior engineer who emphatically denied that further explosions would be as serious as the first explosion. No, he didn't know what had caused it. No, he would not comment until the Assistant Scientific Adviser had completed his preliminary inquiries.

The newsreader promised more information as it became available.

Maggie switched off the radio and picked up one of the prints. 'It doesn't look as if there's anything left to explode,' she commented.

Mitchell took the photograph and looked at it for some seconds. 'Exactly the same thought was going through my head.' he said.

She picked up another picture. It was one of the first photographs Mitchell had taken just before they reached the refinery to clear possible fogged film at the start of the roll. In the foreground were the Vulcan Hall nuclear cooling towers.

'I wonder what my father is doing there,' she said.

Mitchell looked at the print over her shoulder. At the edge were the two helicopters standing near the petrol tankers. The registration letters on the American-built JetRanger were clearly visible. The figure of a man seemed to be running towards the tankers.

'Is he friendly with Patterson?' asked Mitchell disinterestedly.

'Much more so lately. I came home one evening a few weeks ago and there were several cars parked outside. One of them was Hugh Patterson's. I went away. It's unusual for my father to entertain.'

'Are you sure the JetRanger belongs to Patterson? I know they're rare over here, but it's just possible that it could belong to someone else.'

'I can easily check,' said Maggie. She crossed to a sideboard and returned with a photograph album. She placed it on the table and leafed through the pages. Some of the prints were not properly mounted and spilled out. She picked up one of the loose prints, compared it with one of the pictured taken that morning, and pushed it in front of Mitchell.

'Look.'

The picture from the album showed a small crowd holding drinks, posing beside a helicopter parked on the lawn before a magnificent Moorish-style house: a St Georges Hill scene.

'I took that picture last year at one of Hugh Patterson's barbecues,' Maggie explained. 'You see? The chopper's registration letters in your photo and mine are the same.'

Mitchell's mind was on the problem of his lost drill-string, but he was sufficiently interested in Maggie to go along with her concern about the whereabouts of her father. He looked at the party photograph.

'Who's the guy sitting in the chopper's door?'

'Oh, that's Ralph Keller – Hugh Patterson's chief physicist or something. He's rather nice. He lives alone and is terribly shy with girls. The woman is Louise Campion. She lives on the other side of the estate. I think there's something between her and Patterson – she's often been over here with him for drinks.'

The girl's voice washed over Mitchell as he stared at the pictures of the devastated refinery.

'Am I boring you, Mitch . . . Mitch?' She put her arm round the American and stood beside him looking down at the pictures.

'Was it worth a lot of money?' she asked gently.

Mitchell nodded. 'It could be the end of my business.'

'I'm sorry. I should have realised. There's me going on about my father while you're–'

'It doesn't matter, honey. I guess I'll sort something out.' He slipped his arm round her shoulder. It was almost an unconscious gesture.

'Are you hungry?' Maggie asked.

Mitchell suddenly realized that he had not eaten that day. 'Yes, I'm starving.'

'Would you like me to cook you something?'

'That would be–' He broke off and grinned. 'Hell, no. I need to keep fit if I'm to tackle this problem.'

He propelled Maggie towards the french windows. 'I wouldn't be a gentleman to let you cook in that mess. You sit yourself down by the pool, and *I'll* cook.'

Maggie laughed. 'That's the sort of proposition I like.'

Mitchell returned to the dining-room. He gathered up the photographs and thrust them into a yellow Kodak print envelope.

16

'Mitchell, Howard Steven, US citizen,' began the Aliens' Register report. 'Born Lower East Side, New York City. No material advantages as a child. Parents deceased, formerly garment workers. PS education. Showed early abilities in engineering. Studied chemical engineering at MIT'.

The Prime Minister skipped the biographical details and turned the page to study the résumé of Mitchell's recent activities while Simpson watched him unhappily.

'Sole stockholder of Oil and Natural Gas Engineering Supplies Ltd. Address: The Centre, Walton-on-Thames, Surrey. According to the Articles of Association (appendix 3), this firm is a shipping and forwarding agent specializing in the supply of engineering materials to oil companies operating in the North Sea. Private address: 'Berrylands,' St Georges Hill, Weybridge, Surrey. Telephone number: Weybridge—'

The Prime Minister stopped reading and looked slowly up at Simpson. Their eyes met.

'This Michell lives at St Georges Hill,' said the Prime Minister evenly.

'It could be a coincidence.'

'Coincidence,' snorted the Prime Minister, and returned to the report.

Simpson wondered if he was going to read the last page.

The Prime Minister read the last page.

'Unmarried. Lives alone. Plays an occasional Sunday morning game of golf with General Conrad Pyne. CR:

Several traffic offenses (Appendix 6). Believed to be friendly with Paul Weiner, Industrial Liaison Controller at the American Embassy'.

The Prime Minister read no further. He dropped the report on his desk and unwrapped a cigar. 'Mitchell appears to have a US Embassy contact,' he observed. 'Paul Weiner.'

'There's nothing unusual about that, sir. The nature of Mitchell's business means that he's certain to have an industrial liaison contact in the embassy and we've no evidence that they've been regularly meeting.'

'Where does this Weiner live?' the Prime Minister interrupted.

'Cumberland Mansions in Seymour Place.' Simpson's fingers drummed lightly on the desk.

The Prime Minister watched him carefully through the flame of his table lighter. He knew Simpson well enough to guess that the report had shaken him too. It was an overlooked detail – perhaps more than a detail. Simpson did not like overlooked details and was usually efficient enough not to have to worry about them. The Prime Minister inhaled on the cigar. 'Has Weiner been kept under normal surveillance?'

'Yes, sir.'

The Prime Minister considered. 'Selective surveillance I suppose?'

Simpson nodded. There were times when he resented the politician's knowledge of security procedures. A neat little trap had been laid; he saw it coming.

The Prime Minister examined the glowing end of his cigar. 'In that case, Simpson, if Weiner has not been watched full time, we cannot be certain that he and Mitchell have not been meeting regularly . . . can we?'

'No, sir.'

'And if I remember correctly, the Industrial Liaison Department at the American Embassy covers a multitude of sins and sinners- CIA sins and sinners especially. Am I right?'

73

Simpson did not enjoy hot seats, even when they were only moderately warm.

'We believe its function is to monitor the behaviour of overseas American firms — to ensure they don't supply strategic materials to the Middle East. It's a negative activity which has suited our book.' Simpson's voice was edged with irritation.

'This fellow flying over Vulcan Hall power station is hardly a negative activity, Simpson.'

'He flew past it, sir.'

The Prime Minister looked faintly contemptuous.

Simpson began to get annoyed. 'It could be merely a coincidence, sir. We don't know for certain—'

'Quite right,' cut in the Prime Minister. 'We don't know for certain. But we will know if we keep a close watch on him. I needn't remind you of the consequences if this business blows up in our faces. So I suggest we keep an eye on him for the time being.'

'Yes, sir.' Simpson reached for the telephone.

'Who are you calling?'

Simpson hesitated. 'Well, I thought the Special Branch.'

'I see. You think we can trust Sir Gordon Clement?'

Simpson considered for a moment and took his hand away from the telephone.

'The only people we can trust,' said the Prime Minister scathingly, 'are one another. There's far too much at stake to involve anyone who has an axe to grind against me. It's going to be a damned nuisance having you out of the office, but Weybridge isn't too far from London, and I only want you to find out what Mitchell knows and what he's passed on.'

Simpson sat alone reading the file on Howard Mitchell for the umpteenth time and decided that he had no intention of being out of London during the crucial hours ahead. On the other hand the Prime Minister was right — Howard Mitchell was a problem: he was obviously working for the CIA, but how much did he really know about the conspiracy? And if he did know anything, how much had he passed on? Simpson sighed. There were so many imponderables. Maybe it was merely bad luck that the CIA had an agent on St Georges Hill where the terrorists had their homes but it seemed unlikely.

Simpson glanced through Howard Mitchell's company returns. It must have taken them a long time to set him up. The thought gave him an idea. Supposing Mitchell was just nibbling round the edge and knew only little of what was going on? There was nothing that could be done about the information already passed, but it would be possible to stop him sniffing out any more. If he was 'deactivated' or otherwise dealt with, it would arouse CIA suspicions, but it would take them months to set up a replacement. Time was the one thing that was vital now.

Time . . . Time . . .

Simpson stared straight ahead, his shrewd brain turning over the problem and possible solutions.

It made sense. Removing Mitchell would kill two birds: it would stop the CIA finding out more than they knew already, and it would mean that Simpson wouldn't have to be out of London to watch him.

Simpson smiled. He was wrong – his plan would kill three birds – one of them being Mitchell. He wondered how it could be made to look like an accident.

17

The afternoon was suffocatingly hot. The fifteen kilometre drive, in what was nothing more than a perambulating oven, from Thames Haven to Canvey Island was enough to make Cox-Spender forget the terrors awaiting him at the power station. The sweat rolled down the inside of his unlaundered collar. The car's air-conditioning couldn't cope. Opening a window didn't help: a vengeful horsefly was sucked into the car and bit him on the back of the neck.

The car crossed the road bridge on to Canvey Island. The army waved it through the checkpoints. Its registration number was on their lists. The barrier puzzled the driver, but he had been trained not to talk to his passengers unless they spoke to him. Holidaymakers and caravan owners were arguing with the soldiers. The troops were indifferent; all traffic trying to get on to the island was ordered into a field for a detailed examination.

The black government car drove across the island towing a cloud of dust. The driver followed the signs that indicated the way to Vulcan Hall power station. The signs were unnecessary because the four cooling towers were visible from every part of the island.

The car stopped before a high steel-framed chainlink gate that stretched across the road. Two soldiers emerged from the guardhouse and checked Cox-Spender's pass. The gate swung open. The soldiers told the driver to park beside an amphibious assault craft, and wait. No one was to leave the car.

Cox-Spender waited as the dark car soaked up solar radiation. A Land Rover driven by General Conrad Pyne arrived just as Cox-Spender was about to tell the driver to leave. Cox-Spender remembered Pyne from meetings when the Oil Rig Defence Force was in the early planning stage. He appeared to have aged since he had last seen him.

'Good day, Mr Cox-Spender,' said Pyne opening the car door. 'Please come with me.' His voice was tired. Neither friendly nor unfriendly. Just very tired.

'I expect you know who sent me,' said Cox-Spender, sitting beside Pyne in the open Land Rover.

Pyne let in the clutch. Cox-Spender had to grab the top of the windscreen to avoid falling out.

'There are several things I should like to see,' said Cox-Spender, opting for the direct approach. 'But first, I wish to examine the reactors to ensure that are safe. Then I should like to see the power-station staff. And then take a look at this high explosive you claim to have placed round the waste silos.' Despite the knot of fear in Cox-Spender's stomach, he felt it was necessary to assert his authority from the beginning and show these people who they were dealing with. The fact that no one had pointed a gun at him gave him confidence.

Pyne drove through the inner camp gate and into the power-station compound. He turned angrily to Cox-Spender. 'The reactor decommissioning programme was started last week,' he snapped. 'You'll see what we've decided you should see. No more, and no less.'

All the fight finally went out of Cox-Spender. He remained silent for the rest of the brief journey.

The Land Rover drove across the shadow of the aluminium containment dome that housed the nuclear fuelling machine perched on top of the twenty-metre-high prestressed concrete reactor building.

Cox-Spender remembered that Pyne used to have considerable dealings with the Prime Minister in the days when the politician had been Minister of Defence. There had been rumours at the time that this had something to do with Pyne's rapid promotion. The two men had much in common – they had come from relatively poor backgrounds and had risen in their respective careers thanks to a combination of logic applied to uncompromising ruthlessness. They were men who liked to get things done.

Pyne swung the Land Rover on to the concrete apron and parked near the two petrol tankers.

A man and a woman emerged from the power station and walked towards them. Cox-Spender guessed that they were Hugh Patterson and Louise Campion. He swallowed nervously. From the way the Sterling submachine-guns were slung casually from their shoulders, it looked as if they knew how to use them.

One of the most beautiful sights man has ever seen is the heavenly blue glow of Cerenkov radiation which occurs when high-energy particles pass through water.

Whenever Cox-Spender had witnessed the strange, ethereal light he felt he was witnessing the hand of God. It was easy to believe that the hypnotic glow suffusing the water in the fuel-element tank beneath the high catwalk held the key to the secret of the creation.

But now Cox-Spender's sense of wonder, which marks the true scientist, was no more. In its place was a sense of deep foreboding that the easy confidence of the three men at his side did not dispel.

'Gamma radiation is at zero.' said Keller politely. 'And we're leaving the rest of the elements in the stand-pipes.'

'You're following the decommissioning programme to shut down the reaction?' asked Cox-Spender.

'Yes, sir. We've continued the staged reduction of boiler pressure so that the coolant absorbs the neutrons and kills the reaction.'

Cox-Spender nodded. 'I understand there's a thermocouple temperature-monitoring computer in the main control room I should like a print-out, please to check the reactor core temperatures.'

'They're cooling nicely,' said Keller respectfully.

'I should still like to see for myself,' said Cox-Spender testily. At least this Keller seemed to know his place.

Keller exchanged a look with Pyne. Pyne nodded.

'And now,' said Cox-Spender, when he had finished examining a fanfold computer print-out, 'I wish to see the hostages.' He tried to make his voice sound insulting.

'I'm afraid that won't be possible,' said Pyne.

'Why not?'

'Because I say so.'

Pyne's grey eyes were hard and cold. Cox-Spender decided not to press the matter. For a moment he could think of nothing to say.

'He's seen the ultimatum,' Pyne said to the others.

'That should make our task easier,' commented Hugh Patterson.

'Terrorism has never achieved long-term objectives,' began Cox-Spender. 'You've only got to look at—'

'I don't think you were sent here to discuss politics,' interrupted Pyne caustically.

'You can't possibly hope to succeed,' Cox-Spender blustered angrily. 'There's only four of you. Eventually, you will tire – your men will turn against you.'

'Perhaps they will,' said Pyne, 'but they've served their purpose, so it doesn't matter. As for tiring, I'll tell you this much, and you can convey this to the Prime Minister when you go back; we will never tire, and we will never give in. I'd sooner commit suicide.'

'It might just come to that,' snapped Cox-Spender.

'And as for long-term objectives,' continued Pyne, ignoring Cox-Spender's outburst, 'they've never been effectively attempted by means of terrorism until now; no one has ever bargained with the lives of fifty million people, with their eventual well-being as the objective. And another thing – you could hardly call the half-lives of some of the isotopes in the silos as 'short-term'. Correct?'

Keller appeared with a sheet of paper which he pushed into Cox-Spender's hand. Cox-Spender gave it a cursory glance before thrusting it in his pocket. It was a list of radioactive materials, beginning with the higher and most dangerous plutonium isotopes.

'The contents of Silo Three,' explained Keller.

Cox-Spender looked at his watch. Determined to sound offensive, he said: 'I've little time to waste talking to you thugs, so if you show me the arrangements you've made with the high explosive, I'll be on my way.'

Pyne gave Cox-Spender a video cassette. 'That's for the Prime Minister,' he said. 'Before we go down, Mr Cox-Spender, there's something you should know if you don't already: the radioactive waste that's in storage here isn't just the power station's spent fuel rods, but waste that's been moved here from all over the country.'

'I know that,' said Cox-Spender frostily.

79

'Including some high-grade plutonium waste from Japan . . . Remember the cargo ship that the press dubbed the 'Flying Dutchman' last month because no port would accept it?'

'Of course I remember!' At that moment Cox-Spender defiance suddenly melted. He stared at Pyne. 'Are you trying to tell me that that cargo's here?'

Pyne nodded and smiled bleakly at the scientist's thunderstruck expression.

18

The Prime Minister looked up from the large-scale map spread out on his desk.

'What about an attack from the river?' he demanded.

'It would be most dangerous, sir,' replied Cox-Spender. 'Even if the attacking group managed to get on to the apron, they'd be detected by the IRIS system.'

The Prime Minister picked up the Racal infra-red sensor that Cox-Spender had placed on his desk. 'How sensitive are these things?'

'The body heat from a mouse can set one off at fifty metres, sir,' Cox-Spender replied. 'They even have automatic daylight compensators so they don't react to the ambient temperature fluctuations between day and night.'

The Prime Minister wondered what Cox-Spender was talking about, but remained silent. He replaced the detector and toyed with his amber paperweight. 'How about launching CS gas grenades through the control-room windows?'

'That too would be most dangerous sir, CS gas or CR gas grenades don't work instantly. There would still be a few seconds for two of the terrorists to operate the main detonator control.'

'Nerve gas?'

Cox-Spender considered. 'It's quicker, but still not quick enough.'

'What about stun grenades? They were effective enough during the Princes Gate siege.'

'You're thinking of an SAS-style assault, sir?'

'Isn't everyone?'

'That would entail a helicopter assault, sir. They've got radar, and besides – the noise of helicopter engines–'

'Yes. Yes,' said the Prime Minister interrupted testily. 'I had realised that.'

For a while neither spoke. The politician exhaled a thin stream of cigar smoke. It spilled across the map and pooled under the table lamp.

Cox-Spender broke the silence. 'With respect, sir, don't you think it would be a good idea to call a meeting of the Policy Review Committee so that the maximum number of brains could be brought to bear on the problem?'

'No,' said the Prime Minister shortly.

'What about the chiefs of staff?'

'The army would want to storm the place, the navy sink it and the RAF bomb it.'

Cox-Spender smarted at the brusque dismissal of his suggestion. It was an unfair generalization, but he was uncomfortably aware of the coolness, bordering on open hostility, that existed between the Cabinet Office and the chiefs of staff over the recent and most sweeping defence cuts. Cox-Spender had even heard rumours that a number of army officers were seriously considering taking direct action to assume power if the threatened talk of a centralised European defence force became a reality. Nevertheless, he decided to press the matter – the events of the day had given him a new-found confidence.

'Even so, sir, there are a number of extremely capable brains on the staff. I'm sure they would come up with something.'

A nerve in the Prime Minister's neck twitched. Cox-Spender would have recognized the danger signal had he known the politician better.

'The important thing at the moment, Cox-Spender, is to restrict knowledge of this business to as few people as possible until we've had a chance to examine all the options open to us. We don't know yet if these people are bluffing. It is possible that the magnitude of their enterprise will dawn on them, and that they will hesitate to press their demands. If that happens, as I suspect it will, then it follows that they will not carry out their threat to blow up the waste silos.'

This was all too much for Cox-Spender. 'Sir, with all due respect, I've seen these people. They won't weaken – I'm absolutely convinced of it. They've committed themselves too far.'

The Prime Minister banged his amber paperweight down on the desk in fury. 'I selected you for this task, Cox-Spender, because I thought you were the sort of man who wouldn't lose his head in a crisis. Obviously, I was wrong. I'm well aware of the situation, but I refuse to be stampeded into taking ill-considered action on the say-so of advisers who've lost their heads!'

Cox-Spender quailed. The sudden tirade was wholly unjustified, but he lacked the courage to say so. All he could manage was a rather shamefaced, 'Yes, sir.'

The Prime Minister relaxed. 'So you agree with me?'

There was no alternative, but to repeat the, 'Yes, sir.'

The Prime Minister smiled. Cox-Spender's acquiescence was safely recorded on tape. 'Did you give them the phone number?' he asked in a more moderate tone.

'Yes, sir.' Cox-Spender resented having to keep uttering the two words. There had been moments during what had been the longest Sunday of his life when he had thought he had finally broken the habit.

'In that case,' said the Prime Minister, 'we'll wait for them to make the first move.'

He glanced up at the eighteenth-century French clock. 23:05.

The Prime Minister tapped the video cassette from General Pyne. 'I hope you haven't played this.'

'No, sir. I brought it straight to you.'

The Prime Minister yawned. 'Very well, Cox-Spender. You've done as well as can be expected so far. I have a feeling that tomorrow is going to be worse than the usual Monday. It's time you and I were in bed – I'm sure you must be exhausted.'

Again Cox-Spender had to say, 'Yes, sir.'

The Prime Minister reached for a telephone. 'I'll have your car sent round to the Downing Street entrance. Save you that long walk, eh?'

The Prime Minister went to bed at 23:25 and slept soundly from 23:40.

Monday

1

Pyne slept badly during his first night at the power station.

He awoke after one hour's sleep and tried to orientate himself in the strange surroundings. His room had been the station superintendent's office. He could hear the throb of a passing ship. He tried to go back to sleep but gave up. He threw back the sheet, swung his feet on to the coarse horsehair carpet tiles and switched on the light.

03:00 hours. Louise Campion would be on duty in the control room.

The corridor was silent apart from Hugh Patterson's snores from the next office. The pan and tilt servo of a heat-guided closed-circuit television camera whirred briefly as its lens swung towards him.

Louise Campion was sitting at the central console with an open vacuum flask before her. She turned from the television monitors and smiled at Pyne's approach.

'Couldn't you sleep, Conrad?'

Pyne sat near her. 'We should sleep in here, Louise – it's cooler.'

Louise pointed to the computer cabinets. 'The air-conditioning is for that lot. Computers are fussy about their comfort.' She held up a technical handbook. 'I've been reading all about them.'

'Didn't you bring some books?'

'About a thousand on CD-ROMs. I'm saving them. Heaven forbid that we should be stuck in here for–'

'Louise,' interrupted Pyne, 'what happened last night?'

'Hugh gave you a report?'

'I want to hear your version.'

The radiation biologist looked puzzled. 'Well. Ralph and I arrived at about 15:30. He drove the first tanker, and I drove the second – just as we planned.'

'Where was Hugh?'

'Holding the staff in here. About thirty of them.' She paused, 'Look, Conrad, if you've any questions about Hugh and Ralph, you should ask them. We agreed that mutual trust between the four of us was essential. Right?'

'Really, Louise? What about the revised ultimatum? Or have you told Keller?'

Louise flushed. 'That's your job, Conrad.'

'It's also my job to find out what happened to the hostages.'

'Ralph sent them across the river by boat when they'd finished helping to position the explosive.'

Pyne watched her carefully. She avoided looking at him.

'Did you see this boat?'

'Of course not. It was dark.'

'Or hear it?'

'I was too busy checking the supplies.' She poured a cup of coffee without offering one to Pyne.

'Did you hear submachine-gun fire?

'There was some noise. Ralph said he'd been testing some detonators.'

'Louise, among the power station staff, do you remember a girl of about twenty? A pretty little thing with fair hair?'

Louise continued to avoid Pyne's gaze. 'I may have seen her. I can't remember.'

'Keller shot her.'

Louise looked up angrily. 'You're being absurd. Ralph could never–'

'I've seen the body. I didn't do it. I'm certain that you and Hugh didn't, so that only leaves Keller, The girl's body is in the inspection tunnels, and only Keller had business down there at the time.'

Louise pushed the coffee to Pyne. 'You think Ralph killed all the staff?'

Pyne accepted the cup and drank. 'I think so. There're plenty of hiding places down there.'

There was silence. Louise shuddered inwardly, then looked steadily at Pyne and nodded slowly. 'I suspected something. But why would he do such a thing, Conrad? Why?'

Pyne shook his head. 'Christ knows. I was going to tell him about the revised ultimatum at the meeting, but decided to hold back for the moment.'

'You're going to have to tell him sooner or later,' Louise pointed out.

Pyne stared at the detonator controls on a nearby console. There were two simple combination switches three metres apart screwed to the plastic work surface. To activate them required two people to set the combinations and throw the switches simultaneously.

'There's plenty of time,' Pyne said slowly. He ran his hand through his hair. 'If only I could understand him – if only he wasn't so damned polite all the time.'

'You should tell him about the changes we made to the ultimatum, Conrad.'

'No, Louise. Let him find out when the Prime Minister announces the new laws. By then it will be too late for him to object.'

Louise frowned. 'I wonder what the Prime Minister is doing now?'

Pyne stood. 'What I should be doing – sleeping.'

'Even with the problem of us?'

'He'll sleep.' Pyne turned to leave.

'You used to know him, didn't you?' Louise said, looking up at Pyne.

Pyne did not like the question. 'A long time ago when he was at the MOD.' Pyne quickly changed the subject. 'Louise, destroy your copy of the ultimatum. I'll tell Hugh to do the same in the morning.'

He was gone before Louise could reply.

2

From 10:00 that morning Howard Mitchell spent an hour
on the phone trying to discover the truth concerning the
cause of the Thames Haven explosion. He desperately
needed to know whether or not his drill-string had been
destroyed or moved. No one could, or would, help him. The
oil company's head office in London said the disaster was to
be the subject of a Department of Trade and Industry
investigation and would say no more. The Department of
Trade and Industry said they could do nothing for the time
being because there was a danger of more explosions. The
Home Office said the area had been sealed off by the police
and would remain so until the site had been declared safe.
The Ministry of Civil Aviation said the prohibited zone
above the Thames Estuary would remain in force until the
Department of Trade and Industry said the prohibition
could be removed.

Despairing, Mitchell made one last call to his old contact,
Paul Weiner, at the American Embassy. He left his office five
minutes later, telling his secretary he would be gone for
three hours.

Ten minutes later he was driving towards London with
Simpson following at a distance in a ten-hundredweight
Bedford van. It was an ideal vehicle for the job – the high
steering position enabled the driver to follow his quarry at a
safe distance without losing sight of it.

Mitchell slid his Mustang tail first into a parking-meter bay
near Grosvenor Square. Simpson cruised past in his van and
was beaten to a bay by a woman driving a Golf who dived in
nose first. By the time Simpson had satisfied his male ego
with horn and invective, Mitchell had disappeared.

Simpson found another parking space and went into a
McDonald's. He had lost Mitchell but at least he could keep

the Mustang under observation from a high stool near the window.

Mitchell found the 'American Dream' without difficulty.

'Mr Weiner says he'll be along as soon as possible,' said a waitress, showing him to a reserved corner table.

Weiner entered ten minutes later as Mitchell was starting his second cup of cup of coffee. The two men exchanged warm greetings. Weiner ordered steak for both of them.

'Long time no see,' said Weiner. 'I was wondering what had happened to you.'

'The political and physical storms in the North Sea have been keeping me busy.'

Weiner grinned impishly. 'And furnishing a new house on St Georges Hill.'

'How the hell do you know that?'

Weiner looked round with a gesture of mock secretiveness. 'We know all there is to know about our boys far from home. Not many make it to St Georges Hill. The oil business must be doing fine.'

'It won't be,' said Mitchell shortly. 'That's why I've come to see you.' He briefly outlined his account of the previous day's flight and his concern about the missing drill-string.

'Wasn't it insured?' asked Weiner.

'Not until today, and, in any event, not if the loss is the result of terrorist activities. British underwriters here have got the jitters at the moment over oil platforms. They're expecting some sort of terrorist action in the North Sea any day now. I've got to pay out a hundred thousand dollars next week for some pumps. I don't want to if I'm going to need the money to cover the loss of the string.'

The waitress brought their steaks.

'I saw on the news last night,' said Weiner when she was gone, 'that there's a danger of more explosions.'

Mitchell opened his briefcase and produced the yellow Kodak envelope. He passed a photograph across to Weiner. 'You don't have to be much of an expert to see there's nothing left to explode. Just look at the place. It's a ruin.'

Weiner examined the print curiously. It was an oblique shot of the devastated refinery taken at a distance of two kilometres. Mitchell was right – there was nothing left.

'There's something else,' said Mitchell. 'You said you saw the television news coverage last night about the explosion?'

Weiner nodded. 'I saw the commercial networks news when I got back after a show. Why?'

'I watched that and the coverage on both BBC networks and on Sky,' said Mitchell. 'None of them had cameras at or even near the site. All they had was a presenter sitting in front of an old blow-up showing the refinery as it was before the explosion. Now I know British television news coverage is crummy, but they're usually pretty good when it comes to a major event just a few kilometres outside London.'

'Sure, but the area has been sealed off,' Weiner pointed out.

'No,' said Mitchell. 'They could've easily staked out cameras with long lenses on the opposite river bank, even though it's four kilometres wide just there.'

Weiner said nothing. Mitchell gave him another photograph.

'If you look at that one, it's possible to tell roughly where the explosion took place. One explosion – right in the middle of the employees' carpark – the last place you'd expect an explosion to happen.'

'Strange,' said Weiner looking up from the picture.

'You're goddamn right it's strange. I'll show you something that's even stranger.' Mitchell gave Weiner a third photograph. 'It's not such a good picture of the refinery – it was taken too far off. That complex looks like a power station, and those two choppers parked in the front belong to neighbours of mine on St Georges Hill: Hugh Patterson and General Conrad Pyne.'

Weiner looked at the prints for some seconds and said: 'Why should that be strange? I've heard of Patterson. His firm manufactures radioactive-waste storage tanks. Maybe he's working extra time on some project.'

'Maybe,' replied Mitchell. 'You once asked me to report interesting developments in the oil business. I thought the information would be fair exchange if you could find out what's happened to my string.'

Weiner gathered up the photographs. 'Can I keep these?'

'Sure. You can have them all.' Mitchell handed him the yellow envelope. 'There's a few more in there that aren't so good.'

Weiner pushed the prints into the envelope. 'I'll see what I can do.' he said. 'I'll check these pictures out, but I can't promise anything.'

Simpson followed Mitchell's Mustang to the roundabout under the Hammersmith flyover and decided he must be returning to Surrey. Simpson had no intention of being out of London that day – not with the events that were looming up. Mitchell continued westward. Simpson went right round the traffic island and headed back to London.

When Weiner reached his office he tipped the photographs on to his desk and examined each one carefully for some minutes. Mitchell's theory about the location of the explosion appeared to be substantiated by the pattern of twisted wreckage, but it was not possible to say with certainty that it had taken place in the middle of the carpark – not without checking the pictures against library covers taken of the refinery on the last UK aerial survey. The pictures were interesting, but Weiner was not certain they were of interest to the CIA – apart from providing another set of covers for the print library.

He decided to make a few inquiries to satisfy Mitchell and then to forget the whole affair. He yawned and pushed the prints back into the envelope. Something was stopping them. He peered into the envelope and shook out a postcard size photograph that obviously didn't belong to the batch taken by Mitchell. It showed a group holding drinks gathered round a Bell JetRanger helicopter. He was about to return it to the envelope, when something in the picture triggered a memory chord.

He placed the photograph on his blotter and stared down at the vaguely familiar face of the man sitting in the helicopter's open door.

Keller . . . Ralph Keller! Jesus Christ!

Weiner picked up his telephone and dialled two digits. He waited, telephone pressed to his ear and the photograph between his elbows.

'Harry . . .Paul. Cast your mind back a few years to Libya. Remember the guy who teamed up with Eric Hoffman and offered to build the Libyans an atomic bomb? . . . Yeah . . . Well, you won't believe this, but I think I've found him.'

3

Two hours after Howard Mitchell had left Paul Weiner following their lunch in the 'American Dream'. James Raven, the duty officer at the Madrid Space Track Center, received a signal from the USAF base at Mildenhall in England. When deciphered, the instructions in the message were simple enough: CYCLOPS was required to take a photographic 'stripe' of southern England.

Raven decoded the positions and wondered why anyone should want to waste the limited amount of film in the satellite's magazines on a series of photographs of the Thames Estuary. Once the magazines were empty CYCLOPS would be useless. Unlike the French SPOT series of satellites which used computer-enhanced high resolution digital TV pictures for remote sensing of the earth, CYCLOPS used film. The problems with film justified the expense: film could resolve down to the granular level whereas the quality of television pictures, even with enhancing, was limited to the line scan rate.

He requested verification in case a cipher clerk had made a mistake. Five minutes later an affirmative clattered out on the center's teleprinter. Raven did not bother to decipher the second message – the code groups were a repeat. He filed both messages in the day book, and decided that whatever happened he wouldn't be held responsible for the expensive operation he was about to undertake.

Raven sat at the CYCLOPS control console and pressed the button which projected the low earth orbit satellite's path on to a fluorescent screen. The illuminated LEO trail was climbing towards the North Pole across Siberia. The computer forecast that in twenty minutes the satellite would be sweeping down the western coast of Greenland – too far west of the required target.

Raven tapped out the course-correction codes. Thirty seconds later a stream of telemetry signals from the Reykjavik relay station triggered CYCLOPS's course-correction vernier rockets.

Raven checked the new orbit.

A few more squirts to orientate the satellite and it was set to pass over southern England only a few kilometres east of the Greenwich Meridian, and exactly over the remains of the Thames Haven oil refinery.

The screen at Raven's elbow showed the required course and the projected course – both lines overlapped exactly. A winking light on the glowing line indicated the satellite's position.

At 15:30 it was over Scotland.

Raven pressed the button that would start feeding the strips of film through the camera-shutter gates and wind the protective visors away from the lenses.

At 15:35 he sent a signal to Mildenhall giving them the position for the recovery of the film capsule. The information was radioed to Colonel Donald Kaufmann, who was flying a Hustler bomber that had left Mildenhall when the instructions to the Madrid Space Track Center were first issued.

At 15:45 CYCLOPS was above its objective.

There was no sound in the still vacuum of space as the shutters on the stereoscopic and infra-red cameras opened and closed.

At 15:48 the satellite passed out of the 'area of interest' determined by the Madrid computer. A final signal stopped the shutters. The rest was automatic: the capsule pulled away from its parent satellite and began its long, five hundred kilometre fall to earth – its tiny rocket motor burning brightly to cancel the orbital velocity imparted to it by CYCLOPS.

The capsule's parachute opened at 16:03. Colonel Kaufmann's navigator detected the faint radar echo at 16:15 and extended the Hustler's scoop net.

A few minutes later the capsule was snatched out of the sky.

The Hustler touched down on the hot runway at Mildenhall exactly five hours after Mitchell had handed his photographs to Paul Weiner in London.

4

At 12:30 Simpson made six anonymous phone calls: five to the editors of the national newspapers and one to the chief commissioner of the Metropolitan Police. Each time he identified himself with the codeword 'Moonflower' used only by the Provisional IRA to distinguish genuine bomb-warning calls from hoaxes. He spoke in a thick Irish accent and announced that the Palace of Westminster was to be the target for a bomb attack during the afternoon while it was being used for the special meeting called by the Prime Minister with the 360 members of his parliamentary party.

The police responded swiftly: the chief commissioner telephoned Simpson urging that the meeting should be called off. Simpson said that the meeting would have to go ahead – 360 telegrams had been sent out to members of Parliament demanding that they should break their holidays and return to London. The best thing, Simpson suggested, would be for the police to clear the Palace of Westminster of everyone – even maintenance staff – and ensure that only MPs were allowed to enter.

The meeting was due to start at 15:00 hours. The police took no chances. They stepped-up their usual security measures to an unprecedented level. Arriving Members of Parliament were subjected to even more stringent searches than usual and their identities were double-checked before they were allowed through the cordon.

Not even ministerial cars, which were checked each day as a matter of routine were allowed into the underground car park; drivers were required to remove themselves and their cars once they had dropped their passengers.

The MP's milled round the corridors trying to find out from one another why the meeting had been called. The chief whip's office checked every new arrival, and telephoned Simpson when the number of MPs present reached 345.

Simpson drove. For once the Prime Minister sat in the front, obliging his bodyguard to travel in the back.

'What have you found out about the American?' The Prime Minister demanded.

Simpson slowed in response to the upheld arm of a shirt-sleeved, armed policeman who wanted to see their passes. He examined it carefully, and the two other occupants of the car, before waving it on to the police equipped with ion charge instruments who carefully checked the underside of the car.

'Well?'

'Nothing, sir. I followed him from Walton to London this morning, but was unable to discover whom he visited.'

A knot of MPs gathered on the steps pressed forward as Simpson brought the car to a standstill. The Prime Minister had his hand on the door lock.

'Don't forget what I said, Simpson. Although I'd prefer to have you with me, it's essential we find out what he knows.'

The MPs, crowded into the largest committee room and spilling into the corridor, fell silent when the Prime Minister rose. He had deliberately avoided speaking to his Cabinet colleagues; today they were all equal. Each man and woman present represented one vote – and that was all that mattered.

'I'm sorry to call you all back from your holidays,' he began. 'I wouldn't have done so, but at this moment our country faces the gravest crises in its history.

'Yesterday a group of terrorists under the command of General Pyne seized control of Vulcan Hall nuclear power station on Canvey Island. They are threatening to blow up the radioactive-waste silos unless the government adopt certain stringent measures which they believe will solve the country's economic and social problems.' The Prime Minister paused. Every face in the room was turned towards him.

'My secretary will distribute copies of their demands, which I received yesterday. I want you to read the measures most carefully during the next five minutes. Each copy is numbered and will be collected afterwards, so don't lose them please. No one is to talk and no one will be allowed to leave this room until all the copies have been collected.'

Simpson handed out copies of the ultimatum, including a copy for Cox-Spender, who had been told to attend the meeting. The gathering read in stunned silence, apart from the occasional rustle of paper. As the minutes passed more and more of the ashen faces fixed their horrified gaze on the Prime Minister. He waited until the last man had finished reading.

'Thank you,' he said. 'Now in case any of you think these terrorists are bluffing, they caused yesterday's explosion at the Thames Haven refinery to show they mean business.'

The silence in the room was total. One MP lifted his feet off a table and lowered them to the floor without making a sound.

'Vulcan Hall is not contributing to the national grid – decommissioning was started when it was seized – but I understand that its waste silos hold an unusually large amount of material at the moment as a result of the Cheshire repository problems. The so-called 'Flying Dutchman' plutonium cargo is also stored there. Indeed Vulcan Hall now holds the largest concentration of waste in the country.

'Yesterday, Mr Cox-Spender visited Vulcan Hall. The terrorists showed him the arrangements they have made to carry out their threat unless the government adopt their proposed measures. I'm no scientist, so I've asked Mr Cox-Spender to tell you about his visit . . . Mr Cox-Spender.' The Prime Minister sat down.

Cox-Spender felt Simpson jab him from behind. He climbed reluctantly to his feet. He always felt hopelessly self-conscious when addressing a crowd – even more so when the crowd was completely silent. He spoke hesitantly at first, gradually gaining confidence with the realization that this wasn't a committee meeting and no one was likely to contradict him. The 345 faces watched him intently. Cox-Spender resolutely kept his eyes on his notes. He spoke for fifteen minutes, gradually lowering himself to his chair on his closing sentences.

'A question, please!' The voice cracked out from the back of the room. Cox-Spender looked at the Prime Minister for guidance, but the politician's eyes were fixed pensively on the floor. Cox-Spender's hesitation was a signal for everyone to start firing questions. The Prime Minister rose to his feet and held up his hand. The babble died away.

'Mr Cox-Spender will answer your questions one at a time. I believe Mr Quentin Brieley spoke first.'

Quentin Brieley, the member for Breckon Park, was a small, pugnacious man. Before becoming an MP he had been a physics master in his home town of Cardiff.

He pushed forward until he was nearly face to face with Cox-Spender.

'What I want to know,' he said, in his thin, reedy Welsh accent, 'is what is the exact nature of the radionuclides stored at Vulcan Hall, and what will happen if they are released.'

The use of the word 'radionuclides' did not put Cox-Spender on his guard. Had it done so, he would not have said, 'They are the radioactive byproducts of the nuclear-fission process.'

Brieley snorted. 'I know that. What exactly are they and what can they do?'

'Well, basically, the flasks in the central silo contain up to two hundred isotopes which have been produced from uranium—'

'Such as?' demanded Brieley.

The MPs remained silent. The small Welshman, with his implacable opposition to the nuclear-energy programme, could be relied on to ask all the pertinent questions.

Cox-Spender frantically tried to recall all the isotopes with short half-lives. 'Er . . . Xenon one-three-three . . . Iodine one-three-three—'

Brieley snapped out: 'Wasn't that the stuff that escaped from Windscale a few years back?'

'Yes.' Cox-Spender inwardly cursed the knowledgeable Welshman and wondered why the Prime Minister wasn't coming to his rescue. 'But it didn't kill anyone,' he added.

'Because it has a short half-life – right?'

Cox-Spender nodded.

'And there's the 'Flying Dutchman' cargo. Anything else brewing in there you've forgotten to tell us about?'

Cox-Spender opened his mouth to protest at the man's offensive attitude, but Brieley was too quick.

'What about strontium ninety, Mr Cox-Spender? There'd be a lot of that wouldn't there? It's got a long half-life.'

'There is a quantity of strontium ninety at Vulcan Hall.' Cox-Spender admitted.

Brieley turned to face his colleagues. 'You've probably heard of the stuff,' he said angrily. 'It has a similar atom to calcium so it is readily absorbed by the body to build bones. It doesn't affect adults much.' He turned to Cox-Spender.

97

'Tell them what it does to children. Tell them what happens to kids who've got bones made of strontium ninety.'

The Prime Minister stood up. 'Mr Cox-Spender didn't invent the stuff,' he said mildly. Cox-Spender thought he was taking over the question-and-answer session, but the Prime Minister avoided his adviser's eye and sat down again.

Brieley remained staring fixedly at Cox-Spender with a mixture of loathing and contempt. 'Iodine and caesium are nothing compared with plutonium. How much of that have you got at Vulcan Hall?'

Cox-Spender looked in vain to the Prime Minister for support. 'I'm not sure. Not much.'

'Christ!' shouted the Welshman. 'It doesn't have to be much!' He held up his fist. 'A lump that size could kill everyone in the country!'

In the world, thought Cox-Spender, but he did not enlighten his opponent.

'Inhale one particle of plutonium, and you get lung cancer. After that, you get dead. Right Mr Cox-Spender?'

'What's its half-life?' asked a voice.

'Twenty thousand years,' said Cox-Spender quickly, frightened that Brieley would use a dramatic simile to express the period of time.

'What does that mean?' asked another voice.

'It means,' said Brieley, 'that after twenty thousand years a few pounds of the stuff can kill only half the world's population, and so on. And they're sitting on tonnes of it.'

No one spoke.

'Shall I tell what will happen if those terrorists blow up the silos?' said the Welshman, turning to the gathering. 'Three Mile Island and Cheynobel will be a kids' chemistry experiments going wrong by comparison. Everyone in the country – perhaps even in Europe, Asia and America – will be dead within a few years, and the land uninhabitable for the best part of a million years. Isn't that right Mr bloody Cox-Spender?'

Cox-Spender nodded. He could argue survival factors, but basically, the Welsh MP was right.

Brieley was no longer angry. 'If the gates of hell do exist,' he said sadly, 'we will find they are made of plutonium.' He looked slowly round at the sea of silent faces. 'It's even named after the Lord of Darkness . . . Pluto . . .'

He sat down.

The silence continued for a few moments, then everyone was firing questions.

The Prime Minister was on his feet again. 'If you will all be patient for a little longer, please, I have something you're all to see. After that, you can ask Mr Cox-Spender as many questions as you wish.'

Cox-Spender sat down. There was a suspicion at the back of his mind that he had been a useful whipping-boy.

Simpson had been busy during the precious few minutes setting up a video recorder and a portable television receiver. He nodded to the Prime Minister that he was ready.

'You are about to see a video recording that the terrorists gave Mr Cox-Spender during his visit,' said the Prime Minister. 'All right Simpson.'

The opening shot showed Pyne sitting at a desk in front of a bookcase. The caption 'MAJOR GENERAL CONRAD PYNE OBE' appeared briefly on the screen.

Pyne interlocked his fingers on the desk blotter and leaned forward, looking fixedly at the camera.

'By now,' he said, in a flat, unhurried voice. 'You will know the truth. You are probably thinking that you face a terrible dilemma. But there is no dilemma, ladies and gentlemen, if you follow the conditions we have laid down in our ultimatum. Indeed you must follow them, because you have no choice.

'Through a mixture of greed and self-interest and a failure to implement straightforward remdial measures, this country is rapidly becoming bankrupt. This is many people's

99

fault – but it is especially yours.' Pyne pointed at the camera to emphasize his words.

'The public broadcasting of Parliament has proved to the British people that the majority of you are an undisciplined collection of self-interested egotists totally unfit to govern a nation of sixty million people. I ask myself – what has this country done to deserve you?' Pyne paused. The MPs sat in shocked silence.

'Perhaps it is not your fault as individuals – it is the fault of your constituency parties who weed out candidates of vision and return to Parliament narrow-minded Union Jack-wrapped Britishers who seem incapable of clear, logical thinking. The sad result that we have a hung parliament of weakness and mediocrity that lacks the drive, initiative, and *courage* to tackle the country's problems with zeal and determination. As a consequence we have rampant infla-tion, unemployment, virtual isolation from our partners in Europe, and a tap-washer and Luncheon Voucher currency that's a standing joke in Europe.

'You've constantly underestimated the British people with your insipid, half-baked measures which merely irri-tate rather than inspire. Just one example but a vital one: look at the mess we are in over house prices. There's no shortage of land or building materials in this country! Making people take out crippling mortgages amounts to a massive self-inflicted wound. We've built on only ten percent of our land! Land is for people! We should use it to allow them to build and extend their own homes over a period as and when they can afford it – not sell them cramped little ready-made hutches on vast, impersonal estates at vast, inflated prices. The amount of land we want released and sold at realistic prices will serve our housing needs well into the next century.

'The housing situation is a symptom of your failure to recognise real needs. Had you had the guts to introduce really tough controls, instead of forever looking over your shoulder at the myth of empty ballot boxes at the next election, you might have won broad support. Instead you've wrung your hands and blamed everyone for our troubles except yourselves.

'While the rest of the European Community has flourished – even former East Germany is now doing better than us – we've had to listen to successive governments prattling on about sovereignty. Substitute the word 'power' for 'sovereignty' in all the political speeches we've endured over the past few years and they begin to make sordid sense. To you political power is more important than jobs, housing, public health – everything. And yet sovereignty does not provide homes or jobs; sovereignty does nothing for our balance of payments; sovereignty doesn't pay mortgages or provide hospital beds or decent schools and motivated teachers. Sovereignty is a negative force – it props up nationalism and greed and inefficiency. To sustain it requires high taxes to pay for independent armies, navies and air forces. It perpetuates the hideous costs of duplication and even jeopardises air safety because sovereignty stands in the way of a Pan-European air traffic control system. For example: sovereignty provided us with the staggering cost of two cellular telephone systems neither of which is compatible with the rest of Europe. The result is that we now have to scrap both systems and write-off *five billion pounds* of capital investment. Sovereignty gave us the absurd MAC television system which no one else wanted and which contributed to the destruction of our television manufacturing industry. Small wonder the Japanese are walking all over us if we tie-up our best engineering brains in electronics to design systems that are useless. Sometimes I think you all forget that Britain is a tiny country that you can drive across in a morning. We can't afford to waste brains and money and resources on senseless duplication in the name of this corrosive enemy of our future prosperity . . . *this sovereignty . . .*'

The last word was almost spat out. Pyne paused and sipped from a glass of water. 'From now on, ladies and gentlemen,' he continued, 'this country is on a war footing. It has worked before against a visible enemy – now we must strive together to ensure that it works against the invisible enemies of greed and inflation which will destroy this country just as surely as Hitler intended to, and just as surely as Vulcan Hall's nuclear fallout will if we are forced to blow-up the silos.'

Pyne paused again and looked straight at the camera. 'I was wrong just now. You do have a choice. You either accept our measures for five years, or destroy our country for eternity.'

The screen went blank. There was a few seconds of stunned silence broken by the video recorder switching itself off with a loud double click. The Prime Minister stood and surveyed the silent faces. 'You now have an idea of the people we are dealing with – utterly ruthless but efficient. But terrorists none the less – no matter what their motives. That is one thing that we must not lose sight of. Questions?'

'What have the armed forces got to say about this?' demanded a voice from the back. 'When are they planning to break in and get these people out?'

I don't think you quite understand,' said the Prime Minister. 'No move has been planned against them. You are the only people in the country who know anything about this. Not even my Cabinet colleagues were aware of the take-over until now. I considered the situation so serious that it must be revealed to all of you, so that we can all discuss what is to be done, rather than recall Parliament and ask you to approve Cabinet action.'

'Easier to get us to agree to something than the Cabinet,' a backbencher remarked.

There were a few guffaws despite the seriousness of the situation. The Prime Minister smiled frostily. 'The diversions within the Party are reflected at all levels,' he remarked. 'Including the backbenches. Right now we need unity.'

'What *are* the chances of launching a successful attack against them?' asked the Home Secretary.

The Prime Minister nodded to Cox-Spender.

'A preliminary examination has ruled out the possibility that any attack is likely to succeed,' said Cox-Spender.

The Home Secretary was unimpressed. It was clear that he resented not being briefed or consulted before the meeting. 'Oh, really? And who decided that?'

Brieley jumped up. 'What the hell are we arguing about?' he demanded. 'We're carrying on as if we've got a choice.' He jerked his thumb at the television. 'You saw that maniac. We've *got* to go along with him otherwise he destroys the country. It's as plain and as simple and as stark as that. We've no choice. We're in what the Americans call a zero options situation.'

His words aroused everyone from their stunned stupor. MPs were on their feet, some shouting that Brieley was right, others yelling that no government should yield to terrorism. The scene was threatening to degenerate into a familiar parliamentary uproar. The Prime Minister had to shout several times to command attention. Gradually the tumult died away and the sea of faces turned to their leader.

'Well now,' said the Prime Minister. 'As Mr Brieley seems to have such a lot to say on the subject, perhaps he would like to suggest a course of action? Mr Brieley?'

The Welsh MP was not inhibited by the Prime Minister's patronizing tone. His entire parliamentary career had been a tirade against nuclear power. Now every embarrassing question and every empassioned speech was vindicated. 'I propose, Prime Minister, that parliament should be recalled immediately to pass an enabling bill before the week is out so that the measures demanded by those thugs can be implemented.'

'Brieley was in good form,' the Prime Minister remarked, as Simpson drove back to Downing Street.

'Well, it was rather expected,' said Simpson.

'He more or less carried the show for us,' said the Prime Minister, relaxing into his seat.

Simpson kept his eyes on the road. A series of shirt-sleeved policemen held up traffic for the car.

'When do you start your intensive surveillance of the American?'

'Don't you think we should get someone else to do it, sir? It's not the sort of work I'm used to.'

'An excellent chance for you to learn, Simpson. Such a talent might come in useful in the future.'

Simpson pressed his lips tightly together and said nothing.

5

Walter Innam's eyesight was such that he could not see the target on a fifty-yard range, let alone hit it. Without thick pebbleglass spectacles everything more than a metre from the end of his nose disappeared into a vague blur of light and shadow.

But for close work, such as staring through the twin lenses of stereoscopic viewers at aerial-reconnaissance photographs, their performance was phenomenal. Innam could pick out fragments of information from the poorest photograph – frequently discovering details that eluded everyone else. It was as if nature had compensated him by giving him the ability to see in reproduction what he could never hope to see in real life.

In the air-conditioned darkness of the CIA's photo-surveillance laboratory he pressed his face to the eyepiece hood of a huge stereoscopic viewer that resembled a submarine's periscope. His left hand grasped a small lever. With this he could move the three-dimensional scene before his eyes in any direction. Pressing down on the lever brought the ground racing towards him with the sensation of plunging earthward in a vertically diving aircraft.

He had been asked to prepare a report on the probable cause of the explosion which had destroyed the Thames

Haven oil refinery the day before. It was the sort of exercise he adored – the opportunity to exercise his talent without having to wonder why anyone should want such a report.

He spent several minutes ranging back and forth over the refinery, merely getting the feel of the place. As far as Innam was concerned, he was not looking at photographs – he was actually there; revelling in the heady sensations of his own private world in which he was flying an aircraft that could dive to within ten metres of the ground or soar to five hundred kilometres at the touch of a lever.

Here, alone in the darkened room, he was the supreme being –far from the painful memories of childhood filled with the cruel, taunting refrains of schoolchildren determined to make the life of a short-sighted eight-year-old abject misery. Here he was God: an omnipotent entity whose penetrating eyes stared down on the puny works of men and sneered in contempt at their feeble efforts to conceal their miserable secrets. He, Walter Innam, had seen all there was to see – couples copulating in cornfields; Libyan engineers building rocket bases in craggy foothills; a European queen and her husband walking in the grounds of their palace – nothing could be hidden from his eyes.

Innam carefully centred himself over the refinery at three thousand feet. The area of devastation filled his field of vision exactly. He twisted a knob and the view was replaced by a shot of the refinery taken before the explosion – it was one of the many thousands of photographs in the CIA library which had been taken on a survey of British industrial installations two years previously. By flicking the knob back and forth Innam was able alternately to destroy and restore the refinery. It gave him the feeling of being a true god, but the purpose of the 'before' and 'after' exercise, with what are known as 'comparative covers' in aerial-reconnaissance jargon was to determine the approximate centre of the explosion.

Refinery – devastation – refinery – devastation–
His hand flicked the knob with increasing rapidity.

An impression began to form on his retinas; he began to see the explosion.

Refinery – devastation–

The coalescing images merged, like the consecutive frames of a film.

Innam could see the explosion. He could see the expanding shockwave racine outwards from the northern end of the refinery –from the carpark. He could see the tall distillation columns splitting open before the massive concussion and slamming themselves to the ground, only to have their remains scooped up and flung hundreds of metres through the air.

The whole fleeting five seconds of appalling destruction was recreated before Innam's eyes in total silence.

He had discovered the position of the explosion in five minutes. Now for the cause.

It would take an expert interpreter as much as two hours. Innam settled more comfortably in his seat and began a painstaking search.

He divided the refinery into a series of squares by superimposing a grid on his field of vision. He centred himself exactly above the square at the centre of the explosion and lowered himself until his view was completely filled by the square. The blur of twisted ironmongery resolved itself into separate but still unrecognizable shards of technology.

Lower. A hundred metres. The unblinking eyes bored down.

Fifty metres. Glittering highlights – undistinguishable from their surroundings at a greater height – suddenly became fractured beams of sunlight captured on the freshly torn edges of sheet steel. The remains of cars.

Innam made some fine adjustments to contrast and lighting levels. He started with the examination of welding seams. The manner in which they had been forced apart would tell him whether the explosion had been inside a particular vehicle or outside.

He meticulously reversed every square centimetre of the grid square, sometimes dictating notes into the microphone of a tape recorder whose reels turned only when he spoke, sometimes pausing to study more closely something that caught his eye – but never blinking.

The irregular piece of aluminium was about thirty centimetres square. It was curved slightly and appeared to have been subjected to an anodizing process during manufacture. It was inscribed with white stencilled stores reference digits that Innam recognized immediately. During the next five minutes he discovered several more fragments from the same piece of aluminium.

Innam stared down in astonishment for some minutes, then relaxed with a feeling of satisfaction, tinged with regret now the operation was over.

He looked at his watch.

Discovering the cause of the explosion had taken him fifteen minutes.

6

Ralph Keller sat alone with his thoughts in Vulcan Hall control room.

For the hundredth time he went over the options open to the British Government, and for the hundredth time he decided there were none: they had to accept the conditions in the ultimatum. There was nothing else they could do – the power station was an impenetrable fortress, sealed on three sides by the army camp and by the river on the fourth side. On the flat roof above his head the radar scanner probed an inviolate bowl that nothing could enter without sounding the alarms. Even high-altitude bombers would have to rise above the horizon. The worst they could do was launch a rocket attack – that would give him thirty seconds warning.

After several weeks' practice he required only five seconds to pull the modified pocket cellphone from his pocket and tap out the five-digit code on the keypad.

He smiled to himself and caressed the little folding phone. The others didn't know about its secondary function. The others were sentimental fools. When it came to action – doing what had to be done – they couldn't be trusted. Their attitude to those men killed in the oil refinery had shown that. It was as well he had taken precautions.

He stroked the keys on the pocket cellphone. They were hard and smooth, yet yielding – like a woman's nipples . . .

His mind drifted back to the Saturday night.

There had been the blonde girl. By the dim lighting in the tunnel he had watched her breasts sway every time she reached down to pick up one of the Cyclonite cartons. He had absolute power over her. This time it would be right.

He pressed the Sterling into her side and gestured down the passage. She didn't understand at first – her eyes were blank when he wanted her to look frightened. Perhaps he should choose another one? No! If he did that, it would mean *they* were controlling *him*.

He prodded her before him and pushed her into a recess in the side of the tunnel and positioned himself facing her so he could also see the power station staff at work stacking the cartons.

She had long silky hair. He liked long hair. He held the gun in one hand and stroked her hair with the other. Perhaps she flinched when he touched her. He didn't know. He was aware only of his own emotions – the blood starting to roar in his ears like an express train. He lowered his hand to her breasts. They had looked so promising when she had been bending down. But now, with her shoulder blades pressed against the concrete, they were unsatisfactory; her nipples were merely a change of skin texture beneath his fingertips. The recurring rage seized him. He grasped her breast, twisted savagely and flung the girl into the passage. Her scream ended with the roar of the Sterling. The impact from the ten shells that poured into her back in one second lifted her bodily and threw her against the sides of the tunnel. She slid to the floor and rolled over.

She had no breasts left.

Which was how it should be.

The late-evening sun streaming into the control room was hot despite the air-conditioning. His eyes closed. Memories of the Saturday night had stirred him

He touched himself.

Then a shadow fell across his face. He cringed.

'You disgusting boy!' screamed his mother. 'Wait till your father gets home!'

But the expected blow never came.

He opened his eyes.

Louise Campion was staring down at him.

'I've brought you some coffee,' she said. 'I'm on watch in five minutes.'

Keller took the mug and thanked her. She was wearing tight fitting jeans and an expensive blouse that had been gathered at the front and tied into a knot.

Keller sipped the coffee. There was a stain on the mug but he said nothing; the anger and tension were slipping away as they always did, but he still felt uneasy in the woman's presence. Why hadn't she sat down? Perhaps she was trying to demonstrate some form of superiority by standing while he sat – taunting him, just as all women did. Taunting him with the pale band of flesh below her blouse. Now she was watching his whitening knuckles as the involuntary tension tightened his fingers round the mug. He forced them to relax. Showing outward signs of stress was a mistake he rarely made, but the recollection of the girl in the tunnel had triggered the roller-coaster rhythms that pulsed through his brain and occasionally threatened to smash the delicate psychological mechanism that managed to keep him teetering on the edge of sanity.

'You look as if you could do with some sleep,' said Louise.

'Did you manage to sleep this afternoon in this heat?' asked Keller.

'Oh yes,' she answered lightly. 'Try counting sheep.'

Keller nodded and stood.

Maybe her bed was still warm.

Her room had formerly been the office belonging to the power station's chief maintenance engineer.

It was locked.

Keller slipped his Access card between the door and the surround. There was a light resistance as the stiff piece of plastic encountered the convex brass tongue of the Yale lock. He wriggled the cord up and down while easing it forwards. The resistance suddenly ceased and the card slid forward. He pushed the door open and returned the Access card to his wallet; the irony of its name escaped him. For a moment he stood on the threshold, savouring the eager sensations of anticipation at what he would find, before stepping into his childhood and closing the door behind him. He would have to be quick – his mother's shopping trips never lasted more than an hour.

But this wasn't his mother's room. She always made the bed before going out and she didn't sleep on a camp bed.

He kept very still for a moment, picking at the clinging barbs of fantasy in his confused mind.

She was using a typist's desk as a dressing-table. It had her things on it; a hairbrush; a silver-framed head and shoulders of a man in RAF uniform – he was leaning into the picture in the style favoured by professional photographers of a past era. So how old was she? Thirty-five? Forty?

He opened the bottom drawer first. It contained an assortment of empty typewriter-ribbon boxes, pencils and bottles of dried correcting fluid. The middle drawer was the same. He opened the top drawer without closing the lower two. It contained a wallet, some letters, an inventory of medical supplies and a plan showing the power station's radiation detectors. The letters contained nothing of interest.

Keller slammed the drawers shut in frustration.

There were two large crates standing in one corner. One contained cartons of tampons and boxes of new shoes. The other was filled with unworn clothes still in the manufacturer's wrappings. He pulled a small suitcase from under the camp bed; it contained brassieres and panties – all clean and unworn. His calm suddenly ruptured under the pressure. In fury he threw the underclothes across the room and flung himself down on the camp bed. For some minutes he wept bitter frustration into her pillow.

Reason eventually asserted itself. He picked up the garments and folded them before returning them to the suitcase. Then he sat on the edge of the bed, gradually calming down.

The carpet tiles with the sun streaming across them caught his attention. They were all of a uniform colour, but a contrasting shade effect had been created by laying them with the pile at alternative angles to the light. One tile was different – its pile lay in the same direction as two adjoining tiles.

He reached down and picked it up by the horsehair tufts with the intention of repositioning it.

Underneath the tile was a single sheet of typewritten paper. It was a carbon copy – possibly a fifth or sixth copy because the words were blurred and the surface was smudged with carbon. Nevertheless the words sprang clearly off the page as he read them:

Government to commit UK to the setting up of a single defence force for the European Community by the end of the century . . .

Public transport to be free . . .

500,000 hectares of land to be made available immediately and sold in quarter hectare plots to enable people to build their own homes . . .

Disbelievingly Keller read the paper right through. And then a second time with consuming fury.

Conrad Pyne and Hugh Patterson were sitting in the common room when the door burst open. Keller advanced

111

into the room, his face white with anger. Before Patterson could stop him he had yanked Pyne to his feet by his lapels and was screaming: 'Bastard! Filthy, double-dealing bastard!'

Patterson tried to grab Keller but Pyne waved him away.

'What the hell's the matter?' demanded Pyne, trying to pull himself out of Keller's enraged grip. But Keller seemed to have lost control and continued shouting 'bastard' over and over again.

'Look, if you'll just tell me what's wrong!'

Patterson lunged forward but was doubled up by a vicious blow in the stomach from Keller who continued to scream his rage. He released Pyne by thrusting him backwards into his chair. He waved the sheet of paper under Pyne's nose.

'We agreed the conditions. We all agreed!' Keller was shaking with fury.

'Don't be stupid,' gasped Patterson. 'What the hell are you talking about?'

Keller held up the sheet for both men to see.

'Communists!' His voice was a hysterical shriek.

'All right,' said Pyne soothingly. 'Now just calm down and let me see that piece of paper.'

Keller quietened but his face was still deathly white.

'We all agreed on the conditions at the planning meetings. Now I discover you've–'

'Now wait a minute,' said Patterson. 'We couldn't get you to agree to half the terms.'

'Because they were communist-inspired!'

'Look', said Pyne in a reasoning tone. 'Some of the right-wing proposals you wanted – which we all wanted – had to be balanced by socialist measures if we were to win broad support from the people. We want to unite the country – not spark off a civil war. The proposals to set-up self-governing Muslim enclaves within the United Kingdom–'

'Which the Asians want!' Keller shouted.

112

'Which *some* Muslims want,' Pyne corrected. 'The proposals were mischievous and you know it. You only insisted on them because you knew it would drive a wedge between Muslims and non-Muslims.'

'We don't want to usher in a system of apartheid,' said Patterson. 'None of us want that.'

'Look, Keller,' said Pyne. 'We're extremely sorry for having deceived you, but it's too late to change the proposals now – even if we wanted to – which we don't.'

'No, general. That's where you're wrong.' Keller's voice was now smooth and drained of anger. He reached into his pocket and produced the cellular phone. 'I suspected there was something I was being excluded from, so I took a simple precaution to make sure I should always have a direct say in what was going on.'

Keller held up the handset. The two men stared at it in bewilderment.

'Who are you going to phone?' asked Patterson.

Keller smiled icily at his former employer. He pushed the slide switch with his thumb and held the handset up so that the two men could see the keypad.

'It's no longer a cellphone, Mr Patterson, but it can still transmit. All I have to do is switch it on – as it is now – press five of the keys in a certain sequence, and it transmits a coded pulse which, when picked up by a receiver I've hidden in one of the Cyclonite cartons, will detonate the carton.' Keller smiled. 'And all the others, of course. Your idea upstairs of two switches three metres apart which have to be activated at the same time by two people is ingenious – but not as ingenious as this.'

Keller turned the keypad towards himself and pressed four of the keys. The tactile feedback bleeps were clearly audible in the quiet room.

Pyne held out his hand. 'Give it to me, Keller.' It was as if he was talking to a small boy.

But Keller did not respond: not now he was in full control of the situation. It was only when he felt that outside forces

113

were dictating to him that the aggressive, repressed half of his personality assumed control. Now he was cold and unruffled – master of the situation. He merely shook his head and held his finger poised above the keypad.

'Take one step near me, general, and I press the key. Possibly not all the cartons will explode, but I've made certain there won't be any doubt about those under Silo Three – the one containing the plutonium.'

Pyne stared at Keller for some moments. It was hard to reconcile the coldly infuriated man standing before him with the usually quiet, always polite Keller. The only time he had ever displayed temperament was during the planning meeting to draft the ultimatum, when he had expressed his dislike of some measures Pyne had proposed.

Pyne decided that Keller was not bluffing – he had the knowledge to modify the cellular phone and build a receiver. Pyne inwardly cursed himself for including Keller in the group. He had never trusted him, but Keller had designed the silos – he knew their weaknesses, and where to place the explosive.

'So what do you intend doing?' asked Pyne tiredly. Suddenly he wanted to put an end to the whole wretched business. He was not even aware that it was his sorrow at what was happening to his country, and how he hoped to halt its decline, that prevented him lunging at Keller: his supreme self-control had taken over.

Keller looked at the sheet of paper. 'I presume the deadline for the government to agree to implement the ultimatum is still midday tomorrow?'

'Yes,' said Pyne dully. 'With another seventy-two hours to draft the legislation.'

'What else is there I should know about ?'

'Nothing.'

'You're sure?'

'Yes.'

Keller nodded. 'Very well, general. But you'd better be telling the truth, for all our sakes.'

114

He spread the sheet of paper on the table and drew a series of bold lines through some of the conditions. He pushed the sheet across to Pyne.

'I want you to call the Prime Minister now, and tell him about those deletions.'

There was a telephone on the table. Keller picked it up and listened before holding the receiver out to Pyne.

'There's a line on this extension. I presume you've stuck to the arrangement of using a secret number?'

Pyne took the receiver and slowly dialled Simpson's direct-line number. He waited, staring down at the floor.

'Don't say anything else.' said Keller. 'Just say what conditions have been deleted, and make sure he understands.'

Pyne wondered if Keller could hear the ringing tone. He pressed the telephone harder to his ear.

'Simpson? This is General Pyne at Vulcan Hall . . . There have been some alterations to the ultimatum we issued on Sunday . . . Yes . . . Certain conditions have been deleted.' Pyne picked up the sheet of paper and read out the numbers of the contentious demands. The conversation took four minutes. Pyne paused occasionally as if the deletions were being read back to him. Finally he said, 'Yes. That's the complete list as it now stands. I want you to see the Prime Minister is informed immediately . . . I'm sorry but I have nothing to add.'

Pyne was about to replace the receiver when Keller spoke:

'Tell him all future communications are to be on the Government's digitally encoded cell phone TAC frequencies, so we won't be overheard.'

Pyne repeated the instructions into the mouthpiece. Keller took the receiver from Pyne's hand and dropped it on to the cradle.

'I suppose you now wish to assume command?' said Pyne.

'No, general. You're the administrative type – you carry on running the power station.' He tapped the handset. 'Just remember that I'll have this little gadget with me at all times,

115

and that I need less than a second to press the keys. Even if you were to shoot me, you can't be certain that I'd die quickly enough to prevent me from destroying the country. And if you were to destroy this gadget with a well-aimed shot . . .' Keller grinned. 'Well – the way I've programmed it, that would be the same as if I'd operated it.'

'Do you expect me to believe that?'

Keller held the handset up. 'Go ahead and shoot it,' he invited.

'What about our guns?' inquired Patterson, bewildered by the transformation in an employee he had known and trusted for a number of years.

For a moment Keller seemed uncertain. Then he came to a decision. 'You'll have to keep them.' He looked at Pyne. 'I want you to issue strict orders to the soldiers that they're not to enter the power station complex under any circumstances. We'll maintain boundary integrity ourselves by increasing the number of IRIS detectors. You and Patterson will have to carry out the morning and evening patrols to check their batteries and reset them, so you'll need your weapons.'

Keller picked up the typed sheet and returned it to his pocket. 'I'm going to move my things into the control room. No one is to go near the floor without my permission.'

He moved towards the door.

'One last warning. Neither you two or Miss Campion is to try escaping. If anyone does, then it's up to the others to stop him. I wouldn't be able to manage things by myself – or even with just three of us, and as you now know – I don't like being a loser . . .'

He left the last sentence in mid-air and was gone.

Two hours later Keller released the safety-catch on his Sterling. He relished the sensation of power that coursed through his fingers whenever they closed round the crude but effective weapon. There was no need to aim at such close range; the soldiers would hear nothing – Pyne had ordered them back to camp and sealed the entrance to the power station with detectors.

He fired from the hip.

The Ericcson switchboard exploded into shards of grey plastic that skittered across the polished floor of the power station's reception area. The thunderous noise was like champagne. He kept firing until the unit was an unrecognizable mass of tangled wire and smashed key-switches. The pine panelling behind the switchboard splintered under the impact of high-velocity ammunition. A few minutes earlier he had sabotaged the communication equipment in Pyne's and Patterson's helicopters.

The noise attracted Pyne and Patterson who had been inspecting the wrecked transceivers in their helicopters. They waited until Keller had gone and stood surveying the wrecked switchboard.

'That's put paid to our first idea,' said Patterson. 'If Keller's going to stay holed up in the control room we won't be able to get near the radiotelephone. So what do we do now?'

'Some how,' said Pyne, 'I've got to escape.'

'What would be the point, Conrad? The Prime Minister will be acting on those changes.'

Pyne shook his head. 'I didn't get through. I was talking to myself.'

The big man looked at Pyne in surprise, and whistled.

'I didn't think Keller would fall for it,' said Pyne. 'Christ – it's such an old hat ruse and yet it worked.'

'Why do it?'

'The opportunity presented itself. I needed time to think.' Pyne gazed across at the far bank, four kilometres away. 'Hugh, you remember we showed Cox-Spender how the detonator control worked, and how it could only be worked by two people? Supposing we're now being watched through high-powered optical equipment on that bank and they notice that from now on there's only one person in the control room – never two?'

117

Patterson stared at Pyne as the implication of his words sunk in.

'They'd . . . They'd plan a lightning strike, not knowing . . . not knowing . . .'

'Not knowing that the silos can now be blown up by one man in less than a second,' Pyne finished.

Patterson looked thunderstruck. He stared across the river, at the haze hanging over the far bank.

'Put yourself in their position,' Pyne continued. 'Wouldn't you be watching us?'

Patterson nodded.

'That's why I've got to escape.'

Patterson nodded.

'That's why I've got to get word to the Prime Minister,' said Pyne. 'Somehow, I've got to escape.'

Patterson roused himself. 'But Conrad, we're in a hell of a cleft stick. If you were to try escaping. I'd have to shoot you to prevent Keller doing anything crazy.'

Pyne nodded. 'Exactly, Hugh. You'd have to shoot me.'

7

The ten eminent members of the Cromwell Two Committee listened in shocked silence as their chairman related what had happened that day at the Palace of Westminster.

'And so,' concluded the chairman. 'Pyne has stolen a march on us.'

For a few moments there was silence.

'It's what I would've expected from him,' said General Sir Richard Markham. 'Pyne often confided in me that he thought this committee would still be unable to deal with the racial problems unless we revised our ideas about the sort of measures we were in favour of.'

'You were the one who proposed his membership,' the chairman pointed out.

We needed that new force he's been given,' replied Markham. 'I wasn't allowed to have any say in its formation and administration.'

The chairman sighed. 'What do we do now?'

'We'll have to cancel the takeover,' said Sir Oswald Fox.

'Impossible,' said the head of the Special Branch. 'We're ready to move.'

'Sir Oswald is right,' the chairman interrupted. 'What point is there in us taking over if we have to bow and scrape to Pyne and his thugs? No, gentlemen. I suggest we play the Prime Minister's favourite game no matter how much we despise him for it – we wait and see. We let him sort out the problem of Pyne, and then we move. In the meantime I'll keep you all informed of Cabinet meeting developments.'

8

There is no organization within the British Civil Service that resorts to killing as a political function; there are no James Bonds or Boysie Oakes subordinate to retired senior officers in the government's machine. Consequently, Simpson was at a loss when he decided that the best way of dealing with Howard Mitchell would be to kill him.

Then he remembered a list of names and addresses the Special Branch had once supplied to his office in the days when they could be trusted.

At 16:00 hours, he was studying that list intently.

He left his office at 16:05 and drove over Westminster Bridge in search of a suitable telephone box. There was one in an inconspicuous position in the Waterloo Bridge Road.

Patrick Reagan was in his garden, spraying the blackfly on his french beans and reflecting that at least the vegetable crop this year was saving a fortune in housekeeping during the hard times that were upon him and his wife.

Reagan was an instrument-maker. His employers, a small engineering firm, had been forced out of business by spiralling costs. During better days Reagan had supplemented his pay packet by using his skill with the watchmaker's lathe to manufacture bomb and timing mechanisms in his small but well-equipped workshop.

119

Now the cells who had used his services had been mopped-up and the new ones operating on the mainlain consisted of smart, well-educated lads who could build their own mechanisms by buying components over the counter from model engineering shops and electronics shops.

Although things were bad for Patrick Reagan they could be worse. He could be in prison. Fortunately the evidence linking him to the bombing of an Aldershot public house had been too flimsy for the Director of Public Prosecutions to proceed.

Reagan was refilling his garden spray when the telephone rang.

'Mr Reagan?' said a voice he didn't recognize.

'Who's that?'

'Are you interested in earning a couple of thousand pounds, Mr Reagan?'

'Doing what?' said Reagan suspiciously. The caller's accent was right but it sounded slightly contrived.

'I want you to provide a special party for a friend of mine. Using your special talents–'

Fucking law, thought Reagan, and hung up.

The telephone rang again.

'If you go to the telephone box outside Raynes Park Station.' said the voice, 'I will ring you there and give you your instructions . . . Two thousand pounds Mr Reagan. Think about it.'

Simpson saw Reagan's Nissan drive past the café. He paid for his undrinkable coffee and crossed to the telephone box. From inside he watched Reagan park his car and enter the telephone box outside the station.

The telephone surprised Reagan by starting to ring just as he pulled the door open.

'Mr Reagan,' said the voice. 'Look up.'

'What?'

'Look up above your head.'

Reagan looked up and saw an envelope secured to the inside of the telephone directory glass by its gummed flap. It contained a number of £20 banknotes.

'Fifty of them,' said the voice, as if its owner was reading his thoughts. 'And another fifty when you've carried out the task.'

'What do you want me to do?' said Reagan.

Simpson told him.

Five minutes later Reagan sat in his car and considered his problem – namely that he had only ten grammes of plastic explosive. It was hidden in his garden under the compost heap to fool the trained labradors. Ten grammes wouldn't kill a man unless it exploded hard against his body. It was the right amount for a letter-bomb, but they only maimed, and the man on the telephone had been quite clear about the results he wanted.

Reagan turned the problem over in his mind.

Ten grammes exploding hard against a man's body . . .

A traffic warden had spotted his car and was approaching.

Hard against a man's body . . . ten grammes . . .?

Yes. The answer was obvious. Reagan grinned disarmingly at the traffic warden and drove off just as she was preparing to swoop.

The large electronics hobby shop was about to close when Reagan entered. The assistant sulkily found the heat-operated switch he wanted – one set for its contacts to close when the body of the switch was heated to 30 degrees Centigrade – just a few degrees higher than the temperature reached during the hottest part of the afternoon.

And a few degrees below the temperature of the human body.

Reagan was pleased with his purchase. The £2000 was going to be the easiest money he had ever earned in his life.

121

9

Corporal Garnet stumbled off the Waterloo train at Walton-on-Thames and was carried along the narrow and incredibly filthy pedestrian tunnel by a wave of desperate homeward-bound commuters all determined to get away from one another and into the metallic lava stream of wife-driven cars flooding out of the station forecourt. The train had been the only one out of London on the line for an hour. The journey had been a nightmare with coaches holding four times their designed capacity.

Garnet stood blinking in the bright sun considering his next move. The suit he had purchased in a menswear shop off Piccadilly had been expensive, but now it felt and fitted like a fetid scrotum. He had been lucky in managing to find a seat on the train. A clerk sitting opposite had suspiciously eyed his scar and the general's crested briefcase. Garnet had divided his attention between him and the girl sitting beside him with her skirt hitched round her thighs to ensnare the cooling draught blowing through the open window.

All but £5 of the money in the general's briefcase was gone.

A taxi took him into Walton town and dropped him outside the Midland Bank.

The cash-dispensing machine spat out £100 in new notes after he had fed it with the general's card and punched out the PIN number he had found pencilled on a piece of paper in the wallet.

The corporal tried for another £100 but the machine refused to oblige. It also kept the card.

He now had £105. Enough for several drinks and one woman.

He badly needed both.

10

Late on Monday evening Pyne kept watch while Patterson worked at a lathe in the power station's workshop.

122

The sweat running down the big man's face was due partly to the suffocating heat and partly to fear of the consequences if Keller discovered what he was doing. His discomfort did not prevent his working quickly. Fortunately his long-neglected skill with a lathe hadn't atrophied over the years.

He gently tightened a nine-millimetre bullet into the jaws of the lathe's bell-collet so that it was gripped evenly round the rim of the case. Next he opened the chuck jaws on the tail-stock and closed them down on the nickel-jacketed slug. The bullet was now firmly gripped at each end.

He carefully rotated the lathe. The entire bullet turned. He cursed and wiped the sweat from his eyes before tightening the tail-stock jaws a fraction. He gingerly turned the lathe again.

This time the jaws held: the slug rotated in its case as the grip between case and slug was broken. Patterson continued turning the lathe by hand, gently winding the tail-stock back at the same time.

The slug was drawn from its case like a tooth pulled from a socket. He removed the empty case and peered inside to ensure the propellent charge was still in place, then used the lathe jaws to crimp the open end shut, taking great care not to distort the case which could jam.

The case could be fired; it would make the normal amount of noise and smoke and that was all.

Pyne studied Patterson's handiwork.

'Okay. Fine. You'd better do enough for a whole magazine.'

Patterson's normally good-humoured face was creased with anxiety. He took the round from Pyne and examined it critically. 'What are the chance's of the magazine jamming, Conrad?'

'It's a chance we'll just have to take,' Pyne replied unemotionally.

123

11

A committee of twenty Members of Parliament and the two government law officers worked for five hours drafting the enabling bill that would become law within twenty-four hours.

They left Downing Street at five minutes to midnight. All the MPs were also practicing lawyers. Each one had been responsible for the wording of a section, which in turn had been passed to two colleagues for careful checking to ensure that the wording was one hundred per cent watertight.

It had been an exhausting five hours.

The Prime Minister bade them goodnight and returned to the Cabinet Office. Simpson was poring over the sheets of paper written in a wide assortment of handwriting. Each sheet was a mass of amendments and deletions. Simpson held one up.

'The last clause. Written by Beresford. It requires the bill to lapse automatically when pressure on the government has been removed.'

The Prime Minister nodded. 'Provocative, wouldn't you say?' Simpson fed the sheet of paper into a shredding machine.

'Do you know what the Attorney-General said when he left?' inquired the Prime Minister. 'He said, 'It's a good job we haven't got a constitution and that the governments have always opposed a Bill of Rights for the people.'

Simpson looked surprised. 'That's exactly what you said when—'

'I shouldn't attach any importance to it, Simpson.'

The Prime Minister yawned and looked at his watch. Midnight.

He went to bed at fifteen minutes past midnight and was soundly asleep ten minutes later.

12

At 23:00 hours Reagan reversed his Nissan behind a large rhododendron within fifty metres of Mitchell's house. The baked ground was too hard to leave tyre marks.

He closed the driver's window against the swarms of disturbed mosquitoes before checking his set of watch-maker's tools and transferring them to various pockets: tweezers into the handkerchief pocket where the spikes would not dig into him; a multipurpose screwdriver with a selection of blades in its handle transferred to a trouser pocket; a diamond file into his wallet with the tungsten-wheel glass-cutters wrapped in a piece of self-adhesive decorative plastic film. The small vacuum flask containing the components to make the bomb made a conspicuous bulge in his jacket. He wound a short length of transistor radio earphone wire round the matchbox containing his precious ten grammes of plastic explosive. The wire was fine enough to be cut with his folding nail scissors.

He removed the car ignition key from his key ring and placed it on the floor. If he had to make a quick getaway he would be able to pick the key up without having to fumble with the other keys on the ring. Leaving the key in the ignition was inviting trouble. One of Reagan's recurring nightmares was being forced to flee from a house he had broken into, only to find that his car had been stolen.

He left the car in gear with handbrake off and the driver's door ajar.

He approached the house by skirting the edge of the lawn, keeping close to the shadows and checking the lawn with quick stabs of light from his torch for signs that meant dog. There were none.

There was a light on in an upstairs room but that did not worry him: his immediate concern was to get into the house as quickly as possible. Once inside he could rely on his skill to avoid detection; outside he was at the mercy of curious eyes.

The area round the kitchen door was screened from the garden and road by rustic woven fence panels. There were no feeding bowls on the enclosed rectangle of concrete, no scraps of meat and no scratch marks on the door.

Reagan relaxed a little. The door was locked. He pressed it at the bottom with his foot. It gave slightly. That meant it had not been secured on the inside with a bolt. It was the same at the top of the door – all he had to contend with was the mortise lock. He shone his torch through the keyhole and noted with satisfaction the gleaming end of the key's barrel pointing at him.

It took him two minutes to inscribe a circle on the door's glass pane with the glass-cutters, peel the backing paper off the self-adhesive plastic film and secure it over the circle. The third blow with the inside of his fist caused the disc to fracture from the surrounding pane. He quickly removed the plastic film with glass attached and reached through the hole to unlock the door.

The first thing he did inside the house was to search for an emergency hiding-place. The instinct of a professional housebreaker when he hears noises that suggest his presence is known is not to flee, but to hide. Most people fondly believe that making a noise is sufficient to cause a burglar to leave – it works with amateurs, but not with professionals. And Reagan was a professional.

He found a broom cupboard leading off the hall. He pushed a child's rubber sucker onto the inside of the door so that he could pull it closed behind him if the need arose.

The telephone was in the living-room on a low coffee-table. Reagan positioned his torch and laid out his tools on a handkerchief so that he could pick them up and put them down without making a noise. He could also gather them up quickly if he heard a sound from the floor above. He unscrewed the vacuum flask and shook the bomb components and crushed ice into a clean ashtray. Next he unscrewed the telephone's earpiece cover and placed it on the handkerchief. Using the tweezers to avoid heating the

126

component, he picked the thermal switch out of the crushed ice in the ashtray and positioned it inside the earpiece cover. He rolled the piece of plastic explosive, the size of a thimble, into a slender sausage shape between his palms and then placed it on the bed of ice for a few seconds to cool before carefully tamping it around the inside of the earpiece so that it held the tiny thermal switch in position, but with its two fine wires protruding. Buried in the ice was the pin detonator, which he fished out with tweezers and dried with cottonwool before pressing it firmly into the explosive. The last component was a Mallory cell battery the size of an aspirin. Like the thermal switch, it had two fine lengths of wire attached to its terminals. There was a plastic cap at the end of the wire which prevented the ends touching one another and draining the current. Reagan left it in place until he had pressed the battery into the explosive. Finally he connected the components together with short lengths of the earphone wire. He held the plastic earpiece cover between thumb and forefinger and screwed it back on to the telephone's handset. He tested the weight of the instrument. He doubted if Mitchell would notice the additional weight when answering the phone.

Reagan replaced the handset on the cradle and surveyed his handiwork. The two contacts inside the thermal switch would now be moving towards one another. But they wouldn't touch until they were exposed to thirty degrees Centigrade – another six degrees – such as the human body was capable of providing. When Mitchell answered the phone the heat from his body would cause the thermal switch contacts to close after ten seconds, thus completing the circuit.

The resulting explosion, though small, smaller than even a letter-bomb explosion, would be enough to blow Mitchell's brains out.

Reagan gathered his tools together and tipped the melting ice back into the flask. He dried the ashtray with his handkerchief.

The next phase of the operation was for him to earn the other £1000 he had been promised.

And that required only a phone call.

13

Reagan was heading back towards the main road when he spotted the orange-striped police car with its cherry-festooned roof lurking in the trees.

He drove past, neither slowing nor accelerating. In the rear mirror he saw the police car's headlights suddenly stab across the road then sweep towards him as it pulled out from the trees. The distance between the two blazing lights widened in his mirror. Reagan tried to remain calm and drive normally despite the dazzling lights reflected into his eyes.

The police car made no attempt to pass and wave him down – it seemed content to sit on his tail.

Reagan began to sweat. If they were after him it wouldn't take them long to find the house with the broken window. It would take them even less time to learn some interesting facts about his spare-time career. They'd go over Mitchell's house with a microscope. They wouldn't find prints, but the bloody junky labradors would soon sniff out the plastic explosive.

Unconsciously, Reagan accelerated. Why didn't the sadistic bastards stop him?

The searing lights were now right behind him and blinding him. If he moved his head more lights mocked him from the door mirrors.

Bastards.

All he could see ahead was a narrow band of glittering flint road surface funnelling briefly into his field of vision before disappearing under the Datsun's hood. He did not see the approaching yellow flares of the main-road street lighting until it was too late.

British Aerospace driver Peter Floyd was ferrying a spare Airbus tailplane to London Airport. The police required that such a load should be moved only at night. The road from the aircraft works was slightly downhill. He was doing forty-five miles an hour when his articulated truck struck the car which suddenly shot across his path from a side road.

There was no time for Floyd to transfer his foot to the brake pedal before the front of his cab smashed into the car's rear. The shattering impact spun the car round in the road, with petrol flailing from its ruptured fuel tank.

Reagan might have lived had he driven straight into the side of the truck instead of suddenly spinning the wheel in panic as the yellow street lighting and the side of the truck burst upon his consciousness.

In the time it took for his hand to drop to his seatbelt buckle the car was engulfed by an incandescent fireball. Reagan was still alive three seconds after impact – clawing at an unyielding door welded firmly shut by the rapidly melting rubber draught excluder. He managed to wind down the heat-warped window a few centimetres; flames syphoned into the car, setting fire to the headlining. Then he was screaming as globules of falling molten plastic set fire to his hair and clothing, and he knew he was going to die.

Tuesday

1

Corporal Garnet was at Reagan's death scene, but took no interest.

He pushed indifferently through the small crowd, making his way to General Pyne's house on St Georges Hill.

He had been thrown out of a Walton pub at closing time. The girl had been pretty; she had said nothing about his scar, which pleased him, and had worn a short skirt, which pleased him even more. Short skirts were rare in England, but the birds in Northern Ireland wore nothing else as part of their cock-teasing campaign against British soldiers.

He had bought the girl in the pub three rum-and-cokes. Then she had leaned forward, kissed the scar and said she had to go to the toilet. That was the last he had seen of her.

He had gone to pay for another drink, and discovered the wallet had gone.

So had the last bus, and he hadn't enough for a taxi.

He had walked the six kilometres to Weybridge, going first to the road where the general's snooty bitch of a daughter had bought herself a house with her mother' money.

She wasn't in.

He waited an hour, planning to slip into the house behind her when she opened the front door. The longer he waited, the more he brooded on the treatment he had received at her hands. Well, he was a civvy now – the Redcaps couldn't touch him. The courts would probably give him six months – civvy style.

It would be well worth it.

He had sweated all Friday cleaning out the swimming-pool at her dad's place. When it was nearly refilled he'd asked her if he could cool off indoors. The bitch had turned round and said, 'Not until you've mowed the lawn.'

Her father was decent enough. The sort of man you could admire and respect. How'd he come to have a daughter like that? Her dad had helped him over the business of the teenage joyrider outside Corry's timber yard in Belfast. The stupid kid had driven straight through an army roadblock. The bloody car had backfired and Garnet, his nerves keyed-up because he hadn't been in the province long, pumped five rounds into the back of the receding Toyota. It skidded, overturned and burst into flames.

It was the third case of joyriders crashing roadblocks and the drivers being wasted that year; they were going to hang everything on him. Make an example of him to appease a bloodyminded populace. Then they decided to hush things up and ship him home. He'd still be rotting in a military prison waiting for a court martial if the general hadn't stepped in and said he needed a driver and Scout pilot.

He had enjoyed the new job until the general's daughter had heard about his past. He had been clipping the grass along the edge of the drive when she had slowed down in her MG and said jokingly, 'Just making sure it doesn't backfire.'

A police car cruised by.

Garnet decided to move. Perhaps she was at her dad's home at St Georges Hill.

Her car was outside the house.

Garnet let himself in through the front door with the keys in the general's briefcase, pulled off his shoes and checked the house downstairs. There was no sign of her, although she'd left the kitchen in a mess and there were photographs scattered all over the dining-room. There was one of her in a bikini. A chinless twit had his arm round her and was trying to get his fingertips round her left tit. Looking at it, and the

131

thought that she was just upstairs, made him tremble with anticipation.

But first a drink.

He found a half-bottle of whisky in the sideboard.

Thirty minutes later it was nearly empty.

Now for the girl.

He took off all his clothes in the hallway and mounted the stairs. The night air felt pleasantly cool against his body after the oppressive stickiness of the suit.

Her bedroom door was ajar. He pushed it slowly open. For a moment he thought she had a bedside light on, so bright was the moonlight streaming into the room.

She was lying on top of the bed, curled into a foetal position, wearing a short nightdress. Her legs gleamed with erotic paleness.

Garnet stood trembling in the doorway – encouraging his erection before following it across the room to the girl's bed.

His hand closed over her mouth. She made a choking noise as he forced her on to her back. Her eyes were twin pools of terror that stared wildly up at him from above his fingers – he could feel her teeth trying to bite at the inside of his palm. Her legs thrashed madly, making it difficult to pin her down. Then she was trying to tear his hair out.

He hit her hard on the side of the face. Her hand tried to slide under his elbow and he immediately pinned it against the bed. He grasped her other hand and forced it back against the headboard.

Christ the bitch was strong.

He ground his knees viciously into her shins. A cry of pain gurgled from deep within her throat, and spent itself against the hand clamped across her mouth. The sound encouraged him to increased effort. He pounded his torso up and down – using his body as a pummelling wedge to force her legs apart. She tried to crush him with her hips, but the feel of the inside of her thighs only increased his excitement.

The girl's hand groped on the bedside table. Her fingers closed round the alabaster table lamp.

She brought it down on his head with a wild blow that glanced off his temple. The body on her relaxed. She smashed the lamp down again with all her strength.

The body rolled on to the floor and lay still.

Only when Maggie had staggered across the bedroom and turned on the light did she realize her assailant was Corporal Garnet. A bloodstain was soaking into her clothes under his head.

Her first thought was that her father had arrived home. She ran downstairs calling for him, but there was only silence and hot summer air in the big, still house.

She managed to reach the kitchen sink before being violently sick. The cold edge of the stainless-sink helped revive her. She drank a cup of water, then went into the dining-room for her father's gun.

There was a bottle of whisky standing on the scattered photographs, and something else. She stared at it – not understanding. It was her father's briefcase.

She found the Webley revolver in the sideboard. The museum piece's heavy coldness gave her confidence. She went upstairs – stepping over Corporal Garnet's clothes as if the untidy heap was a dead cat.

He was lying in the same position – completely naked. The bloodstain was spreading to the carpet. Fearful that he might suddenly arise to renew his attack, she crept nearer. His chest appeared to be motionless. There was something she remembered from a television play. She held a hand mirror in front of the corporal's face, above the leering scar.

The glass remained clear.

Suddenly her body was racked with pain. Still clutching the revolver, she went downstairs. She sat in the living-room staring at the telephone, nerving herself to call the police. She had heard about the way police dealt with rape cases, or attempted rape. There was the heap of clothes in the hallway; she'd have to say that Corporal Garnet was not a stranger; Christ – they'd want her to be examined.

Her father's solicitor was someone called Meredith. She opened the address book and punched his number. A bloody answering machine replied. She slammed down the handset and tried to think calmly. She saw Howard Mitchell's name and address on the open page. He would help. He would know what to do.

She called his number, praying he would be at home.

The ringing tone chirruped in her ear. She almost wept with relief when it stopped with the click of a receiver lifted off its cradle.

'Mitchell,' said an American accent, heavy with sleep.

'Mitch! Thank God!' Her voice nearly broke into hysteria as the tension of waiting for the telephone to be answered suddenly snapped. 'This is Maggie Pyne. I—'

She got no further as Garnet grabbed her from behind. She dropped the telephone and clawed desperately at the hand that threatened to choke her.

'Bitch!' screamed Garnet. 'Stinking, cock-teasing bitch!'

The receiver was swinging by its cord. She could dimly hear the puzzled, reedy, distorted voice:

'Maggie . . .? Maggie . . .?'

Garnet let go of Maggie's throat and hit her.

She fell to the floor, twisted round and snatched up the revolver.

Garnet was about to lunge at her. He froze.

Maggie looked up in terror at the livid scar, and aimed the revolver with both hands. She pulled the trigger as Garnet dived sideways.

The hammer fell on an empty chamber.

Bloody hell — an army daughter and she hadn't the sense to check if the damn thing was loaded!

Garnet threw himself at her, but she rolled sideways. He grabbed hold of her hair, screaming obscenities as he tried to tear her nightdress and climb on top of her. She tried to hit him with the gun. He knocked it from her grasp so that it skated across the floor. She doubled her legs under and pushed him away. The nightdress come away in his hands

134

with a loud, tearing noise. Garnet grinned at her. Blood was steaming down his chest from his matted hair. He wiped himself with the nightdress – his eyes never leaving the naked girl cowering on the floor.

She started to crawl away. He jammed her ankle painfully to the floor with his foot so that she cried out.

'Come on, you bitch,' snarled Garnet. 'Let's see you fight.'

She answered by doubling forward and sinking her teeth into his calf. The corporal drew back his other foot and kicked her hard in the crutch – a lethal kick had he been wearing shoes.

Maggie's teeth did not relax their grip. She could taste Garnet's blood.

He swore and dragged her head back by the hair. He slapped her hard across the face. She moaned in pain.

Garnet laughed. He dropped beside her and put his hands on her thighs. Maggie tensed, and drew her legs tightly together. The corporal lifted his fist menacingly. She winced as Garnet dug his fingers into her legs and forced them apart.

He moved over her, the hideous scar now above her face. She stared up at him, unable to feel him because he had kicked her so hard.

He began moving rhythmically, his elbows splayed out on the carpet and his hands crushing feverishly into her breasts.

Garnet's pace quickened. His whisky-laden breath rasped against his teeth and the blood flowed faster from his torn scalp.

Maggie forced her hand down slowly between Garnet's body and her own.

Garnet felt uneasy as the gently questing fingers closed softly, first round the base of his penis before moving delicately down to encircle his testicles.

Maggie crushed, twisted and pulled with all her strength in one smooth, totally devastating movement. Garnet released a shrill, almost feminine scream, arched backwards off the girl as if his spine was a crossbow and Maggie had

135

pulled the trigger. He continued screaming hideously and rolled himself into a tight, protective ball of personal agony.

Maggie pulled herself to her feet. She looked quickly round, grabbed the revolver by the barrel and raised it above her head to hit the corporal.

He looked up at her – his eyes glazed with pain – and pushed himself on to one knee. Maggie dropped the revolver in panic and raced into the hall. For a moment she was uncertain what to do. Garnet was crawling towards her. She flew up the stairs and locked herself in the bathroom. She could hear Garnet crashing about in the kitchen before he came staggering up the stairs after her, bellowing like an enraged bullock.

Then he was outside on the landing.

The lock on the bathroom door was designed to inform rather than to withstand a determined assault. The door splintered away from the surround on Garnet's first charge.

The last thing Maggie saw before losing consciousness was the flash of light on the raised breadknife Garnet was clutching in his hand.

2

The Prime Minister tossed Cox-Spender's phoney report on the cause of the Thames Haven disaster on to the desk and lit a cigar. He watched Simpson covertly through a cloud of blue cigar smoke.

'What are you working on now, Simpson?'

Simpson looked up from his desk and wished the Prime Minister would return to his own office. 'I'm dealing with the discontented families of Vulcan Hall staff who are complaining that their relatives haven't returned home since Saturday night.'

'What are you going to say?'

'I don't know,' said Simpson sourly.

'Unusual for you to be at a loss, Simpson.'

Simpson said nothing.

The Prime Minister stretched luxuriously and watched his cigar smoke define the beams of early-morning sun shining into the room.

'You know, Simpson, were this not such a deadly serious business, I might be tempted to enjoy it. Does that sound callous?'

Simpson met the politician's gaze. 'How much longer do you think we can keep the Civil Service at bay, sir?'

The Prime Minister grinned wolfishly. 'Just as long as I can keep up the pretence that I'm dealing with party business.' He paused, watching Simpson struggle with the report. Simpson's trouble was that he had little imagination.

'Supposing you tell the families that there was an accident with one of the reactors and that the staff have been quarantined?'

'That would bring the press swarming around our ears.'

'A row is inevitable, Simpson. Rows we can deal with once the full story is out. What worries me at the moment are the imponderables.'

'Such as?'

'Such as that American – Howard Mitchell. What's happening on that front?'

Simpson braced himself. 'I've organized a private investigator to watch him'

The nerve in the Prime Minister's neck twitched. 'Dangerous, Simpson.'

'I've arranged everything by phone,' said Simpson evenly.

'Not only dangerous, Simpson, but contrary to my orders.'

'I wanted to be near at hand to assist you, sir. I thought the Nelson touch seemed appropriate.'

The Prime Minister watched Simpson through a cloud of cigar smoke. Simpson knew too much. It would be wiser not to push him too far.

Simpson smiled thinly at the politician. 'I'll be calling him each morning and evening for a progress report.'

Simpson found it easy to lie. His whole life was one huge, complex web of deception.

3

It had been a dream.

Maggie hovered for some minutes in the half-world between sleep and consciousness while one partially open eye and her drugged brain sluggishly co-ordinated their respective images and sensations in an effort to assemble the familiar surroundings into one continuous tapestry, so normal that her reason, struggling up from the depths of sleep, told her that the recent, hideous events uncoiling in her memory had been a dream.

She pushed her feet into the cool corners of the bed and immediately sensed that two things were wrong: the dull ache in her pelvis and the smoothness of the sheets. They were smooth only on Sunday mornings because Saturday was the one day in the week when she made her bed properly.

Then there was something else – she was wearing one of her mother's nightdresses. She sat up and screwed her face up as a lance of pain probed behind her temple. Her fingers traced the outline of a sticking plaster taped to the side of her forehead.

The bedside lamp was missing. It hadn't been a dream. Or had it?

Then she saw the bloodstain on the bedroom carpet and the flood of vicious memories dropped into their slots.

Garnet was still in the passageway outside her door. She pulled the sheet protectively up to her chin.

The door opened.

Mitchell entered the room carrying a tray. He looked at her in concern and said: 'I've been looking in every fifteen minutes to see if you were awake.'

He set the tray down on the bedside table and poured her a hot sweet drink.

'It's tea. Don't try to say anything – just drink it.'

The drink scalded the back of her throat, burning away the taste that lined her mouth. Her hands began to shake. Mitchell sat on the edge of the bed and leaned forward to steady the cup and saucer.

'I'm sorry,' she began, but Mitchell raised a finger to his lips. 'You don't have to say anything. The doctor said you were to get as much sleep as possible.'

'What time is it?'

'Nearly 8:30,' said Mitchell, and added as an after-thought, 'In the morning.' He took the cup and saucer from her and placed them on the tray. 'You need some more sleep, Maggie.' Mitchell gave her an encouraging chuck under the chin and left the room, closing the door softly behind him.

An hour later, with unanswered questions crowding out sleep, Maggie went downstairs. Mitchell was eating a sandwich in the kitchen. He smiled warmly at her.

'How are you feeling now?'

'Awful.' She sat at the table opposite him.

Bruises had appeared on her face that Mitchell hadn't noticed before.

'Maggie, you don't look well. You ought to go back to bed.'

His tone irritated the girl.

'I always look like this in the morning,' she snapped, and immediately regretted it. 'I'm sorry, Mitch. Is that coffee?'

He poured her a cup. 'That was some party you were having last night. The doctor said you were suffering from shock. He's going to look by this afternoon.'

Maggie avoided Mitchell's eye. 'You know what happened?' she asked.

'The doctor told me. You were in a helluva state when I found you.'

'You found me?'

'You called me, remember? I don't know how long you'd been ringing when I answered the phone. I can sleep through

139

anything – even with the extension ringing by my ear. I could hear you yelling so I dropped the phone and got here as quickly as I could.'

'Thank you.' said Maggie.

'He was standing over you with a breadknife, shouting about his crown jewels. I hit him from behind and dumped him in here. I guess I should've tied him up, but I was more concerned about you. By the time I'd cleaned you up, he'd gone.'

God, thought Maggie bitterly. You're attacked by one man, and end up being pawed by two more. It was an ungrateful thought, but she couldn't help it.

Mitchell sensed her embarrassment. He went to the sink and pretended to wash his plate.

Maggie watched him. She remembered the flashing breadknife. She went across to him. 'Mitch, I'm sorry. I didn't mean to sound rude. It was good of you to come so quickly.'

He put his arm round her and steered her back to the chair. 'Don't worry about me, honey. You just sit down and drink your coffee. Then you should go back to bed. I'll stay if you like.'

Maggie allowed herself to be pushed gently on to the chair.

'Do you want to have him charged?' asked Mitchell hesitantly. 'There would have to be an examination by a police doctor'

Maggie shook her head. 'I don't know.' Then she remembered her father's briefcase.

Despite Mitchell's protests, she rushed out of the kitchen. She returned, reading the various papers.

Mitchell read the letter Pyne had written to his bank about Corporal Garnet. 'Why would he want to do a thing like that?' he asked.

Maggie shook her head in bewilderment and held out another paper. 'He's given him the boat, and told him to sell it for whatever he can get . . . And these . . .' She held up an envelope, ' . . .are Corporal Garnet's discharge papers . . . And look – a cheque. Made out to the corporal – for *five hundred pounds*!'

Mitchell took the papers and studied them. 'Why would your father do a crazy thing like that?'

Maggie stared at the cheque. She looked up at Mitchell. 'He's blackmailing him,' she said, her voice low. Then she was screaming, 'That filthy little trigger-happy runt's blackmailing my father!'

Mitchell calmed her down. 'Now, honey. You don't know that.'

The telephone rang. Maggie pulled away from Mitchell and went to answer it.

She returned a few minutes later looking thoughtful. 'That was Weybridge Marina. They said Garnet had just taken the boat out and were checking to see it was okay . . . Mitch, you've got a boat, haven't you?'

Mitchell looked at her. The doctor was right – she was tough. There was a hard light in her eyes.

'Now look, Maggie. Don't you think you should wait for the doctor?'

'I want to find out about my father.'

'We should call the police.'

'No! Not until we know what hold that bastard's got over my father!'

Mitchell decided not to argue. He sighed. 'Okay. I'll go home and get the boat keys. Give me thirty minutes.'

There were a police car and a dog handler's van outside Mitchell's house.

His first thought was that Maggie had changed her mind and had telephoned them.

'Mr Mitchell?' said the senior officer.

'Yes? What's the matter?'

'We've been waiting for you, sir. Were you aware your house had been broken into last night? Your paperboy reported it.' The policeman sounded suspicious, as if people

141

who allowed their houses to be robbed were instrumental in the crime.

The police spent fifteen minutes checking the house. They even let the labrador loose. It sniffed round every room, returning to the living-room several times, but found nothing.

Mitchell finally persuaded the policemen to leave, promising to call them if he later discovered anything missing. They drifted reluctantly back to their vehicles and sat watching the house for some minutes before driving off.

Mitchell ruefully examined the broken kitchen window. He couldn't leave the house empty without carrying out some sort of temporary repair. As he finished hammering the last piece of wood into place he realized that the living-room telephone was ringing.

4

The meeting in a cool, north-facing room above the reservation offices of Mid-European Airlines in Oxford Street was due to start at 10:00 hours.

Walter Innam arrived at 10:05 carrying a briefcase and wearing a ten-year-old suit. The receptionist pointed to the lifts and told him he was expected in Room 101. Innam spent an unhappy five minutes peering at room numbers until he was rescued by a typist.

Paul Weiner arrived by taxi at 10:10.

A man in his early forties, wearing a check suit, arrived on foot. He nodded to the receptionist and went straight to Room 101. Weiner and Innam were already seated at the long conference table. One wall of the room, was occupied by a beaded glass screen with loudspeaker enclosures mounted on each side. A selection of film and slide projectors stood on a long shelf at the opposite end of the room.

'I presume you've converted the pictures to slides?' was the first thing the man in the check suit said to Weiner.

'Yes.' Weiner nodded to Innam. 'Mr Innam has them.'

The man in the check suit seemed to notice Innam for the first time. Then he smiled, and shook Innam warmly by the hand.

'Good to see you again,' he said. 'How are you keeping?'

'Very well,' said Innam, trying to peer closely at the vague face without appearing to be rude.

'We met in Washington a couple of years back. You did some verification work on some suspicious construction work in Iraq.'

'Oh yes,' said Innam politely.

'And now you've found some more surprises for us right here in England?' The man in the check suit looked at Weiner expectantly. 'Right. Shall we start?'

'I think we should wait until Hendricks arrives,' replied Weiner. 'He should be here any moment.'

The man in the check suit looked surprised. 'He's in the country?'

Weiner nodded. 'He flew in from Langley two hours ago.'

'What made him decide to come?' The man in the check suit regarded Weiner accusingly.

Weiner shrugged. 'Hendricks is entitled to do as he pleases.'

'Something must've touched a nerve to drag him across the Atlantic.'

'I sent him Mr Innam's report as a matter of routine,' said Weiner.

'Which I haven't seen yet,' the man in the check suit said pointedly.

'I thought Hendricks should see it first.'

The man in the check suit looked at Innam speculatively. 'It must be something pretty spectacular you've got in that briefcase.'

'Pretty spectacular,' said Weiner, answering for Innam.

The door opened and Hendricks entered. He was a tall, gaunt man with a long craggy face completely devoid of humour that inspired profound gloom and a deep sense of foreboding in everyone with whom he came in contact. There was a rumour circulating in the 'firm', the headquarters of the CIA at Langley in Virginia, that he had once smiled. But it was one of those events, like the falling of Jericho's walls, for which the evidence was slight and largely circumstantial.

Weiner's attempts to introduce him to the other men were waived brusquely aside. He sat at the head of the table facing the screen, positioned his gold pen carefully parallel to the sheets of paper already provided and looked up at the three men.

'Good morning, gentlemen. Shall we begin?' The question was expressed as a command.

Weiner and the man in the check suit looked uncertainly at one another.

Weiner cleared his throat.

'Well, sir, as you know, last Sunday the big oil refinery here at a place called Thames—'

Hendricks held up his hand. 'Quite right, Weiner. I do know. Therefore there seems little point in going over it. I've come all this way to see your covers because I couldn't make much sense of the faxes. I want to hear your interpretation and decide what should be done. So I suggest we get on with the task in hand without preamble.' The sentences were delivered in short, grating bursts in a Harvard accent.

Weiner looked uncomfortable. He muttered a 'yes, sir' and crossed to the windows to close the venetian blinds so that Innam had to grope in near-darkness as he struggled to load his slides into the projector.

The first picture showed the remains of the refinery from an apparent height of a thousand feet. It had hardly been on the screen for five seconds when Hendricks clipped accent rapped out: 'Next.'

It was the same with the following three slides. Each one was allowed barely five seconds on the screen, and the long face would say, 'Next!'

The fifth slide was a close-up of the piece of aluminium which had first captured Innam's attention the previous day. The stencilled white characters were indistinct.

'Do you have a closer picture?' Hendricks asked the darkness.

'There's a zoom attachment on this projector, sir,' said Innam.

'Then use it, please.'

The picture sprang at the audience – the edges spilled on to the ceiling and over the loudspeakers. The white letters and numbers were now much clearer and could be read without difficulty.

'That, gentlemen,' said Hendricks waving his bony hand at the screen, 'is a Federal Stock Number issued from a block of numbers assigned to the Marine Corps by the Defense Logistics Center at Battle Creek, Michigan. The first two digits – one-four – are, as you correctly pointed out in your report, the Federal Supply Classification group for guided weapons. Before leaving, I was able to establish that the rest of the number is the stores identification reference for the after-fairing of an Honest John missile. The number was stencilled on the section in accordance with the Marine Corps normal policy for the identification of spares.'

Hendricks paused, leaned back in his chair and hooked his long fingers behind his head. 'The general consensus of opinion at Langley is that it was most astute of you gentlemen to detect this peculiarity, for which I am asked to thank you.'

A nice back-handed compliment, thought Weiner.

'My own opinion,' continued Hendricks, 'is that fulsome praise should be reserved for when you find out who has been firing American-made missiles. Among other things, you are paid to solve mysteries – not merely find them.'

There was a silence in the room, then Weiner spoke:

'According to the statement issued by the British government, the explosion was an accident.'

'All part of the same mystery,' said Hendricks slowly. 'There's no doubt that the destruction of the refinery was the result of terrorist activities, and that the British government know that. Terrorists do not keep their acts a secret.' Hendricks smiled thinly. 'Otherwise there wouldn't be much point committing them. The questions we must ask ourselves, gentlemen, are – firstly, who and what are these people who have fired an American-built missile; and secondly, what are the demands they are making on a friendly government? Demands that the government is apparently keeping secret.'

'Do we know how the missile came to be in the country in the first place?' asked the man in the check suit, wondering what all this had to do with power stations.

'Yes,' said Hendricks unhelpfully. He paused, and continued:

'We believe it must have been one of ten that were sold to the British government some years ago. Very old stock. A truck taking two of the missiles to a Royal Ordnance Factory for decommissioning was hijacked three months age.' Hendricks looked at Weiner. 'You may remember the incident.'

Weiner nodded. He remembered submitting a report to Langley that had resulted in a sharply worded note being sent by the United States Secretary of State to the British government. It criticised the lack of security arrangements for the transport of missiles by road.

'Normally,' said Hendricks, 'I am reluctant to draw conclusions, but it's reasonably safe bet that the missile used to blow up Thames Haven was one of those that disappeared.' Hendricks looked round the room, as if inviting a challenge. None came. 'It would be interesting,' he continued, 'to know where the missile was fired from. We can draw a radius of thirty kilometres around the site of the explosion, which gives us an area of about four thousand square kilometres as a hunting-ground. We need suggestions on probable sites we can work on first.'

This was the opening Weiner had been waiting for.

'Mr Innam has discovered more information from his study of the covers since he filed his report,' he said quickly.

Hendricks turned to Innam.

'Is that so?'

Innam saw a patch of light above Hendrick's shoulders facing in his direction. 'I think I can tell you exactly where it was launched from,' he said nervously.

'Please do,' said Hendricks.

'If I could change the slide . . .' Innam clicked rapidly through the slides. A succession of images flashed on the screen until he reached one that showed the Thames Estuary in strange contrasts. The river was bright green, and the surrounding countryside was a mottled patchwork on various shades of red ranging from pale pink to vivid scarlet.

'An infra-red picture converted to false colours,' Innam explained. 'The shades of red are caused by foliage. If we zoom in closer . . .'

The strange scene moved nearer the four men. Weiner experienced the god-like sensation that Innam enjoyed whenever he plunged towards his reproduction earth.

Weiner looked at the screen with professional interest, but could make no sense of the riotous hues spread across the landscape.

'That's Vulcan Hall nuclear power station in the middle of the picture,' pointed out Innam. 'It's only ten kilometres from the refinery. Those squares are two tanker trucks.'

Weiner studied the picture closely. He could distinguish a stain round one of the vehicles.

'What's that mark?' asked Hendricks.

'A heat blister,' said Innam. 'The sort of thing you get following an explosion. There's a much bigger one around the refinery.'

'And this . . . heat blister was caused around the tanker when the Honest John was launched?' asked Hendricks sceptically.

Innam sensed the disbelief in Hendricks' voice, and bristled – his professional ability was being challenged. 'Yes, sir. I'm absolutely certain of it because there's an unfired Honest John in the tanker on the right. There's a gap along the top of the tanker if you look closely. Inside it's just possible to see the nose of an Honest John. It must be an Honest John because the measurements fit exactly!'

There was a silence following Innam's outburst.

Innam's hand was shaking. He wondered what would happen to him.

Hendrick's craggy face turned away from the screen. 'Okay. Let's have some light in here.'

Weiner rose and flicked the blinds open.

'Tell me about this power station,' said Hendricks.

The man in the check suit opened a manilla file and pushed it towards the long talons drumming impatiently on the table. They stopped drumming and picked up the plans and photographs in the file.

'It's a thirteen-twenty megawatt unit powered by two gas-cooled fast-breeder reactors,' said the man in the check suit. 'It's only just been pulled from production and was scheduled for de-commissioning. Yet according to the infra-red pics, two of the cooling towers are still chucking out heat – more than the residual heat you'd expect from even recently closed-down reactors. There's a heat cloud spreading right across the North Sea. My guess is that the British have shipped a helluva lot of nuclear waste to Vulcan Hall for temporary storage. They've run into political problems with their repositories in Cheshire.'

Hendricks tapped the plans. 'In that case, how much waste do you reckon there is at Vulcan Hall?'

The man in the check suit hesitated. 'I've only been able to make a rough calculation based on the size of the heat cloud, but I'd say in the region of two-point-five billion curies, plus.'

'What does that mean in terms of quantity?' Hendricks demanded. 'I'm not a nuclear physicist.'

148

'It means the largest concentration of nuclear waste in the world,' said the man in the check suit.

No one spoke. The walls of Jericho suddenly cracked: Hendricks smiled.

'I have formed a theory, gentlemen,' he said, 'one which ties all these seemingly disjointed facts neatly together.' He turned to the man in the check suit. 'What would be the effect of releasing all that waste into the environment?'

The man in the check suit scribbled on his paper and looked up. In a tightly controlled voice he said, 'It would be another Cheynobel only worse . . . Much worse . . .'

5

An hour later Hendricks was sitting in Paul Weiner's chair studying the photograph of Ralph Keller taken at a St Georges Hill garden party.

He dropped the picture on to the desk and looked up at Weiner. 'Odd that he should turn up.'

'We don't know that he's involved,' Weiner replied.

'We do if my uncanny sixth sense says he is,' said Hendricks, picking up the St Georges Hill electoral register and idly turning the sheets. His shrunken eyes flicked down the printed columns of names and addresses. Several entries were underlined. He pointed a gnarled finger to one and raised a questioning eyebrow.

'People with strong right-wing views,' explained Weiner. 'Strong right-wing views – not extreme. We've eliminated the crackpots and only classified those possessing a degree of sobriety – those who have the ability to form the nucleus of a resistance movement.' Weiner paused. 'Should the need for such a movement ever arise.'

Hendricks studied the list is silence. 'Where's Pyne's name?' he inquired at length.

'Sheet seven. Patterson's name is on sheet five. Louise Campion's name is on the same page. She's the woman in the photograph.'

Hendricks turned the pages. 'What does Pyne do?'

'He's the British government's Logistics Liaison Officer – their hatchet man for supervising the run-down of the armed services. All the defence-cut recommendations carry his signature. He's a leading advocate of a central European defence force.'

'A carpet warrior?'

'A pretty efficient carpet warrior. The Treasury Department like him – that's why he's made the rank of major-general at forty-five.'

Hendricks nodded. 'And it's definitely his helicopter at Vulcan Hall?'

'Yes.'

'How well does your contact – this Howard Mitchell – know him?'

'He plays golf with Pyne on Sundays. Nothing more than that. Howard never used to make friends easily.'

Hendricks stood up. 'I want to see this Howard Mitchell. Call him up and have him come here . . . Like now, please.'

6

It was a woman's voice who answered the phone.

'May I speak to Mr Reagan, please?' said Simpson.

There was a pause, then the woman said: 'Who's that?'

'A friend ,' replied Simpson.

Another pause. 'I'm taking messages for Mrs Reagan,' said the woman. 'If you could tell me who you are . . .'

Her tone worried Simpson. 'I want to speak to Mr Reagan,' he interrupted, keeping his voice calm.

'Mr Reagan . . . He was killed last night in a road accident.' The last sentence came out with a rush.

Simpson placed his hand on the coin box. 'Really? How?' The shock in his voice was genuine.

'It's terrible,' said the woman. 'Mr Reagan was such a careful driver. Always so careful with everything he did. The truck driver said he came straight out of a side road . . .'

150

'Where did this happen?'

'Weybridge. None of us can think what he was doing there. His wife's in a dreadful state, poor soul . . .'

Simpson let the woman continue for some moments – his mind racing, as one improbable theory after another clamoured for attention.

'Can I say who it was?'

'No. It doesn't matter.' He replaced the handset and stared at the telephone for some seconds, considering his next move.

He called Directory Inquiries and asked for the telephone number of Weybridge police station. Two minutes later he was talking to the desk sergeant.

'I can give you no more information than we've released to the press,' the police officer told him. 'A Patrick Reagan was killed last night at the junction of Brooklands Road with St Georges Hill Road. I can give you the exact time if you hold on a minute . . .'

'Can you tell me which way he was heading at the time?' asked Simpson.

'He was turning out on to the Brooklands Road from St Georges Hill. His car was struck by a British Aerospace truck.'

'Thank you, officer,' said Simpson, and hung up.

He left the public telephone box looking uncharacteristically worried.

7

Keller was woken by the hot morning sun streaming into the control room. He had slept badly during his first night in charge at the power station. Several times he had woken suddenly and reached for the cellular phone in the belief that someone was approaching his camp bed but each time there had been no one.

He crossed to a control console and bent the gooseneck microphone stalk to his mouth. 'I would be most grateful if someone would kindly provide me with breakfast,' he announced with impeccable manners. He could hear his voice booming through distant corridors as a variety of loudspeakers reproduced his nasal accent with varying degrees of accuracy.

'Perhaps Miss Campion would oblige, please?' said the speakers in the staff rest-room where Pyne and Louise were eating a cold breakfast.

Louise looked up at a speaker and grimaced.

'He can get it himself,' she said.

Pyne carefully replaced his cup on the saucer and placed his hand over Louise's wrist. 'It might be a good idea, Louise. Especially if you could get him to eat it near one of the front windows.'

She looked down at the hand covering her hand, and up at the grey eyes. Pyne pulled his hand away.

'How would I do that, Conrad?'

Pyne looked faintly embarrassed. 'Well . . . feminine guile.'

Louise smiled. 'Have I got any, Conrad?'

Pyne avoided her gaze. 'Well, of course.'

'Perhaps I should practise on you first?'

Pyne began to wish he hadn't made the suggestion.

Louise said nothing. She crossed to a small counter and began cutting some corned-beef sandwiches.

'Perhaps we could poison him?' she said.

'We could.' agreed Pyne. 'But you'd have to cook something that could kill a man in one second flat.'

She looked up at Pyne, but the remark was made without humour. His hands were clasped together on the table. He was staring at the far wall with an expression of utter dejection. Several times during the night, when the three had discussed possible ways of overpowering Keller before he had a chance to use the cellular phone, she had wanted to comfort him – to tell him that he was not to blame for the unexpected turn of events. But his unresponsive facade and complete acceptance of responsibility deterred her from making such an approach, Even Hugh Patterson had tried to persuade Pyne against an escape attempt by volunteering to shoot Keller, but Pyne had rejected the suggestion.

'All we've got is these Sterlings.' Pyne had said.

'I thought they were lethal.' said Louise Campion.

'Not lethal enough. The first round has got to kill him outright and you can't be a hundred per cent certain of that with a Sterling. They slay rounds all over the place. Okay in close combat but not much use for picking a man off with a hundred per cent certainty of killing him.' Pyne had paused. 'And we have to be a hundred per cent certain.'

The debate had dragged on all night. By 8:30 when Patterson left to check the IRIS detectors on the western perimeter, it was decided that Pyne's original plan, using a Sterling filled with blank cartridges, was the one that offered the only chance of success. Pyne had stressed the importance of someone escaping to warn the government of the changed situation in the power station in case they were planning a break-in.

Hugh Patterson entered the rest-room as Pyne was finishing his second cup of coffee. He perched his massive frame on a chair and looked in alarm at the sandwiches Louise Campion was preparing.

'They're not for me . . .?'

'They're for Keller,' said Pyne. 'He wants Louise to take him some breakfast. Have you checked the detectors along the river front?'

'No. I've come back for some batteries. I thought I smelt coffee.'

Pyne stood. 'It's time to put the plan into operation.' He picked up a Sterling and held it by the open frame towards Patterson. 'Come on. You can have your coffee later.'

Patterson looked first at the offered submarine-gun and then at Pyne. He shook his head slowly. 'Now?' he queried.

'We all agreed to move when the first opportunity presented itself. Louise will take his breakfast up and get him to eat it near the windows so he can watch you and me checking the detectors.'

Patterson took the weapon and examined it in concern.

'It's too dangerous, Conrad. Supposing it jams?'

Louise Campion finished preparing Keller's breakfast. She watched the two men, making no attempt to intervene.

Pyne shrugged. 'I've never pretended the idea was without risks. I'd rather take a chance that sit about doing nothing.'

'You must let me do it.'

'It was my idea,' Pyne replied firmly.

'And my fault Keller was included in our group.'

Pyne looked at his watch. 'We'd better synchronize. I make it 9:17.' He looked at Louise. 'Do you think you could get him to the windows by 9:30?'

Louise checked her watch.

'Yes.'

'That's settled then. Come on, Hugh.'

Patterson sighed and followed Pyne out of the room.

Louise Campion stopped outside the door leading to the control room and set Keller's breakfast tray down on the floor. In the stillness of the corridors she had heard the faint whirring of the heat-guided closed-circuit television cameras following her progress from the restroom. Now she was standing directly underneath a camera and, she hoped, out of its field of vision. Its lens was tilted towards the floor at the maximum angle the tilt head would permit. It was not the thought that Keller had been watching her that made her tremble, but what she had to do next.

Her fingers fumbled at her blouse until the top five buttons were unfastened.

She looked at her watch.

9:21.

She knocked loudly on the double doors leading to the control room, picked up the tray and pushed the doors open with her hip.

Keller was standing a few metres away holding his Sterling at a casual angle with the cellular phone hanging from his wrist by a short strap. He smiled and came forward.

'Miss Campion. This is extremely kind of you. Let me take that for you.'

Louise moved towards the windows.

'Here?' she asked, watching Keller's eyes to see if they dropped to the unfastened blouse. They didn't.

He took the tray from her and sat at one of the consoles. 'It's much too hot to sit in the sun, don't you think?' he answered with his customary politeness as he sipped his coffee appreciatively. 'This is excellent, Miss Campion. I am most grateful.'

Louise pushed a strand of hair away from her face so she could look at her watch.

9:22.

She had eight minutes to get Keller over to the window.

8

At 9:22 Howard Mitchell dropped the hammer he had been using to nail pieces of timber across his broken window and raced into the living-room to answer the telephone. It stopped ringing just as he picked up the receiver. It started again as he was halfway up the stairs.

He answered it in his bedroom. 'Hello?'

He could hear breathing over the line.

'Mr Mitchell?' said a man's voice.

'Yes. Who is this?'

The line went dead.

Mitchell frowned to himself and replaced the handset. He went into the bathroom for a quick shower and shave before returning to Maggie with the keys to his boat.

The telephone rang for the third time as he was returning his electric razor to its case. As before, he took the call on his bedroom extension. It was his secretary, wondering why he had not put in an appearance at the office.

'It's nearly half past nine, Mr Mitchell,' she said reproachfully. 'You said yesterday you wanted to make an early start . . .'

Mitchell cut her short. He said he had changed his plans and wanted to spend the morning on his boat. Urgent calls could be referred to him via the boat's cellphone.

He drove away from the house a few minutes later with the boat keys digging into his hip.

Simpson walked thoughtfully away from the public telephone box. Obviously Reagan had failed in his mission. The Howard Mitchell problem would have to be shelved. If the CIA did find out about the power station . . . Well, it was a problem the Prime Minister could sort out.

9

'I suppose,' said Keller, finishing the first sandwich, 'that we'll have to eat the corned beef first because it has the shortest storage life?'

'I suppose so,' said Louise.

Six minutes.

Keller saw her look at her wrist. He smiled. 'I wonder what being cooped up in here will do to us?'

She realized that his eyes were fixed on her. It took a supreme effort of will-power to resist the automatic impulse to close the partly open blouse and so reveal her embarrassment. 'I don't know,' she replied.

Keller continued eating in silence.

'May I sit down?' she asked.

He looked surprised. 'I'm sorry. I should have said.' He waved his hand round the control room. 'I didn't think you would want to stay. Be my guest.'

Always perfect manners, she thought. It was hard to believe the man was unbalanced. But then, he had fooled everyone – even the shrewd Hugh Patterson. She wandered to the windows overlooking the river and sat down.

Five minutes.

Keller seemed to have lost interest now that she was some distance away. General Pyne and Patterson emerged at the far end of the apron to check the first of the IRIS detectors that guarded the power station's waterfront. Each one was mounted on an aluminium pedestal about two-metres high. The pedestal bases were weighted with a lead plate.

Louise pursed her lips and blew a stream of air up her face so that it ruffled her hair. 'Ye gods, it's hot.'

Keller started on the second sandwich.

'It certainly is,' he said noncommittally.

Four minutes.

She fanned herself with her hand, and pumped her blouse. She stretched her legs and repeated the gesture – enjoying the brief surges of air against her hot skin. She was careful to pull the material out far enough so that Keller would have a glimpse of her body. The behaviour was alien to her nature. It reminded her of her girlhood when she had discovered the sexual powers that girls could exercise over boys. She closed her eyes. Those days were now far away. There had been Clive when she was in her late teens. The halcyon days with him had ended and the memories had begun when he had misjudged an approach, and his Tornado jet fighter had become an incandescent ball of fire in some thick trees at Biggen Hill RAF base.

'Yes, indeed, Miss Campion. Very hot.' The refined, polite voice was immediately behind her.

She opened her eyes and turned slightly. Keller was standing over her staring down. His Sterling was drooping towards her pelvis. A feeling of nausea rose like a poisonous vine in her throat and blossomed into a smile. She glanced casually out of the window. Pyne and Patterson were checking the third detector. Patterson disguised a glance up at the window in a general survey of the power station.

'What are they doing?' asked Keller lightly.

'Checking the IRIS detectors, I suppose.'

'They checked them last night.'

157

'I think they have to be reset each day because of the heat.'

Three minutes.

Patterson paused to tie a shoelace while Pyne moved on ahead.

'Odd.' said Keller casually.

'General Pyne likes to be careful,' Louise replied, hoping her voice was calm.

'I wasn't thinking of that.'

Two minutes.

'You look frightened, Miss Campion.' The voice was flat with a disinterested tone. He rested his hand gently on her shoulders so that his fingers were resting near the top of her arm.

She tried not to shiver, and dared not look up to see if he was looking at her or at the two men below. The sun was glinting on her watch face making it impossible to read the time. She tilted her head slightly towards Keller's hand.

One minute.

The movement was a mistake; Keller thought it was one of affection. His fingers tensed and moved down to the start of the soft skin below her collarbone.

Patterson straightened from tying his shoelace. Pyne was thirty metres from him, walking along the top of the concrete-capped pilings and the water five metres below.

Thirty seconds.

She was certain Keller must be aware of her increased pulse rate beneath his fingertips.

'Can you remember the type of shoes Patterson wears?' said Keller. His voice was soft and gentle, but his nails were now sinking into her flesh like the claws of a mechanical grab.

Twenty seconds.

Pyne was looking down at the water, waiting for Patterson to catch up with him.

'I've worked for him for five years now,' said Keller. 'He wears nothing but expensive elastic-sided shoes.'

158

She risked a quick glance up at Keller. He was no longer interested in her but watching the two men intently. He suddenly released his grip on her shoulder, swung his Sterling up by the webbing strap and grasped the magazine. For a wild moment, as his attention was fixed on the scene below, she considered trying to snatch the weapon from him. There was a metallic click as his finger released the crude safety-catch.

Then Pyne was running as Keller stepped nearer the window.

'Stop!' screamed Patterson, his alarmed yell carrying plainly into the control room. 'For Christ's sake, Pyne! Stop, you bloody idiot!'

But Pyne didn't stop. He raced along the pilings with Patterson running after him. Patterson stopped chasing Pyne and raised his submachine-gun. His next shout was drowned by the sound of breaking glass as Keller slammed the open frame of his Sterling against the control room window.

'Stop him!' Keller screamed at Patterson through the jagged hole. 'I can't do it at this range!'

Patterson looked quickly up at the broken window and took careful aim at Pyne. He fired a long burst which used two-thirds of the ammunition in the magazine. The impact seemed to spin Pyne round; he teetered on the edge of the pilings before falling out of sight to the water. Patterson ran to the edge and poured a stream of fire into the river.

Two minutes later Keller stood panting beside him at the water's edge.

'Where is he?' demanded Keller, squinting at the dazzling sunlight reflected off the water.

Patterson shaded his eyes and pointed downstream towards the low sun. Keller could just distinguish a shapeless form drifting past the edge of the pilings.

He raised his submachine-gun.

'That's not necessary,' said Patterson sharply. 'He's dead.'

159

Keller ignored him. He fired a single shot. The water spat near Pyne's body. The recoil jerked the suspended cellular phone strapped to his wrist, but he was unable to see clearly the miniature plumes that spluttered round the floating shape.

Keller lowered the smoking Sterling and turned to Patterson at his side, who seemed too paralysed to move or speak.

'You've employed me long enough, Mr Patterson, to know that I always like to be certain. Just as you like to be sure you're not walking about with loose shoelaces.'

Patterson said nothing. He turned on his heel and walked towards the main entrance, where Louise Campion was staring at the two men in horror. As he walked towards her he half-expected Keller to shoot him in the back. He stopped and looked back at Keller. The nuclear physicist was shading his eyes and staring across the bright water at the lifeless form drifting towards the sea.

It was then that Patterson decide that somehow he would kill Keller before nightfall.

10

'What does your father's boat look like?' asked Mitchell as he inserted the key to start his Chris Craft's diesels.

Maggie surveyed the rows of boats at their moorings.

'Like that one over there. A Freeman.' She pointed to a smart blue and white fibreglass cruiser. 'Except ours has a white hull and a pale-green cabin.'

Mitchell nodded and pressed the starter buttons in turn. He grinned at a boat owner sitting in a nearby cramped cockpit and called out to Maggie:

'Okay. Untie up front.'

He liked to use non-nautical expressions just to irritate the pretentious yachtsmen, some of whom even wore peaked caps to sail pram dinghies.

160

The two engine temperature gauges were nearing the normal mark as the big cruiser slipped through the marina gates and out on to the Thames.

Mitchell settled into the comfortable helmsman's seat on the flying bridge, while below in the wheelhouse, the stainless-steel wheel and Morse engine-control levers appeared to move of their own accord – as if a ghost were at the helm.

Maggie joined Mitchell and perched on the navigator's seat beside him.

'Do you like boating?' he asked, to make conversation.

'Yes.' Her answer was flat.

Mitchell looked sideways at her. Her face was still lined with the tension of the previous night's ordeal. There was an ugly red mark across her cheek where Garnet had hit her. She had made no reference to the attack during the short drive to the marina.

'How are you feeling now?' It was a stupid thing to say. Why was he always so nervous with women? Why wasn't he able to bubble over with witty remarks that would make her laugh and help her forget?

'Better,' Maggie answered.

'Would it help if you talked about it?'

'No.' Then: 'Can I navigate for a bit?'

The question provided an opening which he seized. 'Do you really think we can get lost on this river?'

Maggie's laugh was immediate and gratifying. 'Idiot. I mean steer it.'

'Sure.' He relinquished his seat and stood behind her. He noticed that she didn't over-correct the steering, as most people do when handling a boat for the first time.

'You've done this before?' he remarked.

Maggie nodded. 'When mother was alive we'd all go on weekend fishing trips to Windsor.'

'With your father?'

'Yes. Always. We were a close-knit family. He always found the time.'

161

'But not any more?'

'He's been too busy lately.'

They passed a Thames Division motor launch riding at its moorings outside the river police station. An overweight policeman was sunning himself on the bank.

The Thames widened and bisected itself against a tongue of land. The left fork led to Shepperton Manor, the right fork was the Desborough Cut.

'Which way?' asked Mitchell.

Maggie considered for a moment. 'We'll go downriver first, and then come back up the cut. That way we won't waste too much fuel.'

'I'm not worried about that. But supposing he's gone further downriver?'

Maggie swung the helm gently to port before replying. 'He wouldn't get through Molesey Lock. The registration plate is out of date. We hadn't bothered to renew it.'

'Maggie, look. There's a police station back there. Don't you think it would be better to let them deal with him?'

'No, Mitch. Not until I find out if he's blackmailing my father.'

She looked determined. Mitchell decided not to argue.

The muted splutter of the water-cooled exhausts and the subdued mutter of the twin diesels steadily easing the long white hull through the water were not enough to disturb the wildlife thronging the wooded banks and small inlets choked with reeds.

Mitchell had journeyed along this stretch frequently – the first time was shortly after his arrival in England. It was that trip, and the discovery of the tranquil magic of the river, that had prompted him to import the Chris Craft when his business prospered. His great regret was that the increased demands of the business did not allow him to make more use of the boat. The business had also prevented him from making friends. The large house on St Georges Hill had been a mistake: with the exception of General Pyne, the neighbours had not been particularly friendly. And as Mitchell now realized, even Pyne's friendship, slight though it was, had been cultivated only because Pyne was keen to learn about the North Sea oil business. Mitchell suddenly realized as he stood beside Maggie that apart from his secretary, who was wrapped up with her own husband and family, Maggie was the first woman he had become involved with since leaving New York. Perhaps if he had worked and lived in London he would have met more people socially. But after a childhood spent on the Lower East Side he had resolved never to live in a city again.

'Would you like something to drink?' asked Mitchell.

'At this time?'

He smiled. 'Okay. How about a Coke?'

'Something stronger might wake me up. Mitch, I'm sorry I'm being so untalkative.'

'It's a virtue,' said Mitchell, and went down the companionway into the well-equipped galley. He was poking at the ice-cube tray welded into the refrigerator when the engines slowed. At first he thought something had fouled the screws. Then the refrigerator door swung shut as the boat gently heeled.

'Look,' said Maggie when he returned to the bridge. She pointed to the reed-encrusted bank where the roof of a cabin cruiser was visible above the tall fronds.

Mitchell placed his palm over Maggie's hand holding the spoked helm. She withdrew it as though she had been stung.

'I'm sorry,' said Mitchell. 'I was steadying her.'

'It's not your fault,' said Maggie shakily.

'Can you manage?'

'Yes.'

The transom of the smaller boat came into view as Maggie nosed the Chris Craft towards the reeds. Corporal Garnet was dozing in the cockpit. A fishing rod had slipped from his fingers. He did not stir at the sound of approaching diesels – it was the shadow falling across his face that woke him. He opened his eyes and looked up at the towering flying bridge, blinking in surprise, and then in alarm when

163

he saw Maggie at the controls. He stood up just as she sent the big cruiser surging forward with a sudden burst of power that jammed its bows into the reeds, cutting off the smaller boat's escape route.

Garnet considered jumping overboard. He had one leg over the coaming when Mitchell appeared in the Chris Craft's lower cockpit.

'I shouldn't,' said Mitchell, menacingly. 'It's about three metres deep here.'

Garnet hesitated. He felt the general's daughter's eyes on him.

'What do you want?'

'A word with you.'

'Fuck off. You're blocking my view.' Garnet tried to cover his fear with belligerence.

Mitchell stepped on to the Freeman's transom. The sudden motion caused Garnet to lose his balance. Mitchell hit him as he jumped into the cockpit.

The exhaust pipes were the first thing Garnet became aware of when he regained consciousness. His legs were splayed wide apart and crooked over the pipes with his ankles drawn painfully together by a length of rope passed under the exhausts.

The Chris Craft's fully soundproofed engine-room was a readymade torture chamber.

He cautiously opened his eyes. The engine-room was illuminated by a single lamp enclosed in a wire cage. Mitchell was standing over him. Garnet closed his eyes and braced himself for a kick in the testicles.

'You'd better answer a few questions,' snarled the American.

Garnet mouthed a profanity, but the outward display of bravado was diminished by the beads of sweat that appeared on his forehead. He tried to pull himself into a sitting position, and grimaced as the pipes dug into the back of his knees.

164

'Why did you do it?' demanded Mitchell.

'Do what?'

Mitchell gritted his teeth and hit Garnet. The corporal's insolent expression eased the surprisingly difficult task of hitting a bound man.

'She encouraged me.' Garnet spat.

Mitchell hit him again. It was easier the second time.

'That's not what she says.'

'Then it's my word against hers. For fuck's sake, why am I tied up like this?'

'You'll find out soon enough if you don't answer my questions.'

'Look,' said Garnet. 'Do you know her? She's nothing but a cock-teasing little bitch.' He paused and glanced round the engine-room crammed with expensive machinery. 'I don't suppose she treats you like she used to treat me.'

'How did she treat you?' asked Mitchell, this time resisting the impulse to hit Garnet.

'Like dirt.'

'Maybe there's a good reason for that.'

The sweat trickled down Garnet's face. 'At first I thought it was because I was only a bloody corporal – not her class, but it wasn't that.'

'What was it then?'

Garnet told Mitchell about the Tuesday afternoon in Belfast – about the joyrider's car that had backfired and how General Pyne had stepped in when he heard Garnet had been trained on Scout helicopters.

'You're fond of General Pyne?' asked Mitchell when Garnet had finished.

'He helped me when I needed help. If you can call having to wait on his daughter hand and foot being helped.'

'If you're fond of General Pyne, why are you blackmailing him?'

Garnet stared at Mitchell. 'Don't talk crap. What the fuck are you talking about?'

165

The third blow jerked Garnet's head back and tore the skin on Mitchell's knuckles.

'For Christ's sake!' Garnet pleaded. 'I don't know what you're talking about!'

The two men glared at one another in the dim light.

'Where's the general now?'

'I don't know,' said Garnet. Blood was trickling from the corner of his mouth.

Mitchell looked at his own bleeding hand. He straightened and lifted an intercom microphone off its hook.

'Okay, Maggie. Start them up. In neutral. Nice and slow.'

As he returned the microphone to its hook there was a loud hiss of compressed air followed by a harsh, metallic grating noise that resonated painfully against the eardrums in the confined space.

The port diesel engine rumbled into life and trembled on its mountings. The noise was repeated until the starboard engine was turning fast enough to run under its own power. The diesels settled down to a regular beat.

The pipes pressed against the inside of Garnet's legs began to get warm. His expression changed from arrogant defiance to fear.

Mitchell forced a smile. There was a difference between hitting a man and what he was about to do now.

'The exhausts are water-cooled so they don't get very hot,' said Mitchell, raising his voice against the reverberating rhythm of the two heavy diesels, 'provided this is turned on.' He pointed to a handwheel. 'But if I was to turn the water off, even slightly, like this . . .' He rotated the handwheel a turn.

Garnet felt the pipes getting warmer. He wondered if the American was bluffing. Mitchell's hard expression was not reassuring.

'Why do you care about the general?'

'His daughter wants to know.'

Garnet was about to risk a grin, when the American turned the handwheel slightly. He felt the temperature increase immediately from the hot gases streaming through the two pipes.

'So why are you blackmailing him and where is he?'

'He told me to say nothing,' Garnet choked out.

Mitchell turned the handwheel a few more degrees. He didn't enjoy what he was doing but the bastard deserved it.

'When did you last see him?'

'I promised to say nothing.'

Garnet sucked in his breath as the pain bit into his tendons.

'Why did he make you promise?'

The handwheel was turned a little more; not much but enough to make Garnet feel that his legs were being amputated at the knees by the searing heat.

'I don't know, for fuck's sake!' he screamed. He tried to arch his back off the engine-room floor, but the tension only pressed his calf muscles harder against the burning pipes.

Mitchell looked at the writhing corporal in concern. He had dropped back on the deck and was twisting his body first one way, then the other, in a fruitless effort to relieve the agony tearing at his legs. Low moans of pain mixed with obscenities escaped from his lips.

Mitchell decided to give up. He was about to restore the cold water when Garnet said:

'All right. Fucking well untie me, and I'll tell you what I know.'

Fifteen minutes later Mitchell dumped Garnet back in the Freeman's cockpit.

'Stay away from St Georges Hill and Maggie, otherwise I'll do a helluva lot worse,' he warned.

'The general said I was to look after his house,' said Garnet sulkily.

'Don't argue with me. Just do as I say!'

Garnet glanced up at Maggie Pyne's cold eyes staring down at him from the flying bridge. He nodded.

Mitchell waved to Maggie to go astern as he stepped over the coaming and back into the cockpit. The screws churned white water under the Chris Craft's hull as they hauled the big cruiser out of the reeds. Maggie swung into midstream and pushed the control levers forward.

'What did he say?' she asked when Mitchell rejoined her.

He related Garnet's scant story about Pyne's Sunday-morning drive to Downing Street. 'He said your father handed a letter to the police officer outside Number Ten. Maybe he's resigned or something,' Mitchell concluded.

Maggie looked puzzled. 'Even if he had, he wouldn't hand it in to the Prime Minister.' She frowned. 'Although, he did once know him.'

Mitchell looked at her in surprise. 'Your father knows the Prime Minister?'

'He used to. I don't think he's got much time for politicians now.' She turned to Mitchell. 'Is that little bastard blackmailing my father?'

'No.'

'You believed him?'

'Yes.' Mitchell paused. 'Maggie, what could your father be doing to be blackmailed?'

She turned her attention back to the river. 'Nothing.'

Her tone aroused Mitchell's suspicions. 'Look, Maggie. If you think Garnet hasn't told me everything, then we'll turn back and- '

'No!' said Maggie sharply.

'Then why—'

'Mitch, if I tell you something, will you swear never to repeat it?'

Mitchell stared at the bruised face turned earnestly towards him.

'Well, sure—'

Maggie paused while she marshalled her thoughts. 'I think daddy's involved with some sort of fraud over government equipment with Hugh Patterson.'

Mitchell looked at her with astonishment. 'Your father? But that's not possible.'

168

'That's what I would've thought. But he's being seeing a lot of Hugh Patterson lately, and I once overheard Hugh mention something about military supplies when I took them a cup of tea in the garden. If something is going on, that corporal could've found out easily.'

Mitchell was silent for a few moments. 'And you really think your father is doing something like that?'

'I don't want to think it,' Maggie replied angrily. 'All I know is that Daddy's been acting differently lately.'

Mitchell shook his head. 'Garnet would've told me. And besides, he respects your father.' He hesitated. 'You're the one he hates Maggie. He said you used to treat him badly.'

Maggie's face went pale with anger. 'He killed a woman. If it hadn't been for my father the ungrateful little bastard would still be in prison.'

Mitchell was unable to think of an immediate reply. He wondered what Maggie knew about service life – real service life, not hunt balls and parties in the officers' mess. Mitchell felt a twinge of sympathy for Corporal Garnet; he had reacted to a car backfiring as he had been trained to. The memory would be with him for the rest of his life.

'Did you hurt him?' Maggie asked.

'Did you want me to hurt him?'

'What do you think?'

'He was drunk,' said Mitchell.

'That makes it all right, does it?'

He was about to reply when the telephone in the wheelhouse emitted a shrill buzz.

It was his secretary. Paul Weiner wanted to see him in London as soon as possible.

'Okay,' he said. 'We're just coming into Walton. Come and pick me up at the Eastwood Marina in ten minutes.'

He explained the situation to Maggie.

'I could take the boat back to Weybridge for you,' she offered.

Mitchell hesitated at leaving his precious boat in the girl's hands. She correctly interpreted his doubtful expression.

'Oh come on, Mitch. I brought it here. You know I can handle it.'

He smiled. 'Sure, better than I can.' He gave her the keys to his Mustang. 'You'll need some transport when you get back to Weybridge.'

'What time will you be back?'

'I'm not sure. Paul's an old schoolfriend.'

'Ring me before you leave London, and I'll try to cook you some supper.' Maggie looked down to avoid his surprised look.

'Thank you. I'd appreciate that.'

Maggie smiled – for the first time that day.

She dropped Mitchell on the towpath at Eastwoods and swung the Chris Craft back upstream, enjoying the sensation of sitting in the sun, controlling a magnificent cruiser on the river she loved, where her father had taken her to feed the Queen's swans when she was a child.

Then she thought of Corporal Garnet also enjoying the river – sitting in her father's boat, fishing with her father's rod. She wondered if Mitchell had hurt him. No, she couldn't imagine it. Mitchell was too kind. It hadn't been him having to stare up at that scar . . .

Five minutes later she came to the island that divided the Thames from the river. She didn't take the Chris Craft up the Desborough Cut but followed the original course of the river towards her father's cabin cruiser.

11

Pyne's immediate concern when he hit the surface was to avoid swallowing the heavily polluted water. The second worry was whether he could swim far enough under water to be out of range of submachine-gun fire if Keller decided to rush out on to the apron. Before his fake fall he had breathed deeply for some minutes so that his bloodstream would be saturated with oxygen, to enable him to remain submerged for as long as possible. The plans he had discussed the night before with Hugh Patterson and Louise Campion – the long underwater swim, the face-downwards drift when he surfaced – began to evaporate as he fought to remain conscious against the numbing shock of the cold water. Luckily the impact had not forced the air out of his lungs as he had feared it might. As he went under he managed a few feeble strokes with no certainty that he was moving in the right direction – he could be swimming against the current and so remaining stationary. Then his brain, with its own indifferent survival instinct, drained his blood of oxygen and clamoured for more. After only thirty seconds beneath the surface he was fighting his way upwards.

As he rolled over he was horrified to see how close he still was to the pilings. He thought he saw Patterson emptying his Sterling into the water. Pyne sucked down one deep breath and allowed himself to drift. He kept his feet low in the water and kicked them in an attempt to move faster than the current.

Another deep breath.

He turned slightly. The pilings had disappeared. He was moving faster than he expected – he was as one with the great mass of water surging towards the estuary.

He felt rather than heard the whack of a bullet striking the water. There was no way of judging how far away it was.

There was no doubt about the next one: it raised a spurt of water a yard from his head. Then he was surrounded by shots smacking into the water. Each one sounded like a thin cane being struck on the surface. He blew the precious air out of his lungs and allowed himself to sink.

There were no more shots.

Pyne surfaced, gulped down air and continued to drift. It was ten minutes before he risked looking back at the power station. He was two hundred metres downstream. The apron, from this angle, was deserted.

And so was the four-kilometre wide expanse of the Thames.

There was a bright orange marker buoy at least four hundred metres downstream and near the far bank. The current was drawing him into midstream. If he could reach the buoy, it would be some thing to hang on to until he was spotted by a passing ship.

He swam with a slow breaststroke – a style he found difficult enough in the ideal conditions of his swimming pool. He dared not risk the faster crawl in case Keller was watching through binoculars. The glare off the water had been one factor in favour of this method of escape, but he couldn't take chances.

He stopped swimming and trod water. The power station was dwindling rapidly now that he was being carried along by the swifter midstream current.

He didn't hear or see the tug hauling a line of refuse barges until it was only thirty metres away and bearing down on him. He stared in bewilderment at the massive coir fender wrapped round the tug's snub bow, and then saved his life by panicking. He struck out for the far south bank just as the tug's bow wave shouldered him aside. He managed to push himself away from the hull as it swept past. Fortunately there was sufficient towline between the tug and the first barge to give Pyne a chance to get clear of the rapidly approaching slab-sided hull. The rusting steel plates tore the skin from his hands as he fought to fend his body away sufficiently to avoid the second barge. He was well out of danger by the time the third barge was passing him. The eddying backwash swept him into the wake behind the last barge. Something caught against his arms and then snaked past his body. It was a long length of mooring rope trailing in the water behind the last barge. He felt it coiling round his ankle. The jerk as the rope tightened would have dislocated his leg had he not grasped it in his lacerated hands to absorb the shock. He held on grimly. The torrent raging against his chest threatened to break his hold. He had to hang on at all costs and drag himself along the rope until his body was clear of the water.

It was that or drown.

By a supreme effort he managed to haul himself four metres along the rope. He tried to rest by wrapping the rope round his body, but it kept pulling straight in the wash from the barge.

Pyne's arms were aching from the strain of hanging on in the boiling wake. He remembered the trick PT instructors had taught him when he was a cadet: he gripped the rope between his instep and ankle, and pushed with his leg muscles.

A few minutes later he was under the barge's raked stern with the rope hanging straight down under his weight. He began to lift his body clear of the water. The rope was dry a metre above the surface; red stains showed where his hands had gripped it.

The motion of the barge swung him from side to side – increasing the load his wrists had to bear. He swung his legs over the remains of a rusting iron pintle projecting from the stern and reached up to grab a bollard before thankfully releasing the rope.

He rested for a few minutes, then carefully balanced on the pintle. As he straightened his head cleared the top of the barge coamings. He could see the other three barges obediently following the tug line astern. Almost fainting with fatigue, he pulled himself on to the narrow side deck. The stench of decaying refuse from the open hold was the most beautiful smell he had ever encountered.

He tried to stand when a sudden heavy wave caused him to overbalance.

It was only a two-metre fall to the refuse hold, but he struck his head on the side of a bottle and lay still. A steady avalanche of wrapping paper, plastic egg boxes and vegetable waste slithered down causing a depression caused by his fall and covered his body.

The crew of the tug were unaware that one of their refuse barges was carrying a passenger.

In five hours they would be in Dover, where a Dutch floating plant would deal with their cargo. Huge vacuum pipes would be lowered into the barge holds and would suck them bare in a matter of minutes. The refuse would be conveyed to hydraulic crushers for compressing into neat one-metre cubes which would end up as back-fill for a Dutch dyke.

12

Paul Weiner introduced Hendricks to Mitchell in his office at the American Embassy as 'my boss'. Hendricks was sitting in Weiner's chair. He waved a gnarled hand at an empty seat.

'Sit down, Mr Mitchell. I'm sorry to have kept you waiting.' He studied Mitchell like a vulture contemplating a piece of meat, and – not being a man to waste time on table manners – got straight to the point. 'Tell me about General Pyne.'

The question surprised Mitchell. 'What about my drill-string?'

'What about it?' inquired Hendricks.

Mitchell glanced at Weiner and then back at Hendricks. 'Isn't that what you dragged me up here for?'

'I daresay it will be possible to see that you're fully compensated for the loss of your equipment, Mr Mitchell,' said Hendricks carefully. 'Provided you tell us what you know about this man Pyne.'

Maggie's right, thought Mitchell. Her father is in trouble. He tried steering Hendricks away from the subject. 'Do you have any idea how much a drill-string is worth?'

'No.' said Hendricks, 'but I expect—'

'More than a million dollars.'

Hendricks nodded. 'Tell me about Pyne.'

Mitchell told him what he knew, but said nothing about Maggie's fears and Corporal Garnet's attack. It was his account of Pyne entrusting his property to Garnet that convinced Hendricks that his theory might be correct.

Hendricks listened carefully, making frequent notes, and produced the photograph of the group standing before a JetRanger helicopter. Mitchell looked at the print in surprise.

'How did you get hold of this?'

Weiner opened his mouth, but Hendricks waved him into silence. 'Do you recognize any of those people?' inquired Hendricks, in an icy tone that discouraged Mitchell from pressing his question.

'No,' said Mitchell, 'But, Mag– General Pyne's daughter showed me an identical picture the day before yesterday. She said the chopper belonged to Hugh Patterson.'

'What about the woman?' asked Hendricks, noting that Mitchell had nearly said, 'Maggie' when referring to Pyne's daughter.

'Louise Campion. A neighbour, and a friend of Pyne's family.'

Hendricks nodded, and turned the picture towards himself. 'And the man is called Keller?'

'Yes. I think that was the name.'

'First name?'

'I don't know.'

Hendricks stroked his nose with a bony forefinger.

'What's all this about?' asked Mitchell.

Hendricks watched Mitchell's fingers on the arm of his chair. 'Mr Mitchell, we would like you to maintain your liaison with General Pyne's daughter, and use it to obtain all the information you can from her about him.' The involuntary movement of Mitchell's fingers confirmed Hendricks' suspicions. 'We're prepared to pay for your drill-string, so you can't complain that we're being ungenerous.' He sat back and smiled frostily at the man sitting opposite him. If he was any judge of character, there would be a reaction now. It came immediately.

'What liaison?' snapped Mitchell.

Hendricks sighed. 'Mr Mitchell, it would be the easiest thing in the world for us to ship you back to the United States, if we so wished. A word in the right ears and the British could withdraw your work permit. I believe you would find it most difficult running your business here from the other side of the Atlantic.' He paused. 'Naturally, I'm confident that we won't have to resort to such measures.'

Mitchell looked at the cold, sunken eyes, and decided that Hendricks, whoever he was, was not bluffing. Also, the promise to cover the lost drill-string would lift a major financial burden.

'Okay then.'

Hendricks stood up. He held out his hand. 'Thank you, Mr Mitchell. You will of course contact Mr Weiner if you have any news.'

Mitchell was at the doorway when Hendricks said, 'Just one more thing, Mr Mitchell. Do you know if Pyne was the sort of man to have strong views on the mess this country is in and how to put it right?'

'Yes,' said Mitchell after a pause. 'His daughter said he often discussed economic affairs with Hugh Patterson.'

Hendricks nodded. 'Not a word to anyone about this meeting, please, Mr Mitchell.'

As Mitchell unlocked his office car he remembered his promise to call Maggie before leaving London. He was about to punch the last digit of her number on his car phone when he suddenly wondered what the hell it was all about, and what he was letting himself in for.

Then the sound of her voice made him forget.

Hendricks picked up the photograph.

'So he's changed his name to Keller?'

Weiner nodded. 'It was the name he used at Oak Ridge.'

176

Hendricks pressed the intercom key.

'I want to speak to the Secretary of State. Tell them it's extremely urgent.'

'Should we tell the ambassador?' asked Weiner.

'I expect so,' replied Hendricks.

13

Police Sergeant Harry Snowdon of Thames Division was resting his fourteen and a half stone – two of them surplus – on the grassy river bank outside his headquarters, having exerted himself for thirty minutes trying to clear the patrol boat's blocked fuel injector.

It was peaceful on the river. On the opposite bank, the Weybridge side, a number of anglers were illegally fishing from the public mooring. Thames by-laws were the province of the water authority, so Harry Snowdon was content to let them continue. A few metres from his large feet the disabled patrol boat rocked gently against the slippery jetty. To his left a weeping willow lazily dipped long tendrils into the water.

It was a perfect afternoon; too hot for messing about in boats.

A cruiser gracefully entered his view. Snowdon recognized it as the Chris Craft owned by the American who lived on St Georges Hill. He watched the boat enviously. In his twenty years with the river police he had learned to judge countries by the luxury cruisers they built. The Americans were high in his estimation, with the Dutch a close second.

There was something familiar about the girl at the controls on the flying bridge. Then he recognized her: General Pyne's daughter. Alone.

Harry Snowdon climbed to his feet and ambled into the headquarters building.

'General Pyne's daughter is out with that big American job from Weybridge Marina,' he announced.

'That's right,' said the duty sergeant, not looking up from his newspaper, 'I saw it go off this morning.'

'With the American?'

'Yes.'

'Doesn't look like he's on board now.'

The duty sergeant stood and looked out of the window over Harry Snowdon's shoulder. Then his face went white.

'Christ!' he yelled, throwing the newspaper on the floor. 'Look!'

Both men dashed out into the sun just as the Chris Craft grazed into the side of the moored patrol boat.

'My boat,' moaned Harry Snowdon.

Maggie cut both engines and leaned over the side of the flying bridge. Harry Snowdon clambered into the patrol boat and fended the cruiser away with a boathook.

'I'm sorry,' said Maggie. 'I'm not used to this boat.'

Harry Snowdon mopped his brow in relief while the duty sergeant made the cruiser secure.

'What can we do for you, miss?' asked Harry Snowdon, looking up at the flying bridge and noticing the bruises on the girl's face.

'I want to report an assault,' said Maggie quietly.

In Harry Snowdon's vocabulary, the journey in the Chris Craft to where the girl said Corporal Garnet could be found was 'hairy'.

The girl had said little during the first ten minutes, then she had turned in her seat and said, 'Would you like a drink?'

Harry Snowdon eyed the approaching bank, and wondered why river users didn't have to take a test like road users.

'You'd better straighten up, miss,' he said politely, noticing that the girl's hand resting on the controls was trembling.

She was suffering from delayed shock. Now that Mitchell had gone, she was unable to ward it off any longer. She didn't want the policeman watching her.

178

'If you'd like a drink, you're welcome to go below and see what there is,' she told Harry Snowdon.

'I think I'd better stay up here, miss,' said Harry Snowdon.

'There're several tins in the fridge,' said Maggie, grasping the helm tightly to stop the shaking. 'I'd like one if you wouldn't mind, please.'

Harry Snowdon looked at her pale, drawn face. He moved to the companionway.

'Thank you very much, miss.'

The roof of the Freeman cabin cruiser came in sight a hundred metres away. Maggie suddenly wanted to be sick.

'Sergeant,' she called out, 'he's over on the left.'

Harry Snowdon shut the refrigerator door. 'All right, miss,' he shouted up to the flying bridge. 'You take her in alongside, and I'll talk to him.' He slid the wheelhouse door open and stood watching the Freeman. He corrected the girl's approach slightly by touching the duplicate helm. The wheel suddenly jerked beneath his fingers and the boat heeled. Harry Snowdon nearly lost his balance.

'Sorry,' Maggie called down. 'Are you all right?'

'Yes, miss,' was the sorrowful reply.

From her position Maggie could see Garnet dozing in the cockpit. She pressed the horn button. The twin-tone blast woke the corporal. He stared up at the Chris Craft in fear.

'You stay just where you are until I come aboard,' commanded Harry Snowdon across the narrowing strip of water between the two boats.

Garnet's terrified eyes went to the uniformed police sergeant and back to Maggie, who was throttling back.

She leaned back and tossed the stern line to Garnet. He was too surprised to react – the rope fell into the water.

'Let me do it,' offered Harry Snowdon, calling up the companionway.

'It's okay,' said Maggie, coiling the line and tossing it again. The rope fell short as the cruiser drifted. Garnet lunged at the flailing end. His hands suddenly lashed out to

179

grab at the coaming to regain his balance, when his foot slipped on the edge of the Freeman's smooth fibre glass transom. He let out a yell as he fell into the deep water.

For the rest of her life, Maggie was to wonder what really happened during the next few minutes.

'Pull her over!' yelled the sergeant's voice from below, as he dashed along the side deck, looking for a line to throw to the man struggling in the water.

Harry Snowdon suddenly remembered seeing the ropes coiled on the flying bridge. As he shouted, the Chris Craft's hundred-horsepower diesels erupted with a roar of unleashed energy. He dived back into the wheelhouse and saw from the positions of the two Morse levers that the girl had thrown one engine into forward gear and the other one astern.

The big cruiser's stern was swinging towards Garnet, who was screaming that he couldn't swim.

'What shall I do?' Harry Snowdon heard the girl cry out.

He grabbed the two levers and tried to reverse their positions.

As the Chris Craft's stern swung towards him Garnet grasped the mahogany rubbing strake protecting the hull where it joined the transom, His feet encountered one of the under-hull brackets that supported the balanced rudders. He braced his weight against it in relief and stretched an arm out to the swimmers' boarding ladder attached to the big cruiser's transom. The enraged water from the madly spinning propellers boiled past his body, threatening to dislodge him. He was only dimly aware of the girl screaming at the top of her voice.

'Let go of the controls!' shouted Harry Snowdon, but his voice was drowned by the girl's hysterical sobbing as she wrestled with her pair of Morse levers.

'There's something wrong with the controls!' he heard her yell.

For a wild moment Harry Snowdon was undecided whether to climb on to the flying bridge and pull the girl

180

away from the helm, or try to gain control in the wheel-house. He decided to stay in the wheelhouse – he was stronger than the girl. He hauled with all his strength on the port throttle lever and managed to drag it back to the neutral position.

The roar of one diesel died away.

By now the Chris Craft had rammed its bows into the reeds and was unable to move forward. Harry Snowdon released the lever. It suddenly slammed to the full astern position. The Chris Craft heeled violently as the engine twisted the hull savagely out of the reeds.

The unexpected motion caused the policeman to lose his balance. He reached out to grab at something, and snatched the starboard lever back.

The Chris Craft seemed to leap astern out of the water. Garnet nearly lost his grip on the boarding ladder. His feet slipped off the rudder bracket, and the wash from the Chris Craft, surging hard astern, swept his legs under the hull.

The bronze three-bladed port screw sliced into flesh, bone and marrow, severing his right leg cleanly from his body just above the knee, and flung the limb aside. His unbalanced body slipped sideways from the boarding ladder and was sucked under the hull. The starboard propeller reaped through his torso.

Starting at his groin, it smashed his pelvis, hacked through his spine in several places and scythed his kidneys, liver, heart and lungs to shreds of pulverized tissue.

The spinning remains of his body thundered against the underside of the hull before being snatched back by the port propeller. It continued its work by threshing his arms and skull to pulp. For an encore, it wound several metres of intestines round its shaft.

A marauding pike, undeterred by the presence of the Chris Craft's hull, snapped up drifting threads of spinal cord.

Sergeant Harry Snowdon and Maggie were taken to a local hospital suffering from shock. Despite a heavy sedative, Harry Snowdon kept repeating that it was all his fault.

Three hours after being admitted, Maggie refused all offers of further help. She made a brief statement to the police and was allowed to return home.

She sat by the telephone waiting for Mitch to call. She shivered occasionally despite the heat.

14

Pyne knew exactly where he was the moment he regained consciousness; the smell of rotting garbage was immediate and overpowering.

He pushed himself into a sitting position. Cans and bottles cascaded from him. He groaned and cradled his aching head in his hands. There was a strange roaring noise that seemed to be getting louder. He looked up at the puzzling shadow snaking about in the darkening sky. The strange shape was twisting and pulsing. He could see the open struts of a crane jib high above him. The refuse was moving beneath him. Suddenly he was sliding deeper into the garbage. Then he realized what the noise was – the shape hanging from the sky and burying itself in the barge's hold was a giant vacuum pipe; the roaring noise was caused by refuse thundering into the pipe's metre-diameter opening.

One of the crewmen, perched on the edge of the hold with a shotgun at the ready to shoot rats, thought he saw a movement in the refuse at the far end of the barge.

He peered into the gloom and raised his gun.

Pyne desperately embraced the massive flexible pipe near its consuming maw and cried out as a frenzied stream of broken bottles and jagged cans hurled into the pipe and swept his feet from under him.

The crewman heard the cry and ran down the barge's side deck. He saw a man clinging to the rim of the pipe. One leg had been sucked into the opening. The man was on the verge of losing his grip.

The crewman frantically waved his arms three times to the jib operator – the signal to cut power. The distant howl from the gas turbine which powered the vacuum pump died away.

The man jumped down into the garbage, and went to Pyne's aid.

15

Simpson's phone rang at 20:35.

He listened to the Permanent Under-Secretary with an impassive expression which he allowed to change to one of surprise because no one was in the room with him.

'Surely he gave some indication?' he said when the civil servant had finished speaking.

Simpson pressed his lips together as he listened to the reply.

'Very well,' he said. 'I'll see if he's free.'

Simpson knocked on the Prime Minister's door and entered without waiting for an invitation.

'I'm sorry to disturb you sir, but the American ambassador wishes to visit you this evening on an urgent matter.'

For the third successive evening the fall in temperature brought the race-rioting mobs out on to the streets of London. This time their numbers were swelled by the arrival of thousands of marchers from Wales – Asians who were demanding their own schools, housing estates and legal recognition of their Muslim courts. The police tried to halt the human tide as it neared Heathrow Airport at a steady three miles an hour along the main A4 trunk road, but a determined vanguard of veiled wives with children in pushchairs and prams forced the Home Secretary to order the police to allow the marchers to pass.

Never had so many children taken part in a march. A journalist phoning a report to his editor said it was as if the entire under-sixteen population of Wales had taken to the road. 'It's their future we're marching for,' the journalist had been told. 'So it's only right they should come.' The journalist completed his story by comparing the four leaders of the march with the Pied Piper of Hamelin.

The head of the procession was within twenty kilometres of Hyde Park Corner when the leaders revealed their closely-guarded secret that the marchers were to invade the gardens of Buckingham Palace for a silent sit-down protest. They deliberately kept their plans to themselves until the last minute to thwart army and police intelligence. They believed that communication along the twenty-mile column would be straightforward and made no allowance for fatigue, which would distort the word-of-mouth message.

By 19:00 hours half the weary marchers shuffling along on the outskirts of London believed they were to occupy Buckingham Palace.

At 19:15 the distorted story was picked up by army intelligence.

General Sir Richard Markham, commander-in-chief of UK land forces, with twenty thousand men at his disposal, decided to act – implementing his powers to take unilateral action when the life of the monarch is endangered. His orders were received and acted on by the Aldershot garrison commander.

The London-to-Guildford road was cleared of traffic to provide a free passage for the tanks, personnel carriers and armoured cars that swarmed out of Aldershot and thundered northwards to London.

A second wave of Chieftain and Scimitar tanks abandoned their exercises near Stonehenge on Salisbury Plain, and returned eastward at the maximum speed they could muster.

The commander-in-chief planned and executed his campaign against the marchers with speed and efficiency. No one was to be hurt if it could be avoided, but protection of the monarch was his paramount duty.

The second phase of the operation was to contain the protesters in a square kilometre of West End streets in an attempt to separate them from a mass of National Front agitators who were planning an assault on the Asians. That the American Embassy was right in the middle of the proposed compound did not worry the commander-in-chief; his main concern was to get his men and armour in position before the head of the procession reached Hyde Park Corner.

He achieved his objective with ten minutes to spare.

By a combination of speed and superbly disciplined co-ordination the army, reinforced by units already in London, succeeded in diverting the marchers along Park Lane, and away from Buckingham Palace. Then the heavy battle tanks, belching clouds of blue smoke and pirouetting gracefully on their tracks with incredible speed for their seemingly ponderous bulks, split the angered column into manageable groups for the anti-riot-dressed soldiers to herd into side streets.

In the ensuing confusion, with parents separated from their children, banners forcibly taken from the marchers, the fighting broke out

The Asians, with their wives, families and supporters found the soldiers to be a different proposition from the police. The troops, professionally trained to deal with street riots, did not hesitate to use tactics entirely alien to those employed by the police. A particularly violent battle in Upper Grosvenor Street ended when the soldiers formed themselves into a 'turtle' – a tight group surrounded by riot shields, which waded into the midst of the rioters, seized the ringleaders by their waistbands and retreated, dragging the leaders backwards.

In Berkeley Square Corporal John Stevens flipped up the rearsight leaf on his anti-riot gun, pointed the weapon at the road in front of a chanting mob of National Front supporters and became the first soldier to fire and kill a protester with a plastic bullet under riot conditions in England. The unstable missile, nearly the size of a Coke bottle, rebounded from the kerb and smashed against the chest of a schoolgirl he had not intended to hit.

The crowd erupted with renewed fury and stormed the line of soldiers that retreated behind a line of army trucks. The ambulance summoned to attend to the girl was set on and overturned.

By 21:00 hours the new CR gas canisters had arrived from a factory at Newdigate and were being issued to the soldiers. The main advantage of the experimental gas was that it could be dissolved in the tanks of water cannons, so that the 'riot barriers' could be created across the path of advancing street fighters, although little was known of its long-term effects.

At 21:45, with the battles raging round Grosvenor Square, a Detroit limousine, with eight men crammed inside, pulled away from the American Embassy.

The ambassador dismissed pleas that he should call off his visit to the Prime Minister, but agreed to wear a bullet-proof waistcoat and have extra bodyguards in the car.

Five men sat pressed together in the back – the ambassador, with two men on each side of him. Hendricks sat in the front between Paul Weiner and the marine driver, his bony frame digging painfully into the two men.

The car had just left Grosvenor Square when the driver was forced to brake suddenly as an armoured personnel carrier roared across his path. Missiles struck the side of the car. The ambassador leaned forward to see who was throwing them.

'Keep back, sir,' said a bodyguard politely.

The car was prevented from turning into Oxford Street by a line of steel-helmeted troops, their batons drawn and riot visors down. There were no markings on their mottled combat uniforms to distinguish officers from other ranks. A soldier approached the stationary car with his rifle resting on his hip. He looked curiously at the USA 1 number plate and the eight men crowded into one car.

'I'm very sorry, gentlemen,' said the soldier in a refined accent, 'but you'll have to turn left here.'

'We want to get to Whitehall,' said Hendricks.

'In that case I think your best plan is to head north, and try and work your way down from there. We're containing the trouble between Green Park and Hyde Park, but it's okay to the north.'

The embassy car was driving northwards when rioters broke through the army and police cordons and charged across Oxford Street. There was a sudden harsh rattle of gunfire.

The driver did not hesitate. He swung the car to the right and accelerated down a side street. A tide of yelling rioters storming down another street forced the car to stop. The driver was about to reverse when a convoy of army trucks roared past the stationary car.

'Follow them!' urged Weiner.

The covered trucks, laden with riot troops, turned left with the ambassador's car close behind, then came to an abrupt halt. The street ahead was seething with street fighters.

The marine driver stopped in response to the upheld arm of a riot soldier. At that moment more army trucks appeared at the far end of the street, effectively cutting off the horde of fighting Asians and National Front supporters. The troops in the trucks near the ambassador's car jumped down and began preparing their equipment. The crowd charged but were driven back by a volley of CR canisters. The pale grey clouds were sucked straight up by the warm air rising off the streets, which had been baked all day by the sun.

'You'd better turn back,' Hendricks said to the driver.

'Wait,' intervened the ambassador. 'I want to see how the British manage.'

'They'll manage,' said Hendricks drily.

'We're late,' commented Weiner.

'Then a few more minutes won't make that much difference,' said the ambassador.

The troops were uncovering their equipment truck to expose a squat, ugly barrel that was like no gun the ambassador had ever seen.

'What is it?' said Hendricks.

'A tasser,' said Hendricks.

'What does it do?'

'Rioters,' Hendricks replied caustically.

More troops arrived and formed a shield-to-shield line to thrust the rioters back. Soldiers suddenly fell back to their former positions. The crowd surged forward. The concealed soldiers charged from their hiding-places, seized the ring-leaders from behind and continued their headlong gallop through the line of their own men.

'Clever,' commented the ambassador.

The loss of their ringleaders did not quieten the mob. A voice boomed out, warning people hanging out of windows watching the battle to get back. Few people took any notice.

The men tending the tasser rammed a large package down its muzzle.

'It'll be over in a minute,' remarked Hendricks quietly.

There was a dull boom. Smoke swirled across the street. Troops dashed forward and disappeared into the drifting clouds, which quickly dispersed to reveal a transformed scene. The rioters nearest the tasser were writhing on the ground, shrieking in agony. The others standing further down the street had stopped fighting and were staring at their fallen comrades in shocked disbelief. The troops quickly snapped shackles attached to long lengths of webbing on to the wrists and ankles of stricken rioters.

'What happened?' breathed the ambassador, not taking his eyes off the troops.

'That gun fired a charge of two or three thousand metal barbs attached to lengths of fine wire,' said Hendricks. 'The electrified barbs snag in skin and clothing.'

188

A power winch started. The webbing straps tightened and began hauling the ensnared rioters towards the trucks.

'It's just like fishing,' Hendricks concluded.

The remainder of unaffected street fighters started throwing anything they could lay their hands on. The soldiers fell back. A large, flat-topped truck loaded with what appeared to be racks of lights and loudspeakers swept past the ambassador's car and stopped near the army trucks.

Hendricks studied the equipment thoughtfully, and turned around. 'Mr Ambassador, I think we should make a move now.'

'What is that stuff, Hendricks?'

Hendricks' reply was drowned by the loudhailer telling people to close their windows. The soldiers had pulled right back to the trucks and were putting on what looked like headphones.

'Ear defenders,' said Weiner in surprise.

The flat-topped truck reversed down the street, its lights and loudspeakers trained on the crowd. There came a deep, disturbing sound that seemed to pervade the air from all round.

'Shut the windows!' snapped Hendricks.

Weiner realized that the terrible noise must be coming from the loudspeaker horn mounted on the truck. A red flashing light pulsed out, illuminating the rioters. Each flash seemed to jar Weiner's brain. The deep, mind-chilling noise and flashing light were designed to induce epileptic fits. The note was rising to a shriek. Weiner began to feel sick. The rioters were collapsing in the road and vomiting; some were screaming as the advancing flashing light dealt repeated hammer-blows to their brains; some were suffering convulsive attacks and were uncontrollably jerking their limbs and emptying their bowels. All were affected in some way.

'Let's get the hell outta here!' snarled Hendricks.

The driver slammed the limousine into reverse and gunned the throttle.

'I told you the British would manage,' Hendricks commented some minutes later when the car was clear of the riot zone.

'What the hell was that device?' the ambassador wanted to know.

'A photic driver and curdler,' Weiner answered, recovering from the waves of nausea that had assailed him when he was within earshot of the ultimate anti-riot weapon.

'An appalling device,' commented the ambassador.

He remained silent for the rest of the journey.

16

After his third swallow of whisky, which Simpson poured for him, the ambassador began to feel better.

Witnessing a proud city on the verge of civil war had shaken him badly.

'I'm sorry you had such a bad journey,' said the Prime Minister, concealing his anxiety to find out what the ambassador had come about. 'I understand it's now quiet, so your return should be less hectic.'

The ambassador replaced his glass on the coffee table and took stock of his surroundings. The Prime Minister was seated opposite in a deep leather armchair. Simpson was standing near the door.

After the initial pleasantries the ambassador had asked if he might speak to the Prime Minister alone.

'You don't mind if my secretary stays?' the Prime Minister had asked.

Hendricks and Weiner were shown to an outer office.

The ambassador picked up his glass and put it down again. He might as well get the business over and done with.

'Mr Prime Minister,' he began, 'the question of terrorism is one which concerns our respective governments. And, of course, both our countries are signatories to the new agreement aimed at stamping it out.'

The two men watched the ambassador in silence. I'm making a mess of it, he thought to himself, wishing he had stayed in industry rather than allowed himself to be tempted by the offer of his present job.

'Mr Prime Minister,' he began again, 'we have information that suggests one of your nuclear power stations has been seized by a group of terrorists.'

There was dead silence in the room.

The Prime Minister smiled warmly, but a nerve in his neck twitched. 'Oh yes. That's right. I heard there was something of the sort, but the police now have the situation under control. Isn't that right, Simpson?'

'Yes, sir,' replied Simpson promptly, although his stomach had turned to water at the American's words.

'Fellows wanted a half million pounds,' said the Prime Minister, drawing on skills acquired during thirty years in politics. 'They'll be in Brixton prison by this time tomorrow.'

Either you're a goddamn fine actor, or Hendricks is getting excited over nothing, thought the ambassador.

He checked himself; what he thought didn't matter. He had a job to do, and Hendricks wouldn't hit the panic button without a good reason.

'The purpose of my visit is to deliver a verbal message from the President,' said the ambassador.

The silence in the room was disturbing. He pressed on:

'The President has told me to say he is most concerned about the possible effects of another power station disaster such as Cheynobel. He has instructed me to say that if Her Majesty's Government is ever subjected to extreme threats or pressures imposed by a fanatical group seizing a nuclear power station, he pledges that the United States, with all its resources, is at the disposal of HM government to help end such threats or pressures.'

'However,' he continued, 'the President has asked me to stress that such whole-hearted, unconditional support can be successfully implemented only if there is the fullest cooperation and frankness between us. Such frankness is essential to enable the President to reject any direct course of action he may be advised to take to safeguard the security and well-being of the United States and her people.'

The Americans left Downing Street at 23:10.

The Prime Minister and Simpson listened to a recording of the conversation. They played the closing words of the message three times.

The Prime Minister sat silently for some minutes after the last playback was over. Then he looked up at Simpson, and said softly, 'Christ Almighty. What the hell have we let ourselves in for?'

It was the first time since he had known him that Simpson had heard the Prime Minister swear.

The Prime Minister went to bed at midnight. For once in his long career he was unable to sleep.

17

The supper Maggie cooked for Mitchell tasted of bomb shelters and abandoned basements, but he ate it cheerfully with a straight face.

The forlorn, elfin face watched him across the kitchen table.

Maggie looked exhausted.

Mitchell pushed the empty plate away and smiled at her. 'That was fine, honey, but you shouldn't have bothered.'

'It took my mind off things.'

'Did you see the doctor this afternoon?'

'Yes.' said Maggie truthfully. She tried to summon up the courage to tell Mitchell about Garnet.

'Mitch . . .'

'Yes?'

'Mitch, will you stay the night, please? You could sleep in Daddy's room,' she added hastily.

'Wouldn't you rather I ran you back to your place?'

Maggie shook her head. 'I want to be here in case he comes home.'

'Supposing he does, and finds me here?'

Maggie exploded. 'Christ! All I want is someone in the house! Can't you understand that?'

Wednesday

1

It was the large, jagged hole in one of the power station's control-room windows, smashed by Keller during Pyne's escape bid, that suggested to Hugh Patterson a method to kill Keller when darkness fell.

At 1:30 Louise helped him climb through a window in the air-conditioning room, which was on the same level as the control room.

She passed him his Sterling submachine-gun, gave him a light kiss on the cheek and held his hand tightly for a moment. Patterson avoided looking at her pale face.

'Good luck,' she whispered, and closed the window softly.

Patterson padded silently along the narrow roof of the visitors' viewing balcony, which extended along the side of the power station, past the base of the fuelling machine towers perched on top of the main building.

Patterson cautiously approached the corner of the building where the balcony roof stopped. The moon shone from a clear sky, carving a path of flecked light across the oil-black river.

He knelt down and sat on the edge of the roof. Twenty metres below the moonlight gleamed on the dummy petrol tankers and on two helicopters parked on the concrete apron. Patterson had a poor head for heights. His confidence deserted him. The twenty metre drop looked worse in semi-darkness. He shone a pocket torch up at the closed-circuit television camera mounted on a projecting bracket three metres above his head. Its lens was staring across the dark Thames. He directed the torch at the horizontal ledge that traversed the front of the building. It was nothing more than a continuous aluminium box.

Higher up, between each window, was a stout window-cleaner's hook. Patterson reached forward, grasped the first hook and transferred half his weight on to the aluminium ledge. He shuffled his foot along until there was room for the other foot. The ledge seemed strong enough, but he preferred to support most of his weight with his hands. He stretched out an arm, reaching as far as possible until his fingers curled thankfully round the next hook. He worked his toes slowly along the ledge – not daring to move them more than a few centimetres at a time – until his body was in the centre of the window section. There were thirteen such sections between him and the broken pane of glass – he had counted them that afternoon when he had first discussed his plan with Louise. She had been firmly opposed to the idea.

'Supposing he's moved his camp bed?' she had asked.

'Why should he?'

'It's a crazy idea, Hugh. And Conrad said you couldn't be certain of killing him outright with a Sterling.'

Louise had paused. Hugh Patterson, normally good-natured, was proposing the cold-blooded killing of a sleeping man. 'You could do that?'

Patterson thought of Pyne's floating corpse.

'Yes,' he said.

'You'd be aiming into a pitch-black room. You'd be using one hand to hang on. You'd be exhausted.'

'Louise, it's a chance we've got to take. The only chance we'll ever have.'

For a while they remained silent.

'What if you succeed?' Louise had asked.

'We give ourselves up.'

Patterson thought she might argue. She had nodded, and said, 'Okay then. How can I help?'

By the time Patterson reached the third window section sweat was streaming down his face. He hung on with one hand and wiped his sleeve across his forehead.

Thirty minutes later, with only three more sections between him and the jagged hole, he rested. His arms were numb with pain. Sweat was forcibly pumped into the palms of his hands, making it difficult to grip the hooks. He wiped a hand on his trousers. The webbing strap on the Sterling suddenly slipped down his body. He grabbed at it. The weapon's frame clattered against the glass. He waited, counting slowly with his cheek pressed hard on the cool window.

Ten metres away the closed-circuit television camera stirred. Patterson did not hear the faint whir as it swung its lens inward towards the power station's facade.

Patterson resumed his shuffling movement, forcing himself to keep going until the sharp edges of broken glass cut into the inside of his fingers. The sudden jolt of pain nearly caused him to lose his footing.

The smashed hole in the window was before him at last. He closed his eyes tightly for some seconds to adjust his night vision to the control room's dark interior.

He opened them. Stray shafts of moonlight gleamed on IBM machines along the far wall. The horseshoe-shaped main console dominated the scene like a surrealist electronic organ. The shapes in the room were regular, with sharp corners. There was one exception – the shadowy, humped outline of Keller's camp bed.

Patterson carefully supported himself by hooking an elbow over the edge of the broken glass. He slipped the Sterling from his shoulder with his free hand and grasped the magazine awkwardly with the other hand. He released the safety-catch and aimed the submachine-gun at the camp bed.

He fired one long continuous burst. His body shuddered with the hammering recoil. The broken glass gripped between his elbow and stomach began to splinter and pull away from the frame. He felt himself falling backwards and was forced to drop the Sterling and grab at a hook in panic. The gun clattered on to the concrete apron twenty metres below. The smoke stung his eyes and filled the control room, obscuring the dark shapes.

A polite voice not two metres away said, 'I should come in if I were you, Mr Patterson, before you fall and have a nasty accident.'

2

Simpson's bedside telephone rang at 3:00, when he was staring at the ceiling trying to sleep.

He picked up the receiver and didn't say who he was; his number was known to less than a dozen people. There was something familiar about the tired voice which said, 'Simpson, I've just discharged myself from Dover General. You'd better get over here and pick me up.'

'Who's speaking?' asked Simpson, mentally running through the list of those who knew his night number.

'Pyne, you idiot!' snapped the voice.

Simpson's mind reeled. 'Pyne?' Then he recognized the voice.

'Listen,' said Pyne. 'And try to grasp what I'm telling you. There's been a major reshuffle. Keller's taken over as chairman. Do you understand?'

Simpson sat up. 'Did you dial through the nine-three-o-level?'

'Yes.'

'You're not on a cellphone?'

'No!'

Simpson relaxed; there was little danger of the conversation being overheard so he risked firing questions. A lot of questions.

Simpson made his way up to the Prime Minister's flat. He could have used the internal phone, but the walk gave him time to think. He entered the private sitting-room and paused outside the bedroom door, wondering how to break the news.

'There's no need to creep about out there, Simpson,' said the Prime Minister from the other side of the door. 'I'm not asleep.'

Simpson entered. The light was on. The Prime Minister knew immediately from his secretary's face that something was seriously wrong.

Simpson started to repeat the conversation with Pyne. He was on his third sentence when the Prime Minister swore, threw back the covers and started to get dressed – his fingers fumbling at his clothes. Simpson helped him while relating the rest of the conversation. The Prime Minister was thrusting his feet into his shoes by the time Simpson was listing the deleted clauses in the ultimatum.

He stopped getting dressed and stared at his secretary. 'We're going to have to get them out of that power station, Simpson. No matter what the cost.'

Simpson swallowed.

'We agreed that was impossible, sir . . .' he began.

The Prime Minister feverishly fastened his tie. 'You're to call a meeting for nine o'clock this morning. Get on to the best brains in the country. Tell them the security of the country is endangered. Don't tell them more than that. Use the police to drag them here by force if necessary.'

Simpson gaped at the Prime Minister.

'What's the meeting for, sir?'

The stocky figure rounded on Simpson in fury. 'To find a way of getting those bastards out, you idiot! You better have about twenty sets of the power station plans made ready.'

Simpson was rooted. 'Whom shall I ask to attend?'

'Christ, I don't know. Use your imagination.' the Prime Minister stopped dressing and glared at his secretary. 'That's one thing we'll need now Simpson. Imagination. People with plenty of imagination. No more lackies. The head of Defence Studies; someone from the Institute of

Oceanographic Sciences; the retired officer who's written that book on terrorism. Get 'em all here. The whole bloody lot.'

Simpson was halfway across the sitting-room when the Prime Minister called him back. 'You better get on to the Americans and tell them the whole story. They seem to know it anyway. Bloody CIA, pretending to be a bunch of morons while running rings round us.'

Simpson looked aghast. 'The *whole* story, sir?'

The Prime Minister gestured in exasperation. 'You know what I mean. For Christ's sake stop sounding like a bloody butler and get moving!'

'Do we ask the Americans to the meeting, sir?'

The Prime Minister paused. 'Yes. We might need that help they offered. Hendricks struck me as a shrewd bastard. He might be useful.'

'What shall we do about Pyne, sir?'

The Prime Minister sat on the bed. 'Christ, yes Pyne.' He thought for a moment. 'We'll have to keep him under wraps. That house at Inverloch or somewhere. Where is he?'

'Dover.'

The same idea occurred simultaneously to both men: the Prime Minister's holiday bungalow at Broadstairs.

'Ideal,' he said. 'The housekeeper is on holiday for three weeks. There'll be a bobby hanging about, but the place is empty. Get the meeting fixed up first and then go down to pick up Pyne and take him to the bungalow. He's to stay out of sight until we decide what to do with him. Try and be back here before the meeting. I don't think there's anything else.'

The Prime Minister finished dressing when Simpson had gone. there *was* something else – something to do with the CIA. He frowned, trying to remember what it was. Normally, his memory never betrayed him. He wondered about Pyne and reflected wryly on the best-laid plans of mice . . .

What the hell was it he wanted to remember about the CIA? He shrugged at his reflection in the dressing-table mirror. Maybe it wasn't important . . .

Even so, it was worrying.

3

The peasant girl had the most sumptuous breasts Cox-Spender had ever seen. They swayed with their own hypnotic life beneath her thin cotton blouse as she crawled across the bistro floor towards his table. Her long dark hair trailed in the bloodstained sawdust strewn on the floor.

Cox-Spender considered her the best so far – much more beautiful than the three girls he had possessed that night. Brutal men in berets and striped jerseys looked on from the shadows with hate and jealousy smouldering in their eyes as the girl slid her long, sensuous fingers up Cox-Spender's legs.

He smiled down, drew back a foot and kicked her. She fell back scowling, her dark eyes flashing angrily as her fingers curled into the sawdust. A gypsy band gathered round Cox-Spender's table, not missing a note of the savage Slavonic dance as they sawed demoniacally at their shrieking violins.

The girl spat at Cox-Spender and reached up to loosen the laces at her throat which held the front of her blouse together.

She was about to rip the flimsy garment open when the bedside telephone rang and woke Cox-Spender.

It was Simpson. Cox-Spender decided he hated Simpson.

'An important meeting at Downing Street,' said the despicable Simpson. 'In five hours. Nine o'clock. Use the Old Admiralty Building entrance.'

'What about a car?' asked Cox-Spender.

'Your local police station will send a car round to your house at eight o'clock,' replied Simpson, and hung up.

Cox-Spender fiddled with his telephone and eventually managed to program a Star Service 07:00 alarm call. He replaced the handset and lay pondering before drifting back to sleep.

But he was too late: the surly, unshaven musicians had packed their fiddles and gone, taking the beautiful peasant girl and the noisy bistro with them.

4

Mitchell was woken by a noise in the bedroom.

It was Maggie standing in his doorway.

'I couldn't sleep, Mitch.'

Mitchell groped for a light switch, but Maggie came forward and placed her hand over his.

'What's the matter?' Mitchell asked.

Maggie told him about the accident with the boat. She talked haltingly for five-minutes, keeping a tight rein on her emotions.

'Jesus,' Michell breathed when she had finished. 'You poor kid.' He put his arm around her. She shrank away from his touch, then relaxed.

'The police will want to see you tomorrow,' said Maggie. 'I told them they'd find you here.'

'What will they want me for?'

Maggie paused. 'I don't know. I suppose because it's your boat. They'll probably ask you if I could handle it properly.'

Mitchell remembered the way she had steered the boat without over-correcting.

'Maggie . . .' he hesitated, but the question had to be asked. 'Maggie. It *was* an accident?'

There was no reply. He wished the light was on so that he could see her face.

'Maggie?'

'I don't know, Mitch. I keep asking myself. But I swear – I honestly don't know.'

Mitchell pulled her back until her head was resting on the pillow. He stroked her hair away from her forehead.

'I'm scared, Mitch,' her voice trembled.

'I'll tell the police the truth – that you had never handled the boat before and that I didn't want to leave you alone with it.'

The girl did not answer. Mitchell moved his arm slightly, and realized she was asleep.

5

'Cox-Spender,' said the Prime Minister, pausing outside the panelled double doors leading to the Cabinet Room and tapping the list. 'Why him? He's incompetent.'

'With respect, sir,' said Simpson evenly. 'I don't agree. He has a capable intellect despite his unfortunate personality. Also, he's the only man who has been into the power station. Exclude him and someone would be bound to ask why. And besides, you'll have someone to steer awkward questions at.'

The Prime Minister grunted and resumed his study of the list of twenty people now waiting on the other side of the door. They included the Ministers of Defence; senior officials from Power Gen; a professor from the Atomic Energy Authority; James Reynolds from the Institute of Oceanographic Sciences; Brigadier Michael Rawlins, who had written the book *Counter-Terrorist*; some well-known engineers, and the two Americans – Weiner and Hendricks.

Simpson noticed the rings under the Prime Minister's eyes. The loss of one night's sleep showed.

'What about the Chief Scientific Adviser?' demanded the Prime Minister testily.

The question surprised Simpson. 'The accident in the Mall,' he said politely.

The Prime Minister folded the list.

You really are losing your grip, aren't you? thought Simpson as he pushed the doors open.

Twenty faces round the long table turned expectantly as the two men entered the room. Only Cox-Spender,

Hendricks, Weiner and the ministers knew what the meeting was to be about.

The Prime Minister greeted the gathering and apologized for the abrupt summons to Downing Street. After introductions had been made he quickly outlined the events since Sunday, omitting Pyne's escape and the revised nature of the ultimatum.

There was no reaction from Hendricks and Weiner when the Prime Minister listed the names of the four holding the power station.

The brigadier was the first to speak, He was about to refer the gathering to his book and say, 'I told you so,' but decided the comment would be inappropriate. Instead he said, 'Why isn't someone from the Special Air Service here? Those boys might have some bright ideas. This sort of thing is right . . .'

'Unfortunately,' interrupted the Prime Minister, 'the Special Air Service has been integrated with the Oil Rig Defence Force under the command of General Pyne. Pyne has been a great advocate of the merging and the rationalization of various armed services units, and has had the drive and personality to push them through.'

'He wouldn't have been able to do so if you hadn't been so keen to rubber-stamp his proposals,' replied the brigadier. 'Damned fellow was a leading advocate of this unified European defence force nonsense.'

The Prime Minister looked frostily across the table. 'I was hoping, brigadier, that you might have constructive suggestions to help with this present problem.'

And then the discussion began in earnest. Simpson distributed sets of the power-station plans. Hendricks and Weiner did not join in. They sat listening as proposals were suggested and dismissed.

'Nerve gas is quick,' said Cox-Spender in reply to one idea, 'but not quick enough for us to be a hundred per cent certain that we could prevent the terrorists from activating the detonators.' He described the system Pyne had shown him during his Sunday visit to the power station. 'A preemptive strike would have to succeed in four seconds,' Cox-Spender concluded.

Less than that now, thought the Prime Minister. Only he and Simpson knew that Keller was now in control. They'd decided that if anyone came up with an idea, that they would insist on certain success in one second as a safety factor before agreeing to the plan.

The arguments and counter arguments dragged on.

'Let's consider the problem on the assumption that they're bluffing,' said Peter Harvey, the Minister of Defence for the Army.

Christ, we're getting nowhere, thought the Prime Minister.

Harvey saw the Prime Minister's expression and said quickly, 'We must look at every angle, Prime Minister. Starting with the improbable . . .'

'I'm not up on these things,' said the Minister of Defence for the RAF. 'My experts would know, but couldn't we use an American laser-guided "Smart" bomb aimed precisely on the quarters occupied by the terrorists?'

Hendricks regarded the speaker with icy contempt. 'Sure. We could drop one from seventy thousand feet with an error of fifty metres. That's pin-point accuracy. But a fifty-metre error is enough to put the bomb plumb through the silos.'

The fruitless discussion went on. After an hour there were ten proposals on Simpson's pad. All had been crossed out.

'Have the Americans got a contingency plan for dealing with similar occurrences in their country?' inquired Peter Harvey.

'Sure,' said Hendricks. 'The main one is making certain all power stations have proper security arrangements. I'm amazed that your nuclear police weren't on duty at the station when it was seized. It's not my place to criticize, but had the British government heeded the warnings of our Atomic Energy Commission, this might not have happened.'

204

'You're quite right,' said the Prime Minister. 'It's not your place to criticise.'

Hendricks' gaunt face was impassive.

Cox-Spender broke the silence that followed. 'Some sort of unmanned attack through the power station's foundations,' he said to himself.

Everyone stared at him.

The sudden silence caused Cox-Spender to look up from his set of plans. Someone must have said something he had missed. He looked round the table and was horrified to discover twenty-one pairs of eyes on him.

'What was that?' someone said.

'Well,' said Cox-Spender, looking down in terror at his plans. 'I thought some sort of unmanned penetration of the galleries round the radioactive-waste storage silos . . .' His voice trailed away.

'Why unmanned?' asked James Reynolds of the Institute of Oceanographic Sciences.

'It's a silly idea. I was merely thinking aloud. It occurred to me that an unmanned machine might be able to cut the detonator wires without activating the IRIS detectors, but then of course, if there was such a machine, it would probably generate more heat than several humans.'

'It would have to be a pretty fantastic machine,' said the brigadier caustically. Something straight out of science fiction.'

'GOPHER,' said Cox-Spender suddenly.

Everyone looked at him again.

'What's a gopher?' asked someone.

'A North American burrowing animal,' said Weiner.

'An acronym,' contradicted Cox-Spender excitedly.

'A what?'

'I don't know what the letters stand for,' said Cox-Spender, 'but I remember reading about it some years ago.'

'What exactly did this device do, and how can it help us?' demanded the Prime Minister.

205

'If I remember correctly, sir.' said Cox-Spender, controlling his excitement, 'it was a one-man machine that could bore through rock.' Cox-Spender leaned across the table and pointed to the Prime Minister's plans. 'If we could get hold of such a machine, we could burrow under the riverbed from the opposite bank, and bore right through the power station's foundation. Of course, we'd have to fix up some sort of inertial guidance system for the pilot so he'd be certain of coming up in an inspection tunnel. He could then leave the machine and cut the wires to the explosives.'

There was a silence.

'You've forgotten something,' said the Prime Minister. 'Surely these IRIS detector things they've installed would sound the alarms as soon as they picked up the heat from the man's body?'

Cox-Spender nodded glumly. Then he brightened. 'Not if we were to dress him in a suit that was a perfect insulator so that none of his body heat escaped.'

'Is there such a suit?' inquired the Prime Minister, looking at each man in turn.

'I've heard,' said Hendricks slowly, 'although I'm no expert, that the spacesuits developed by NASA are perfect insulators.'

'No machine is capable of boring such a distance,' said James Reynolds. 'The river is four kilomtres wide at Canvey Island. And there's another problem. This machine, if it exists – which I doubt – wouldn't be able to bore more than a few metres.' He looked at Cox-Spender. 'Presumably it loosens soil or rock and pushes it behind as it moves forward?'

Cox-Spender nodded.

'Then after a few metres,' concluded James Reynolds, 'there wouldn't be any more room behind for the debris it had removed from in front? Yes?'

Hendricks was scribbling as Cox-Spender nodded sadly.

'Shall we move on to the next idea?' asked the Prime Minister.

But the ideas that followed were variations of schemes already suggested. All were rejected after a further hour's discussion.

'So what do we do now?' asked the Prime Minister.

Hendricks looked up from his notes. Without humour he said, 'I suggest we look for gophers.'

6

Mitchell woke up at 9:00 hours.

Maggie had gone. The bedroom was filled with sunlight and the smell of burning breakfast.

He went downstairs.

'Good morning, Mitch,' said Maggie brightly across the smoke-filled kitchen. 'I thought I'd surprise you with breakfast.'

Mitchell was so pleased to see her looking much better that he raised no objection to bacon that looked like fragments of the Dead Sea scrolls and toast like little squares of midnight. The bruise on her face was subsiding. She chatted away during breakfast as if she were making a deliberate attempt to sever herself from the events of the previous day.

Mitchell was nerving himself to taste the coffee when she said, 'I'd like to go to London to find out what's happened to Daddy.'

'I think you should rest, Maggie.'

'It would be best if I did something,' she said with a trace of defiance.

'The police are coming today you said,' said Mitchell, adding quickly, 'I'll do a deal with you. You rest today and I'll call my secretary and tell her I'm taking the rest of the week off, and I'll go with you to London tomorrow. How does that grab you?'

Maggie smiled and nodded. 'You can take me to an expensive restaurant.'

The electric fan the Prime Minister stood on his desk cooled his coffee in two minutes so it was undrinkable. He sipped it, swore and picked up his telephone to order some more.

There was a tap on his door. Simpson entered.

'I've spoken to Keller by radiotelephone,' he said. 'He's agreed to no more than a seventy-two-hour extension to the deadline from midnight tonight.'

The Prime Minister groaned.

'What use is seventy-two hours?'

'I did my best,' said Simpson, 'I explained that a lot of clauses needed rewording to make them watertight. He was extremely polite and accepted that the bill was the most complicated piece of legislation in history, but insisted that it should receive the royal assent and become an Act of Parliament by midnight on Saturday.'

The Prime Minister stared down at his blotter and twiddled nervously with the smooth amber paper weight. His palms were soaked in sweat despite the cooling air from the fan. The paperweight skipped across the desk and fell to the floor. He made no attempt to retrieve it.

'Hendricks wants a week,' he said dully, 'and then he wants us to bluff Keller into agreeing to another week.'

Simpson smiled thinly and noted the proximity of the electric fan. The old rogue was gradually losing his cool. 'Seventy-two hours from midnight might be enough. The CIA have found the magazine article Cox-Spender remembered seeing,' he said.

The Prime Minister frowned. Simpson's mention of the CIA – what was it he was trying to remember that morning? Suddenly it came to him.

'Mitchell!' barked the Prime Minister. 'Howard Mitchell. How is it the CIA haven't mentioned him? What's happened to him?'

The question took Simpson by surprise. 'Nothing, sir.'

Simpson realized he had made a mistake. He was about to amend his answer hastily, but the Prime Minister was too quick. He pounced with all his old parliamentary skill.

'Nothing? What the hell do you mean? How could anything happen to him if you've only had him watched?'

'What I meant was . . .'

'What the hell have you done with him?'

'Nothing, sir.'

'Did you have him watched? Well?' The Prime Minister sighed. 'Look, Simpson. It would take me an hour to get the truth out of you, and time is precious.'

Simpson decided that he might as well tell him about Patrick Reagan.

The Prime Minister listened.

'Why?' he said when Simpson finished.

'We needed time. Just as we need time now. If Mitchell was working for the CIA, as we know he was, then it was important that I should have him dealt with before he learned too much.'

'Christ Almighty! Didn't it occur to you that removing him would only arouse CIA suspicions still further and bring them crashing down on our necks?'

'Mitchell was a plant – a resident, I think they call them. It would take them many months to establish a new one – fix him up with genuine cover. I thought that having Mitchell out of the way would give us the time we needed. Anyway, what does it matter? Reagan was killed in a genuine road accident.'

'Reagan was a bomber?'

'Yes.'

'You gave him Mitchell's address?'

'Yes.'

'Then how the hell do we know there isn't a bomb sitting in Mitchell's house?'

The interrogation irritated Simpson. 'I'll make an anonymous call to Weybridge police and tell them there might be a bomb in Mitchell's house.'

The Prime Minister lost his temper. 'You'll do no such thing, you bloody idiot! We'll keep this to ourselves. You're to go to Weybridge and check Mitchell's house and car yourself! Understand?'

Simpson's face was white. He clenched his fingers together and kept his voice steady. 'I don't know how to look for a bomb, and what if Mitchell is in the house or using his car?'

'That's your problem. You created it. But I'll tell you this much, Simpson, if anything happens to Mitchell at this stage – there'll be one hell of a row with the Americans and I'll see that you carry the can. After that, I'll make damned certain you're finished. Now get out.'

Simpson made no attempt to move. 'With respect, sir. I don't think you could afford to do that.'

He turned on his heel and stalked out of the office.

8

Cox-Spender hated flying.

He knew it was irrational, but he couldn't help it. The most civilized form of transport was the TGV express that carried him four times a year from Paris to Marseilles, to his beloved bistros and the girls lying topless on the beaches.

Knowing he was going to New York didn't help. He had never been to the United States, but he knew all about New York from the television cop series which he watched religiously and found utterly convincing. He would be mugged as he stepped off the aircraft.

Consequently, by the time he was sitting next to Hendricks in a British Airways Concorde at Heathrow waiting to take off he was a nervous wreck.

Hidden loudspeakers welcomed Cox-Spender aboard and advised him that he would be landing in New York in three and a half hours.

'Great airplane,' said Hendricks.

'Yes,' said Cox-Spender weakly.

A few minutes later he prepared himself to meet his maker as the spindly-legged monster hurled down the hot runway and lifted its drooping nose to the darkening sky.

9

By the time Simpson had purchased new shoes and socks, his inner rage at the way he had been treated was beginning to die down.

He paid the shop assistant out of the £1000 he had drawn for Patrick Reagan and added the purchases to the new suit, shirt, gloves and underwear crammed into the second hand travelling bag.

He went by bus to Waterloo Station and changed into his new outfit in the men's toilets. His original clothes went into the travelling bag. He went to the British Rail Red Star counter and arranged for the bag to be sent to his flat. There was nothing on him that would link him to the Prime Minister's secretary should he be caught breaking into Mitchell's house at Weybridge: no keys, no credit cards or letters – nothing. Even the wallet holding £620 in old notes was new.

The only available train was packed. Every time it stopped passengers had to disembark so that those who wanted that station could struggle off.

He found a second hand car dealer within a hundred metres of Surbiton Station. One of the offerings outside the seedy parade of shops was an elderly Sierra. He examined it with a calculated lack of enthusiasm. He argued the price with he salesman and secured a reduction of £200.

He told the salesman that he would have to draw the money from the bank and would be back in an hour. The salesman promised to have the car ready but insisted on Simpson leaving a 10 per cent deposit.

Simpson went away and sat in a cheap café drinking coffee. He decided that he would wreck the Prime Minister as soon as the three terrorists — if they could be called that — were out of the power station.

He had known the Prime Minister for twenty years; he could tell stories to the press — especially the latest story — that would bring the whole rotten structure crashing down about the Prime Minister's ears.

And why not? Why not pay back the old bastard for not even giving him a lousy OBE?

But he would need General Pyne's help.

He would drive down to Broadstairs that evening as soon as he had finished at Weybridge.

Simpson finished his coffee. He found a public telephone and called Mitchell's home. There was no answer. He rang Mitchell's Walton office. His secretary did not know where her boss was — only that he wouldn't be in the office for the rest of the week.

Simpson gave the car salesman a false name and address and paid the balance owing on the Sierra. The car had seen better days, but it handled well and seemed to be in reasonable mechanical condition. He drove cautiously to Weybridge, observing the speed limits.

By the time he was driving into the outskirts of Weybridge he had worked out a detailed plan of action against the Prime Minister with which he felt certain Pyne would agree.

Simpson was pleased with himself.

It was, he thought, an extremely clever plan.

Mitchell's house was deserted.

Breaking in was not the problem Simpson expected: there were several pieces of rough timber nailed across a broken window in the kitchen door — probably where Reagan had broken in. Simpson pulled on his new gloves and prised the lengths of wood away with a garden fork. He levered the remaining pieces of glass out of the frame and climbed into the kitchen.

Simpson set about looking for the bomb. It was a terrifying business: he pulled doors open with pieces of string; he threw books into rooms before venturing in just in case there was some sort of detonator under the carpets; he even turned the electricity off at the mains switch and went round turning on every electrical gadget, pausing occasionally – listening for the sound of a returning car. He restored electric power at the mains switch. The house filled with the sound of radios, televisions, a food mixer, tape recorder and several fans.

Nothing happened.

After two hours' painstaking search Simpson was convinced that there was no bomb in the house. Reagan must have planted it in Mitchell's car – if indeed he had planted a bomb at all.

Simpson left the house by the kitchen door. He was about to walk down the drive, when he saw two men unloading a new television from a van parked outside the house opposite. He quickly returned to the house and watched them from Mitchell's living room – standing well back from the window. The men disappeared into the house. Simpson decided to wait until they drove away. The bitterness he felt at being put in such an absurd situation was offset by the thought of his plan to pay the Prime Minister out. The nagging doubt was, would Pyne agree?

There was a telephone on a low coffee table. He sat in one of Mitchell's armchairs and picked up the handset.

Supposing Mitchell had itemized phone bills? If so it would be certain to show the number he had called and the time. It could be very embarrassing.

Simpson replaced the handset.

What the hell – the chances were that Mitchell wouldn't be receiving his phone bill for several weeks. He lifted the handset and sat with it pressed to his ear while fumbling awkwardly through the dialling code booklet with gloved fingers, looking for the number of the exchange near Broadstairs.

Thirty seconds later, he discovered Reagan's bomb.

He also discovered that death could be a mind-blowing experience.

A kilometre away, Mitchell lifted his head off the aluminium and plastic bed beside General Pyne's swimming pool. He reached out a foot and prodded Maggie.

'Did you hear that?'

She didn't move.

'Did you?' prompted Mitchell.

She yawned.

'What?'

'A bang,' said Mitchell.

'Later,' said Maggie, and went back to sleep.

Thursday

1

Summer was upon New York like a ravening beast that devoured the slight breeze that barely stirred the fringed sunshade above Cox-Spender's head.

He was sitting at the nearest table to the Prometheus Fountain in the Rockefeller Center. Even at 10:00 the appalling heat seemed to be rising out of the ground. The orderly lines of United Nations flags surrounding the humid sunken basin seemed to be too exhausted by the physical effort of hanging from their poles to make any unnecessary move.

Cox-Spender looked at his watch. Hendricks had been gone fifteen minutes. He squinted up at the dazzling golden statue of Prometheus beneath the soaring RCA Building and reflected that had the god known about New York summers, he might have reconsidered his plan to steal fire from the heavens.

A waitress served him with his morning coffee.

Cox-Spender watched the people milling round the Plaza's perimeter. Not one of them was being robbed, except those buying pretzels and ice-cold Cokes from a stand.

He was beginning to like New York: his room a few streets away at the Hilton, was comfortable, and the television seemed to have an inexhaustible number of channels filled with his favourite cops. What little he had seen of the city suggested that it had everything he could wish for, maybe even a bistro. After London, Midtown

Manhattan was surprisingly clean, littered with fountains, crammed with plenty of buses and taxis. And there were no piles of dog shit on the sidewalks. It was very different from London.

Hendricks returned and sat down.

'Delmar Hydraulics is now run by one of Jack Delmar's sons – Henry. He knows nothing about the GOPHER so I've fixed up for us to fly up to see old Jack Delmar at his lodge in the mountains.'

Cox-Spender hung grimly on to his seat as the helicopter threatened to shake itself to pieces in what appeared to be a desperate battle to remain airborne.

He was forced to jam his tongue against his false teeth to prevent the terrifying vibration from dislodging them. Hendricks sat next to the pilot. He turned his craggy face round to Cox-Spender.

'Are you okay?'

Cox-Spender nodded and mumbled something past his mouthful of tongue and oscillating dentures.

'The flight will take a couple of hours. We'll be there by two.'

Cox-Spender looked down and wished he hadn't. The helicopter was flying due north, gaining height as it followed the valley of the Hudson River. He looked longingly back at the Manhattan skyline, dominated by the bland twin towers of the World Trade Center.

Straight ahead was the distant smudge of the Adirondack Mountains.

2

In a land of rich men, Jack Delmar considered himself to be one of the richest.

He had six sons – one to run each of his corporations; several homes across Europe; an apartment on Park Avenue; a photographic memory and a powerful sex drive. Both

216

the latter were still in good shape despite his seventy years. He also had an engaging personality, which he used on the two visitors sitting on his veranda overlooking the lake.

Normally he never entertained strangers, and he wouldn't have been seeing these two had it not been for a call from the White House asking him to meet them. The White House rarely asked favours these days. Maybe they were too scared, or didn't trust so many as used to. An hour before his guests had arrived Delmar had called up some friends in the Pentagon and given them the names the White House had given him and asked who the hell they were; it was a simple request from an old buddy. He was surprised when they refused to oblige. It also aroused his curiosity.

'Sure I remember GOPHER,' he said to Cox-Spender. 'Must be all of twenty years ago – maybe more. When I was fifty. Crazy things we do when we're young.' He grinned disarmingly at his visitors.

Hendricks showed him the magazine article. Jack Delmar laughed at the pictures.

'Isn't that the weirdest machine you ever saw? This magazine promised to send me some complimentary copies. They never did. A few words to some friends and the editor suddenly found his advertising space hard to sell.' Jack Delmar paused. 'Why are you interested in my GOPHER, Mr Spender?'

Cox-Spender had a story ready. 'A sonar check has revealed what may be an unexploded wartime bomb under Greenwich Observatory. We're hoping it will enable us to recover the bomb without having to disturb the observatory's instruments.'

Jack Delmar threw back his head and laughed. 'GOPHER wouldn't be any good to you. That thing couldn't even cut through warm butter.'

Cox-Spender looked at the industrialist in alarm.

'But these photographs show . . .'

'They show GOPHER drilling down and coming up a few metres away,' said Jack Delmar, grinning broadly. 'That demo was staged on a rented construction site. I had a few hundred tonnes of debris spread around and levelled so GOPHER wouldn't find the going too difficult.'

'What happened to it?' asked Cox-Spender despairingly.

'It was blown up.'

'Do you still have the drawings?'

'Drawings?' Jack Delmar's blue eyes twinkled in amusement. 'In those days we built a prototype first and only drew it up if it worked so we could make another one.'

Hendricks looked at this watch. 'I guess we'd better get back to New York.'

'Do you still have any of the major components?' asked Cox-Spender, frantically casting about for even a slender straw.

'Some went into GOPHER 11.'

Cox-Spender gaped at the old man. 'GOPHER 11.'

Jack Delmar's grin broadened. 'Worked like a dream. Could bore its way through twenty metres of Manhattan rock. No problem.'

Hendricks had half-risen. He sat down again, letting Cox-Spender ask all the questions.

'Have you still got it?'

'Sure thing. And I'm still sitting on the patents. I figured they might come in handy some day.'

Cox-Spender sat on the edge of his chair. 'Mr Delmar, could GOPHER 11 Bore under a four-kilometre-wide river, and then through, say . . . two metres of rock?' Cox-Spender nearly said 'concrete'.

Jack Delmar shook his head. 'Four kilometres? That would be asking a lot of any machine.'

'But the article in that magazine said that a later version would be able to bore under the Hudson or East River to rescue trapped subway passengers.'

Without looking at the magazine Jack Delmar said, 'If I remember rightly, it said, bore *through* the riverbed.'

'Then how . . .?'

218

'When we got GOPHER 11 working properly, we presented the Port Authority with a complete scheme, and laid on a demonstration. We made several dozen thirty-metre lengths of two-metre diameter plastic pipe – once we had the mould we could punch out as many lengths as we wanted. They were made to be easily joined together to form a watertight seal. A team of scuba divers fitted them together on the bed of the Hudson. They started on the West Side and pushed out until they were over on the New Jersey side. They sealed a prefabricated dome to the submerged end of the pipeline with the open base of the dome held against the riverbed by water pressure. Takes some doing. Once everything was ready the City Fire Department pumped the pipeline and dome dry.'

'So after that, you were able to take your GOPHER along the pipeline to the dome, and bore down from there?' said Cox-Spender excitedly.

Jack Delmar grinned. 'You've got it. The GOPHER operator went straight down, levelled out and broke through into the side of the Lincoln Tunnel within a few metres of the spot marked by the railroad engineers.'

'When was this?'

'Fifteen years back.'

'I never heard about it,' said Hendricks.

'Washington asked me to put the lid on the story as a favour. They were worried in case someone thought of using the idea to break into bank vaults – or even missile silos. I was angling for a big government contract at the time, so I agreed.' Jack Delmar grinned at his visitors.

'Have you still got GOPHER 11 and the pipe sections, Mr Delmar?' asked Cox-Spender, trying to control his eagerness.

'Sure. And the prefabricated dome. They're in our West Fiftieth warehouse, unless Henry's had them shifted. I don't run things now.'

Cox-Spender mentally crossed his fingers before asking the next question. 'Can you remember how many lengths of pipe there were, Mr Delmar?'

Jack Delmar looked curiously at the British civil servant. He wondered why everyone was getting so excited over an unexploded German bomb. It had to be one helluva bomb. He noticed that the Englishman's hands were clenched tightly together. Hendricks was gazing boredly across the lake.

'A hundred and sixty lengths,' said Jack Delmar. 'Enough to construct a five kilometre line. The sections split into halves so they can be stacked and not use too much room. They snap together under water with special latches on the inside.'

Cox-Spender edged forwards until he was nearly falling off his chair. 'Mr Delmar, the British government would like to purchase your GOPHER and its ancillary machinery together with the pipe sections and the prefabricated dome. I'm empowered to negotiate on their behalf.'

Jack Delmar shook his head. 'I wouldn't sell it.'

Cox-Spender goggled at him. 'But you must!' he blurted.

Annoyance flicked across the industrialist's wrinkled face.

'Now see here . . .' he began.

Hendricks intervened. 'I think the British government would be willing to pay substantially for the equipment.'

Jack Delmar gestured round him. His hand encompassed the air-conditioned lodge, the lake and a twin Mercruiser boat.

'When you get to my age, you discover that friends, and maybe a little excitement to relieve the boredom, are more important than money. I was about to say you can have the stuff in return for two small favours.' He studied Cox-Spender. 'Have you the authority to grant favours, Mr Spender?'

Cox-Spender nodded.

Jack Delmar sat back and gazed up at the trees. 'One of my boys – Carl – runs Delmar Instruments in the UK. Carl's been having a struggle lately to keep the business going. It's not his fault – he's a good kid, works hard – but he can't raise cash for investment, and he won't come to me. But he would accept a two million dollar grant from the British government – without strings, and without my name being mentioned. Okay?'

'Okay,' said Cox-Spender, using the affirmative for the first time since he was a boy. 'And the second condition?'

'That you ship me to the UK with the equipment and two of my engineers to help run the operation.'

Cox-Spender agreed with alacrity; Jack Delmar's condition was to have been a Cox-Spender proposal. He felt he had scored a point over the shrewd industrialist.

'One thing, Mr Delmar. How long did it take to break into the Lincoln Tunnel?'

'Twenty-six hours from starting to put the pipeline together to when GOPHER showed her nose to the Penn railroad engineers. Do you know what GOPHER stands for? Geophysical Orbital Power Head Earth Explorer.' He grinned and stood up – eager for action. 'When do we get to ship the stuff?'

'Within the next twenty-four hours,' said Hendricks, uncoiling his frame. 'Sooner, if I can get the transport fixed in time.'

The featureless concrete prongs of the World Trade Center were in sight when Jack Delmar yelled to Cox-Spender above the noise of the helicopter's motor, 'That story about a German bomb is a load of crap?'

'Yes,' Cox-Spender agreed solemnly. 'A load of crap.'

Jack Delmar grinned delightedly at the British civil servant.

The police were very considerate to Maggie and even allowed Mitchell to be present when they questioned her about the accident with Mitchell's boat.

The detective-sergeant closed his notebook and stood up. 'Thank you, Miss Pyne. We'll have this typed out then we'll be asking you to sign it.'

'What will happen next?' Maggie asked.

'There'll be an inquest early next week. The coroner will no doubt have something to say about the responsibilities of river users, then record a verdict of accidental death. It won't take more than fifteen minutes.'

'What happened to the river policeman?'

The detective-sergeant looked levelly at Maggie. 'Sergeant Snowdon? He's still suffering from shock.'

When he had gone, Maggie said to Mitchell. 'I'd like to go to London now, Mitch.'

'Why not call his office and ask them where your father is?'

'You promised, Mitch.'

Mitchell looked at his watch. 15:00 hours. 'Yes, but look, honey. We didn't know the police would be so late coming. It's going to take at least an hour to get into London – there are probably road blocks after yesterday's rioting.'

But Maggie was determined. 'In that case, we'd better leave now.'

She marched out of the room.

Mitchell sighed, and followed her out to the car. He wanted to go back to his place and change, but decided against upsetting her.

It took two hours of driving along nerve-racking police and army diversions before Maggie and Mitchell reached the Ministry of Defence overlooking the Thames in London. The rioting was over but obviously there was still a major alert on.

'Sorry,' said the security officer. 'But everyone's gone home now.'

'But you can at least call his office!' said Maggie angrily. 'Room 1702.'

'It's gone half past, miss. They've all cleared off.'

'Look,' said Maggie calmly, 'my father often works late. You could at least ring his extension.'

The security officer glowered at the angry girl, and decided it would be best not to have a row with a general's daughter. He called the extension. No one answered.

'Do you know where this new camp is that my father's in command of?' demanded Maggie.

'I wouldn't know things like that, miss. Your best bet would be to come back first thing tomorrow morning.'

Mitchell and the girl walked out into the early-evening sun. They crossed the Victoria Embankment and stood leaning against the parapet, looking down at the Thames, swollen with drifting islands of rat-infested refuse.

'God. Just look at it,' said Maggie bitterly.

'What?'

'Everything. When my father came back from a visit to Singapore, he said how clean it was because they had such tough penalties for dropping litter. He said that that was half the trouble with this country – that we don't crack down hard enough to solve problems.'

Mitchell slipped his arm round her and steered her back to the car. 'Come on, honey. We'll find a hotel, and give those bureaucrats hell in the morning.'

4

New Yorkers are more accustomed to helicopters than most inhabitants of large cities. At most times of the day the air space above and round their city is thick with twenty to thirty helicopters either pleasure-tripping tourists round Manhattan, ferrying mail and passengers to La Guardia and

Kennedy airports, or just hanging about making a noise. But the spectacle of fifteen in-line Sikorsky S61s, painted in the mottled green and brown camouflage of the US Air Force Recovery and Rescue Service, thundering across Manhattan from the direction of Queens caused many of the late home-going crowds thronging the sidewalks to look up. The immense machines ignored city ordinances controlling the movement of helicopters; they swept across Central Park, turned sharply above the Parks Department Boat Basin on the Hudson and formed an orderly line of disciplined, hovering thunder between the basin and the Dwight Eisenhower Passenger Terminal.

The Circle Line Ferry nosing towards its berth after the last trip of the day listed dangerously to port as excited passengers swarmed to one side.

Ex-Sergeant Dean Forester from Colorado Springs, pointed out the machines to his son.

'Know what they are, Ben?'

'A lot of noise and lot of pollution,' said Ben distastefully.

'Jolly Green Giants, we used to call them. One of those whirly-birds picked up your Pa when he was shot up bad. If it wasn't for them, you wouldn't be here. What do you think of that, hey?'

It was one of those statements that parents are wont to make for which their unsuspecting offspring have no ready answer.

The first Sikorsky swung towards the West Side water-front, lowering its cargo hoist to the men clambering over the stacks of thirty-metre pipe sections. It hovered for thirty seconds. The whine from its turbines deepened. The heavy machine lifted, swinging away from the waterfront with a cluster of pipe sections suspended from its hoist. The helicopter thrashed down river and the second machine in the line moved in to take its place.

Don Marchant of Oklahoma was on second honeymoon with his second wife and his three cameras. Even on the balcony of the observatory on the eighty-sixth floor of the

224

Empire State Building there was no wind to upset his shutter finger. The second honeymoon had been a disappointment, but he was amply compensated by his magnificent Polaroid shot of fifteen big helicopters flying in line towards Kennedy with the setting sun flashing on their twisting, suspended cargoes.

Operation GOPHER was underway.

5

Paul Weiner was shown into the emergency operations room at five minutes to midnight. His heart sank when he saw the number of people present. Senior army officers were gathered round a large plotting-table bearing a huge large-scale map of the Thames Estuary. Engineers were aiming spluttering soldering irons into the maze of coloured wires sprouting from the end of a massive cable that entered the room through a ragged hole in the wall. A man was mounting a public address speaker on a wall bracket. Girls were hovering near the officers with shorthand pads at the ready. The Prime Minister was at the centre of a huddle grouped round a television monitor showing a surprisingly clear picture of the Vulcan Hall nuclear power station. Another engineer had the back off a second monitor and was probing its innards with a test meter. Two senior police officers were playing StarGlider III on a microcomputer.

No one took much notice of Weiner. He had passed through five security checks to get near the room. He stood looking round. The windows were shut and the blinds pulled down. There was no air-conditioning.

Weiner pushed his way across to the Prime Minister.

'May I have a quick word with you, please, sir?'

The Prime Minister looked up from the monitor. Weiner was surprised by the transformation in the man's face since he had last seen him. He had an expression of elation – the look of a soldier eager for battle.

'Ah, Weiner. What do you think of the picture from opposite Vulcan Hall? We've set up hidden cameras fitted with something which lets them see in the dark. Image intensifiers or something.' The politician left the huddle and drew Weiner into a corner. 'How's everything going?'

'All the equipment has left New York. It's on its way.'

The Prime Minister looked surprised. 'Already? I'll introduce you to the Marshal of the Royal Air Force so you can arrange for Biggin Hill . . .'

'It's all arranged,' said Weiner. 'But we're not using Biggin Hill. It can't handle the long-range strategic heavy transports we're flying in.'

'We agreed it was the best place.'

'Our aircrews were against the idea. They've suggested Dunsfold.'

The Prime Minister had never heard of the place.

'It's owned by British Aerospace and has one of the longest air strips in the South of England,' explained Weiner. 'So we'll need all the helicopters diverted to Dunsfold.'

The American's attitude had annoyed the Prime Minister all through the day during their frequent telephone conversations. The Americans were trying to take over the entire operation.

'We've decided against helicopters,' said the Prime Minister firmly.

The statement astounded Weiner.

'But we decided . . .'

'*You* decided.'

'But Prime Minister, helicopters are the most logical way of transporting the pipe sections to Chatham Dockyard.'

The Prime Minister grasped Weiner gently by the elbow and steered him into the corridor. 'Listen, Weiner, dozens of helicopters buzzing across the country with thirty-metre lengths of pipe hanging from their hoists will start a whole spate of rumours which it will be impossible to suppress. If the story about the power station gets out, it could easily

226

start a panic. Naturally, we're extremely grateful for all the help your country is giving us, but we're the ones who have to govern here when this business is over. Not your President, and certainly not the CIA.'

The Prime Minister gave Weiner no time to reply.

'You give Sir Dudley McBryan full information on when and where your transport is expected, and he'll arrange for them to be met by the fleet of trucks and low-loaders he's laid on. How far is Dunsfold from Chatham?'

'About a hundred miles.'

'What time will your transport be arriving?'

'Ten hundred hours.'

'Then there's no problem. The navy say the ship won't be ready until sixteen hundred hours so there'll be plenty of time to shift the stuff from Dunsfold. There's no point in a lot of unnecessary panic, Weiner. We British are used to keeping cool in adverse circumstances.'

And being offensive, Weiner wanted to say, but he managed to remain silent.

'What about this GOPHER contraption and the space-suit? When's that arriving?'

'They'll be on the transports arriving at Dunsfold in the morning.' said Weiner. 'The team of technicians will be arriving with them; two men to look after GOPHER; the NASA spacesuit experts and, of course, the GOPHER operator. He's our only astronaut who's also a first-class marksman.'

'I've changed my mind about that, too. The operator who breaks into the power station will have to be British.'

Weiner was appalled. 'We can't change the plans this late in the day, sir. besides, he's on his way.'

'Maybe you can't change the plans, Weiner, but we can,' said the Prime Minister smoothly. He was gratified by Weiner's expression. The CIA man was badly shaken.

'We can't substitute the operator,' Weiner nearly shouted. 'Jesus, he's a trained astronaut. He's accustomed

227

to working in a spacesuit. He's been shown how to operate the machine—'

'According to Cox-Spender's last instruction,' the Prime Minister interrupted, 'operating the machine is relatively simple.'

'You don't understand. We have to use an old pattern spacesuit because they've got a hundred per cent heat-insulating properties. Those spacesuits were individually made. You can't just get anybody to wear one!'

'I'm sorry, Weiner. But my colleagues and I have made up our minds. The man who breaks into the power station must be British. On that we are firmly decided.'

The American shook his head in disbelief.

'Christ. What does the man's nationality matter?'

'It matters to us.' The politician paused and patted Weiner patronizingly on the shoulder. 'As a matter of interest, I've already made a personal choice of the officer who is to break in. He's a capable man and, I understand, an excellent marksman.'

Weiner saw no sense in arguing further. He merely said, 'The agreement was that we supply the equipment and the specialized personnel. In view of this change, we will have to revise downward our estimates of the probable success of Operation GOPHER.'

The Prime Minister grinned. 'So you've taken it upon yourselves to allocate a code name?'

'It's necessary for communication purposes.'

'Have you read Churchill's memoirs on the Second World War?'

Weiner moved towards the operations room.

'No.'

'I think it was Volume Two,' said the Prime Minister, now enjoying himself. 'In it, he published the directives he issued to be applied when deciding the code names to be used for wartime operation. He stressed that the name selected should not be trivial — it would not do, he said, for the relatives of those killed in a particular action to have to recall an operation with an absurd name. He also said the name should in no way reflect the nature of the operation.'

'I'm surprised that you should concern yourself with such minor points, sir.'

'Churchill also said that the greatness of an organization manifested itself in its attention to detail.'

Weiner choked back an impulse to tell the Prime Minister what he thought of a country that allowed its nuclear power stations to be seized by a handful of terrorists. Instead he said coldly, 'If it's detail you're concerned about, you'd better let me have the measurements of your operator so we can have another spacesuit flown in from Houston.'

With that, Weiner turned and walked away.

The Prime Minister spent another hour in the operations room. He left at 2:30 and went to bed at 3:00 hours. As he undressed he reflected that here were only forty-five hours left before Keller would carry out his threat.

He lay awake for some minutes wondering what had happened to Simpson, and then fell soundly asleep.

Friday

1

The Lockheed Galaxy's wings drooped as it lost speed, lowering its twenty-eight landing wheels to Dunsfold's runway. By the time it had rolled to a standstill the tips appeared to be touching the ground. Then the massive transport kneeled by partly retracting its undercarriages into their vast pods.

The load master wasted no time.

The Galaxy's nose swung upwards like the visor on a suit of armour, and the two Queen Mary vehicles reversed smartly up to the yawning cavern.

Beads of sweat rolled down the soldiers' faces as they laboured to load the curious lengths of half-section plastic pipe on to their long trucks. The vehicles were quickly loaded to safe height and moved away to allow two more to take their place. After thirty minutes under the dawn sky eight low-loaders were loaded to capacity. The last two pulled clear as the great visor swung down. The ponderous bulk of giant freight aircraft heaved itself up from its kneeling position and taxied away to the far end of the long runway. A few minutes later the great shadow swept over a farmhouse, its engines bellowing at the sustained effort required to keep the improbable mass in the air.

The next arrival at Dunsfold was a flying nightmare: a hideous bloated Super Guppy owned by Aero Spacelines Inc. of Santa Barbara, California.

The Super Guppy had started out to be a graceful Boeing Stratocruiser, and then things had gone badly wrong for it.

The wings and the underside of the fuselage were Stratocruiser, but its upper half was a grotesque swollen balloon that swept up from the nose until its height matched the tailplane. The sides bulged sickeningly over the wings and continued bulging until they reached the tail, where sanity was restored. The weird aircraft had been designed to transport the top stage of the Saturn/Apollo moon rocket, and was now available to anyone with a bulky load that required urgent transportation.

The monstrous creation sat pregnantly on the runway while its crew performed a Caesarean section on its fuselage. The opening disgorged more of the pipe halves, a large crate, several giant reels of flexible hose, a number of smaller crates and ten passengers. All were spirited away in the remaining trucks.

The Guppy waddled to the end of the runway and waited while the airfield-control officer nerved herself to give it permission to take off.

2

Hendricks arrived in London at 8.00 hours. He went straight to Paul Weiner's office. Weiner was asleep on a folding bed. Hendricks shook him roughly.

'What's this bull about the British wanting to use one of their own men?'

Weiner sat up yawning and rubbing his eyes. Hendricks repeated the question.

'National pride,' said Weiner. He looked at his watch. 'Jesus, I need more sleep than this.'

The long bony fingers hooked the covers on to the floor 'You've had some, which is more than I've had. Come on. We're going to make them change their minds.'

Weiner shook his head. 'We'd be wasting our time. I've tried. The Prime Minister won't budge.'

Hendricks sat in Weiner's chair. 'You told him we had someone lined up?'

'Sure.'

'An astronaut who's a marksman?'

'Yes,' said Weiner wearily. 'He said he too had picked an ideal man.'

'The British don't have astronauts.'

'You tell him.'

Hendricks drummed his talons on the desk.

'Does it matter?' asked Weiner. 'The machine isn't difficult to operate. All we need is for NASA to get off their asses and fly out a spacesuit that matches the measurements I've faxed them.'

'That's the whole goddamn trouble,' growled Hendricks.

'Haven't they got one?'

Hendricks gazed at Weiner sadly. 'Sure they got one. But nothing less than a personal directive from the President will persuade them to part with it, even for a week. I got their message an hour before I landed. I thought, in a moment of rashness, that I could leave you to look after things at this end.'

'What's so special about one lousy spacesuit?' demanded Weiner, stung by Hendricks' comment.

Hendricks picked up the phone and fished in his pocket for a piece of paper, which he tossed to Weiner.

'*That* is what is special about it.'

Weiner read the slip. He looked at Hendricks with a mixture of surprise and dismay. All he could think of to say was, 'Oh shit.'

'My reaction precisely,' said Hendricks, and gave the switchboard the day code that would put him through to the White House.

3

By noon, the seven-thousand-tonne ore-carrier *Barrow* lying at the navy dockyard at Chatham was beginning to look like a ship again. Most of the two hundred skilled

232

dockyard workers who had been swarming over her since she had been commandeered the previous night had completed their frenzied operations and were clearing up the mess. They had laboured first under floodlights and then under the hot morning sun to cut a three-metre diameter hole in her side into the midships hold. The position of the hole had been carefully calculated so that it would be well below the waterline when the forward and aft holds were laden with gravel and equipment.

When everything was ready the signal was given to the cranes that were holding the *Barrow* at a thirty-degree list. The ship slowly righted herself. Water roared through the gaping hole. A steel hawser parted with a sudden twang, The *Barrow* heaved herself over on to an even keel and settled lower and lower as water continued to flood into the midships hold. The engineers looked on anxiously. Their main concern was whether the reinforced bulkheads separating the hold from the rest of the ship would withstand the water pressure normally directed on the hull.

The *Barrow* stopped sinking and rode serenely at her mooring. No one went near her for thirty minutes – there was a chance that a bulkhead might collapse without warning.

Two dockyard engineers ventured cautiously aboard. They looked down at the flooded hold.

'Just like a bleedin' swimming-pool.'

'I reckon there's enough freeboard for the gravel.'

'I wouldn't go out on it. Bloody dangerous with this lot sloshing about in any sort of chop.'

'I've heard they're taking it up river – not out to sea.'

'Why do they want them extra anchors then?'

'Nice ship until we buggered her up.'

'Wonder what it's for? I've not heard there's a market of ships with bleedin' great three metre holes in their side.'

'Maybe it's a new method of fishing. They sit up here waiting for a fish to swim through the hole them chuck gavel at it.'

The first engineer spat into the brimming hold.

'Why should we worry? Just so long as they pay us that bleedin' treble time they promised. Come on. Let's get the gravel loaded before that stuff turns up.'

'Do you know what's it's all for?'

'Dunno. Who cares?'

The first engineer nodded to one of the many closed-circuit television cameras recently installed on the *Barrow*'s bridge. 'Not me. But someone does.'

4

'I'm sorry, Miss Pyne,' said the principal officer at the Ministry of Defence. 'But I'm afraid I cannot disclose where your father is.' He smiled sympathetically at Maggie, finding it hard to believe that she could have been responsible for all the scenes throughout the building which resulted in him agreeing to see her personally.

The American with her seemed to be embarrassed by the whole business.

'General Pyne is in command of the new oil and gas platform defence force?' said Mitchell.

The principal officer nodded. 'Quite right. There's no secret about that. But I'm afraid I'm not at liberty to disclose where the camp is. Not until the minister decides to release the press statement.' He nodded to Maggie. 'As the daughter of a senior army officer, Miss Pyne, you must be accustomed to your father being called away on business.'

Maggie stood. 'He's always told me when he would be away, and when he would be returning. If you won't help me, then I'll find him by myself.'

She turned and marched out of the office.

Mitchell looked at the principal officer in embarrassment. 'I'm sorry.'

The civil servant smiled good naturedly. 'Don't worry, Mr Mitchell. You'd better go after her. A few more like her and we wouldn't need an army.'

'Take me home Mitch,' said Maggie when they were outside the building.

'Hey. I thought you were a fighter?'

'I'm sick of London. I never thought I would be – but I am.'

'It's possible,' said Mitchell slowly, 'that Paul Weiner might know where your father is.'

'Your friend at the American Embassy? How could he?'

Mitchell considered telling her about his interview with Hendricks and Weiner and their interest in Maggie's father. He recalled Hendricks' threat and decided against it. Still – it wouldn't hurt to take Maggie to see Weiner.

'Maybe not,' he said in answer to Maggie's question. 'But it might be worth looking him up.'

Mitchell steered Maggie back to the Mustang.

5

The officer the Prime Minister had selected to break into Vulcan Hall nuclear power station was one of the few in the country who knew about the terrorist takeover.

He was watching a television programme when two plain-clothes men called for him. They were polite, but firm. They allowed him to change out of his shorts, then pushed him into the back of a two-door sports car.

'Where are you taking me and why?'

'We only know where, sir.'

And that was all they said during the entire journey.

They took him to a drab, inhospitable mansion in a tree-lined road off the Bayswater Road and left him to contemplate the view across Kensington Palace Gardens from a comfortable flat on the top floor.

He sat on a window seat wondering what was going to happen next.

He was a lean, muscular man with grey eyes and dark wiry hair that was beginning to go grey at the temples. After five minutes in the flat he crossed to the door. It was unlocked. two soldiers were standing on either side of the door.

'Can we help you, sir?' one of them asked.

The officer returned to the window seat. He was still sitting there when the Prime Minister walked into the room, sat in an armchair and proceeded to unwrap a cigar. The officer gaped at him in surprise.

'You know about the power station takeover, of course,' said the Prime Minister, as if unaware of the impact his appearance had had on the officer. 'What you don't know is that with a little American help, I've devised a scheme to get them out.' The Prime Minister paused to light his cigar before explaining about the *Barrow*, the prefabricated riverbed tunnel and the GOPHER boring machine. The Prime Minister concluded by saying that the officer would have to go to the Royal Aircraft Establishment at Farnborough to be shown how to use the spacesuit and to check that it was effective against the IRIS detectors. He was about to enlarge sightly, when the officer interrupted him:

'You said "me", sir.' The officer was puzzled.

The Prime Minister examined the glowing end of his cigar.

'That's right. As one of the most loyal officers in the country, you're going to be the one to break in.'

The officer stiffened. 'Whose idea was this?'

'Mine,' said the Prime Minister, grinning. 'Rather ingenious, don't you think?'

The officer's face relaxed. He nodded slowly and allowed himself a faint smile.

'There is one thing,' said the Prime Minister. 'If you were unable to cut all the detonator wires, you'd have to find this Keller and be absolutely certain of killing him with your first shot before he saw you. There'd be no second chance. Could you do it?'

'Yes. I'm a good shot.'

236

The officer had misunderstood the question, but the Prime Minister let it pass. There was a silence, then the politician said, 'I've told my Cabinet colleagues that the identity of the officer carrying out this task must remain a secret known only to me. If you succeed – well and good. But if you don't . . . Well, I don't think it fair that your name should be remembered in history, if there is any history should you fail, as the man partly to blame for the death of millions of people.'

The officer nodded. The explanation made sense. 'And that view has been accepted?'

'Yes,' said the Prime Minister. 'For that reason, I've decided you should have a code name – Phoenix.' He paused. 'Your identity will never be known. You're prepared to accept that?'

'Yes.'

The Prime Minister nodded. Loyalty was a commodity to be exploited first, and respected second.

The two men discussed details for an hour. At the end the Prime Minister crossed to a cocktail cabinet and poured drinks. They drank a silent toast to their plan's ultimate success.

'I must go now,' said the Prime Minister, 'and you must get down to Farnborough to see about that spacesuit.' He paused at the door. 'One thing, for God's sake be careful with it. The Americans are rather attached to it. It was the suit worn by Neil Armstrong when he took his giant leap for mankind.

6

Cox-Spender dragged his suitcase off the circulating conveyer and tottered towards the customs hall.

He was not feeling his best. He had persuaded Hendricks to allow him to return on a slower aircraft than Concorde. The flight from New York had taken nine hours instead of the usual seven. There had been storms all across the Atlantic. Belts of severe clear air turbulance from all over the ocean had gathered in the path of his Boeing and lain in ambush – arranging themselves so that each succeeding air pocket was worse than the previous one.

On top of that a baby had been sick all over his suit.

Two men approached him. One was wearing a sailcloth suit which Cox-Spender thought he must have purchased in a dark boutique during a power cut.

'Mr Cox-Spender?' Sailcloth suit smiled disarmingly.

'Yes?'

'Will you come with us please.'

It was an order, not a question.

They were very kind to Cox-Spender. They told him that they had been told to say what a magnificent job he had done, and that he was to be rewarded with some well-earned leave at Inverloch in Scotland.

'Inverloch?' echoed Cox-Spender. 'You mean the safe house?'

'I expect so, sir,'

'But it's been closed since the war!'

'Deliberate rumours, Mr Cox-Spender. You'll find it cooler that London.'

'What would I do there?'

'Well, there's golf.'

'I don't play golf.'

'We'll teach you.'

'And Commander Crabbe will teach you fly fishing,' said the second man. 'He's an expert now.'

'A trout stream prima donna,' said sailcloth suit, taking Cox-Spender's case.

Ten minutes later Cox-Spender was sitting between the two men on a flight bound for Edinburgh.

7

The navy dockyard at Chatham had not seen so much activity since the war.

At 14:00 hours a convoy of low-loaders, with tarpaulins covering their loads, rumbled along the naval town's sun-blistered streets and into the dockyard, where cranes transferred their loads on to the thousand tonnes of gravel spread evenly in the *Barrow*'s forward and aft holds.

The level of the gravel was three metres below deck, so there was plenty of room for the pipe sections, the pumps, the prefabricated dome and the GOPHER boring machine.

A team of shallow-water divers arrived from the navy's HMS *Vernon* underwater training school, followed by trucks loaded with oxygen rebreathing sets and additional equipment delivered from Westlands in Yeovil.

The Prime Minister watched the final preparations with ill-concealed satisfaction on the monitor screens in the operations room.

Hendricks was standing beside him.

The politician waved a hand at the tiered television screens fed from cameras mounted on the *Barrow*.

'Supposing all this hadn't been possible, would you have carried out that veiled threat?'

'I can't speak for my government,' replied Hendricks.

'Your ambassador had no inhibitions on Tuesday night.'

Hendricks watched a crane lowering a cluster of plastic pipe sections.

'That was Tuesday night,' he replied.

8

'Would you wait in the outer office please, Miss Pyne,' said Weiner.

Maggie made no attempt to move. 'So you won't help?'

Weiner glanced at Mitchell. 'We don't know where he is. I'd like to speak to Mr Mitchell alone. It won't take a minute.'

Maggie regarded Weiner coldly. She left the room without speaking.

'Now see here Mitch,' said Weiner when the door closed behind her. 'Do you want us to cover your drill-string or not?'

'Sure.'

'Then why bring her here? You heard what Hendricks said.'

'I've told her nothing. We were in town, and I thought you might be able to help. Why *are* you interested in Pyne?'

'I can't tell you that.'

'This fraud or whatever it is he's mixed up in, does it involve American equipment?'

Weiner came around from his desk. 'Listen Mitch. Take the girl home. Take her away on vacation somewhere – anything to stop her worrying about her father. She'll find out soon enough, but I can't tell you anything at this point.'

'Can I tell her that?'

Weiner shrugged. 'Why not. Just take her away somewhere where the press and the crackpots won't be able to give her a hard time.'

'So he is involved in a serious crime?'

Weiner nodded. 'In a way – yes. But don't for Chrissake tell her.'

Saturday:
The final hours

1

'Phoenix' arrived at the Royal Aircraft Establishment at 00:15 hours.

The untidy test laboratory was busy with technicians milling round a spacesuit suspended from a frame. A long bench against a wall was strewn with the component parts of the suit's backpack. A loud Texan accent was yelling for a six-mill wrench. A white-coated man was chipping at a block of ice.

Earl Kramer's name was embroidered on his coveralls. Phoenix introduced himself. Kramer stared at Phoenix, then yelled, 'He's here!'

Everyone stopped work and gathered around.

'How's it going?' asked Phoenix.

'Lousy,' said Kramer. 'Come back next week.'

'What's the trouble?'

'Heat absorption.' Kramer looked at Phoenix curiously. 'This thing you've got to do. Could you do it in an hour?'

Phoenix was surprised by the direct, no-nonsense approach. 'I don't know. Why?'

'We have a problem with your body heat. Come over here, and I'll show you what I mean.'

Kramer stepped across to the bench and picked up a garment that resembled long underwear to cover arms, legs and torso.

'Feel,' he said, as if he were a tailor trying to convince a customer about the quality of some material.

241

Phoenix could feel minute tubes sandwiched into the material. The entire garment was a mass of them.

'Water-cooling tubes,' explained Kramer. 'You wear this next to your skin over the absorbent underpants, and these tubes carry your body heat to the PLSS on your back, where it's pushed through an exchanger out into the environment. Now as I understand it, we can't do that.'

'That's right,' said Phoenix. 'No heat must escape.'

'So what the hell do we do with it?' demanded Kramer.

Phoenix shrugged. 'I'm sorry. I'm not an engineer. What do you do with it?'

'Instead of getting rid of it, we absorb it – into crushed ice. We've modified the PLSS–'

'PLSS?'

'Personal Life Support System,' explained Kramer patiently. 'The backpack. We've modified it so you'll have a an insulated flask containing thirty pounds of ice. Ice can absorb a helluva lot of heat, but as soon as it's all melted, its temperature starts to creep up. That's why you only have a hour to do whatever it is you're going to do. Maybe two hours if you take it easy, but we can't be sure, so we've fixed you up with an ice-weight indicator. That way you'll know when you're heading for trouble.'

Phoenix frowned. No one had mentioned this problem during his long telephone conversations with various experts.

'Couldn't you provide more than thirty pounds of ice?' he asked.

Kramer shook his head. 'We've tried, and run up against a law of diminishing returns. The more ice you carry, the more heat you generate having to hike it around, and the faster the ice melts. Besides, thirty pounds is half the weight of the suit. You'll have ninety pounds over your body weight to shift around. It's enough.'

'One hour?'

'Two if you don't rush around. Okay, let's get you suited up. The guys in the next lab want to run some tests.'

Phoenix found the spacesuit, or 'extra vehicular mobility unit', as the NASA technicians called it, was surprisingly comfortable and permitted an unexpected freedom of movement – the one thing that had worried him since he had learned he was to wear one. The only uncomfortable feeling was caused by the urine tube fitted to his penis and leading to a bag on the right leg of the suit above the knee.

'The absorbent underpants will cope with anything else,' Kramer said.

Phoenix commented on the crude arrangement.

'If you can come up with an improvement on diapers,' said Kramer, grinning, 'then we'd be glad to hear about it.'

The first garment had been the one-piece cooling suit. This was followed by he eighteen-layer 'integrated meteoroid suit' with an outer covering of non-flammable Beta cloth, finally the abrasion-resistant Teflon fabric covering designed to protect the suit against mishaps on the rugged lunar terrain.

Tinted pull-down visors were provided on the helmet to protect the astronaut against ultra-violet and infra-red radiation, and micro-meteoroids. It was impossible to see the wearer's face when they were lowered.

Kramer secured the backpack and connected the water cooling, oxygen purge and communication umbilicals. He guided Phoenix's gauntleted hands to the control box on the suit's chest.

'I'm going to switch you on now,' he said into a two-way radio.

Phoenix suddenly felt water flowing through the tubes next to his skin. It was like being plunged into a cool bath. The sensation was a welcome relief from the heat building up in the suit.

'How does it feel?'

'Great.'

Kramer grinned. 'For the first time in your life, you're completely independent of Mother Earth in your own little self-contained space-ship. If this planet was to blow apart suddenly, you'd outlive everyone. But only for a few hours.'

Kramer checked the suit's controls. 'Okay. Try moving about a little, but lean forward – remember, you've got a high centre of gravity.'

The backpack was a deadweight on Phoenix's back. The straps dragged at this shoulders. He took a few unsteady steps. Sweat streamed down his face despite the cooling system.

'Well?'

'God, it's heavy.'

Kramer nodded sympathetically. 'Yeah. They're not designed for EVA in one gee. And you've got an extra thirty pounds of ice.'

'Why are you using pounds instead of kilos?'

'Because all this kit was designed before NASA adopted the metric system. What's the gauge reading?'

Phoenix looked at his right wrist – holding it high in front of the visor.

'Twenty-nine pounds.'

'You see? You've melted a pound of ice already, and you've hardly started moving about.'

Kramer's easy-going manner annoyed Phoenix. 'Why the hell couldn't you arrange something better than this ludicrous system? Christ, even a sixth-former would've thought of refrigeration.'

'Easy on,' said Kramer's voice inside the helmet. 'All refrigeration does is move heat from one place to another: it doesn't get rid of it. Ever put your hand down the back of an icebox?'

'I'm sorry.'

Kramer brushed the apology aside. 'Don't let it bother you. You'd better get next door.'

'Just as I am?'

'Sure. It's meant for moving about in. Through the door. First door on the right.'

As Phoenix swayed unsteadily towards the door, he heard a click in his helmet as Kramer cut communications. He did not hear him say loudly into a telephone for the benefit of everyone:

'One astronaut on the rocks coming up, fellers.'

Phoenix turned in the corridor and saw the technicians mouthing silent laughter.

The spacesuited figure shuffled towards an IRIS detector. His external microphone was switched on so he could hear the sounds in the laboratory. Four men and a woman doctor were watching his progress from behind a glass panel set into the wall. A loud speaker relayed their talk.

The detector was mounted on a pedestal. The dome on top of the unit discarded ambient heat radiation, and concentrated on any dense sources of heat that moved.

'Hold it a minute,' said the loudspeaker.

Phoenix paused.

'Okay. Carry on. We thought we were getting a reading.'

Phoenix moved nearer the detector until he could reach out and touch it.

'What do you want me to do now?'

'Move a hand in front of it.'

Phoenix waved a gauntlet up and down a few centimetres from the detector.

'Fine,' said the loudspeaker. 'Now turn around slowly, and put your face near it.'

Feeling slightly ridiculous, Phoenix did so.

'Now push one of the visors up.'

Phoenix complied.

'Now the other one.'

He had only just pushed the visor halfway when the loudspeaker shrilled with a continuous, discordant note.

'Just thought you'd like to hear the result,' said the loudspeaker.

'How much ice is left?'

'Nineteen pounds.'

'Right. There's just one more test, then you can get some sleep.'

The four men and the woman entered the laboratory. They guided Phoenix to a cycling machine and helped him on to the saddle. He had to hang grimly on to the handlebars to prevent the backpack's weight from toppling him off. He was unable to see his boots, so they secured them to the pedals with straps.

'Just pedal slowly,' said the doctor. 'As if you were cycling along a flat country lane and enjoying the view.'

While Phoenix busily pedalled nowhere, the laboratory staff surrounded him with a fence of detectors before returning to their booth.

'How much ice now?' said the loudspeaker ten minutes later.

'Thirteen pounds.'

'Slow down a little.'

The needle on the wrist gauge crept downward. After twenty minutes it was hovering over the figure five.

'Ease up little,' said the loudspeaker after Phoenix had relayed the information.

Phoenix slowed the pumping action. The movement of his legs was causing the urine attachment to chaff painfully on his penis.

Fifteen minutes later the needle was on zero.

'It'll take a while for the water to warm up and trigger the detectors,' said the loudspeaker.

Phoenix continued pedalling. The heat in the suit began to rise.

'Speed it up a little,' said the loudspeaker.

He pedalled faster, tightening his abdomen muscles against the desire to urinate.

Another five minutes passed. There was no sound in the laboratory apart from the creak and whir of the cycling machine and the rustle of Teflon fabric.

Then the room suddenly filled with a violent shrieking tone from the loudspeaker. The mind-numbing noise caused

Phoenix to relax his stomach muscles. Hot urine coursed through the tube and gurgled into the bag on his thigh. The shrieking rose to a deafening crescendo.

'Christ,' breathed one of the men in the control booth. 'He's set them all off. Every fucking one.'

2

At 2:00 hours, Jack Delmar was hardly able to contain his excitement. He leaned on the bridge rail beneath a bright moon and breathed deeply, savouring the feeling of anticipation now that the operation was about to begin. God, how he hated retirement.

There was a flooding tide, the *Barrow*'s navigation lights were switched on and her mooring lines singled up. A tug eased across the still water and between the dark shapes of mothballed warships.

The shallow-water divers sat in orderly rows on polythene sheeting spread over the gravel in the aft hold. They were dressed in neoprene wetsuits and wearing oxygen rebreathing sets. Their masks hung down on their chests. Some passed the time threading weights on to their quick-release belts, a few smoked. None talked. A chief petty officer checked the spare lithium hydroxide canisters the divers would be using to purify the oxygen in their rebreathing sets. He was unhappy having so many men on oxygen. He preferred aqualungs, which used compressed air and were much safer. Oxygen under pressure could kill a man in a few minutes, especially if he had to be dragged out of a four-kilometre long underwater pipeline.

'Scubas are out,' Jack Delmar had told the chief petty officer. 'We don't want exhaust bubbles pooling in the pipeline and forcing it to the surface before we've pumped the gravel in.'

The chief petty officer moved across to his men. 'You okay, Jones?'

The diver he addressed nodded nervously. 'Fine, thanks, chief.'

The chief petty officer grunted and moved on. Jones was recovering from a perforated eardrum after diving with a head cold he had not reported. Normally he wouldn't be allowed near a pair of flippers for another month, but those in charge, whoever they were, sitting God knows where, and watching every move with the television cameras, wanted every diver they could lay their hands on.

The tug left the *Barrow* when the two ships reached the widest part of the River Medway. The bridge rang down 'slow ahead both' to the engine-room. White water boiled under the ore-carrier's stern. Black water heaved in the flooded hold as she moved downriver alone.

In one hour she would be entering the Thames Estuary; and another hour's steaming up river towards London would bring her to Canvey Island.

Keeping well over to the south bank, away from the power station, she would gradually lose way, pay out her anchors and use her engines to drag their flukes deep onto the mud until the *Barrow* was held firmly fore and aft. Then, below the high sides of the holds and screened from the distant power station, everyone on board would start work. Even the *Barrow*'s original crew had a task to perform: they were to laze in the sun in full view and show no interest in the power station whatsoever.

While *Barrow* was lifting her bows to the gentle waves, Phoenix was in a sedative-induced sleep at the Royal Aircraft Establishment.

A pilot boat would take him to the *Barrow* when everything was ready. That would be at 14:00 hours if everything went according to plan.

Ten hours before Ralph Keller's Doomsday Ultimatum deadline.

3

Phoenix raised the M1 automatic rifle and fired three times.

The first round tore a piece off the top of his target's skull, the second smashed through the back of the neck and the third shattered the remains of the head.

'Not bad,' said the major grudgingly. 'You're getting the hang of it now. The first one would've been enough.'

'I like to be certain,' said Phoenix, pulling off the space helmet and gauntlets. They were the only part of the spacesuit he had been wearing. He examined the rifle. 'Sawing off the trigger guard was a good idea.'

The major looked curiously at the strange gauntlets.

'Damned difficult shooting with those things on. Is it absolutely essential?'

'Yes.'

The major walked down the indoor firing range and collected the fragments of wax. He assembled the skull in his hands and showed it to Phoenix. There was a neat hole where the second shot had penetrated the back of the neck, but at the front was a crater the size of a man's fist. The major put the skull down and examined one of the unjacketed bullets disapprovingly.

'Nasty things,' he said. 'Don't know why MOD buy them. A bullet goes in and an express train comes out.'

A nice way of putting it, thought Phoenix.

'I suppose you'll be shooting the real target from behind?'

The telephone rang.

'For you,' said the major, holding out the receiver.

Phoenix took the telephone and waited for the major to move away.

'How's it going?' asked the Prime Minister.

'Very well indeed, sir.'

'You're now going to have to deal with Keller no matter what happens. The Americans know something about him. It's his presence which has caused all the trouble.'

Phoenix was intrigued. 'What do they know that we don't know?'

'A hell of a lot. It seems he was involved in some mischief concerning nuclear fuel when he was working in the United

States. It's something we should've known about. Anyway, the important thing now is for you to deal with him so that we can make them a present of his body. That way, they'll lose interest and go home. Do you understand?'

'Yes, sir.'

'I'll wish you the best of luck,' said the Prime Minister. 'See you on television.'

The line went dead.

The major lifted the space helmet off his head.

'Will you be wearing the rest of it? A full spacesuit?'

'Yes.'

'Where exactly is the target? On the moon?'

'Somewhere just as difficult to get to,' said Phoenix, and changed the subject.

4

With six anchors dragged deep into the riverbed, the *Barrow*'s captain was satisfied it would be impossible for the ship to move, apart from up and down with the tide.

He glanced at the bridge chronometer: 4:45 hours. Fifteen minutes ahead of the operations schedule on the chart table.

He gave the order for work to begin.

On the word from Jack Delmar, the chief petty officer herded the first team of twenty divers into the flooded hold.

The black-clad figures guided the lower half of the first pipe section into the hold and through the hole in the *Barrow*'s side without difficulty. Three divers swam out into the Thames and supported the end of the pipe while their fellow-divers pushed out the upper half and allowed it to settle on the lower half. A diver swam along the inside of the pipe fastening the latches that pulled the two halves tightly together against their seals.

An inflatable collar was pushed round the pipe so that it was trapped evenly between the pipe opening and the side of the hole in the hold. The collar was inflated slowly, with divers pulling out the creases until a tight seal was formed.

The *Barrow* now had a flooded thirty-metre length of plastic pipe protruding from her side into the Thames three metres below the surface.

'Current's dragging it a bit,' said Jack Delmar. 'Get another five sections in position right away so we can anchor them to the riverbed.'

The first team worked well. By 5:20 ten sections were in place and the pipeline was three hundred metres long.

'I'm going to have to rest them,' said the chief petty officer.

'Okay, chief. Put your next team down,' said Jack Delmar.

'I'm sorry, sir. But I've put my most experienced divers into the first team so they'll know all the snags that are likely to crop up. Each one of them is to be a divemaster for the other teams, so I can't put any more men down until they've rested.'

Jack Delmar nodded. 'How long do you need?'

'Thirty minutes, sir.'

'Thirty minutes then chief. But no more.'

The second, less experienced team tired in forty-five minutes and managed to increase the pipeline by only five sections. It was exhausting work: each new length added sixty metres to the distance the divers had to swim from the *Barrow*'s hold to the end of the pipeline, and back again.

The third team tired in thirty minutes and succeeded in adding only four sections.

'It's this business of having to shove the sections along the tunnel,' said the chief petty officer despondently. 'Each section makes it more and more difficult. It's a six hundred metre swim as it is, without having to handle the pipes.'

'The pipeline is going to be four thousand metres long, chief,' Jack Delmar pointed out.

The chief petty officer nodded glumly. 'We'll have to think of another way of getting the sections out to the end,

251

sir. At this rate, all the men will be exhausted with only half the sections in position.'

The American considered the problem. 'Okay, chief,' he said. 'You carry on, I'll see if I can up with something.'

5

As each new section disappeared into the hold a girl in the operations room stretched a rod across the plot-table and pushed another length of plastic on to the end of the line that was creeping from the model of the *Barrow* towards a replica of the power station. The Prime Minister, Hendricks and senior officers watched the agonizingly slow process in concern.

Weiner had disappeared in response to an urgent telephone call from his office.

'Ten past nine, Prime Minister,' said Hendricks. 'There should be fifty sections out.'

The Prime Minister picked up a telephone and pressed the button that would sound the buzzer on Jack Delmar's two-way radio. They talked urgently for five minutes.

'They need another two hundred divers,' announced the Prime Minister when he had replaced the receiver.

6

There was very little of Simpson's face left, but enough for Paul Weiner to recognize him as he gingerly turned the body on to its back in Howard Mitchell's sitting-room.

'Do you know who it is?' asked Mitchell.

Weiner stood up and stared down at the body, baffled. Mitchell repeated his question.

'No,' lied Weiner.

'I thought you might,' said Mitchell coldly. 'That's why I called you.'

'Why should I know who it is?' demanded Weiner.

'Come on, Paul. I wasn't born yesterday. You call me up to London. You tell me I'm to spy on General Pyne in return for covering my drill-string which would cost you a helluva lot of money.' Then Mitchell was shouting, his face a few centimetres from Weiner's. 'And now I find this on my carpet, and my telephone blown to bits by what looks like a bomb!'

Weiner groped for words. The bedroom telephone rang. He followed Mitchell upstairs and stood in the doorway. The telephone call had given him time to think.

Mitchell picked up the receiver. 'Yes?'

It was Maggie. Excited. 'Mitch! I've found Daddy! I was an idiot not to have realized before. Those photographs you took last Sunday. I've just made another print from one of the negatives. You remember all those huts and things at the back of that power station that I thought was a holiday camp? Well, it's an army camp! Daddy's new camp! It must be!'

Weiner could hear an excited voice from where he was standing but was unable to make out what was being said. He was grappling with the mystery of Simpson's body, and suddenly realized that Mitchell was speaking to him – his hand cupped over the mouthpiece.

'You know London, Paul. That power station near Thames Haven: is it called Vulcan Hall?'

Weiner was too shaken by the question to speak. He could only nod dumbly.

'Yes,' said Mitchell into the mouthpiece. 'And you couldn't? Sure you dialled the right number?'

Weiner tried frantically to attract Mitchell's attention. Mitchell turned his back on him.

'Sure. I'll take you there, honey.'

Weiner thought he was going to have a heart attack. 'You can't!' he shouted.

Mitchell finished talking and replaced the receiver. He looked up at Weiner. His friend's face was ashen.

253

'You can't go to Vulcan Hall, Mitch.'

'Sure I can. Who's going to stop me?'

Weiner grabbed his arm.

'Mitch! You can't! You've got to keep away. Both of you!'

Weiner was scared. Mitchell knew him well enough to know that he didn't scare easily.

'Supposing you tell me what all this is about, Paul? Right from the beginning.'

Weiner hesitated, then nodded. 'Okay,' he said reluctantly, and sat down.

Half an hour later Weiner was driving fast back to London, wondering if he had done the right thing. The car clock said noon. Weiner shrugged inwardly. In twelve hours it wouldn't matter what Mitchell knew. It would all be over.

One way or the other.

7

Charlie Davidson was the secretary of the West London branch of the British Sub-Aqua Club. The police called for him at his Ealing office and drove him home through the streets of Acton with sirens howling and lights flashing.

He searched through his club papers and gave the police a list containing the names and addresses of every first-class and second-class diver who was a member of the branch.

'Are any of these people experienced in the use of oxygen rebreathing sets?' asked the police officer, reciting a question he had been told to ask.

Charlie stared at the policeman.

'Hell, no. We only use compressed-air aqualungs. Oxygen sets are too bloody dangerous.'

Charlie followed the policeman out to the car.

'Look,' he said, as the officer called his headquarters. 'None of these people will be any good to you. They know nothing about diving with rebreathing sets.'

'Looks like they're going to get the chance to learn,' said the policeman, and started reading out the names and addresses.

8

The spacious modern bar on the lower deck of the Thames pleasure boat *Chay Blyth* was crowded with over a hundred bewildered members of the British Sub-Aqua Club who had been ruthlessly press ganged into leaving their homes or places of work and driven to Westminster Pier.

The *Chay Blyth*'s master cut his engines and allowed the vessel to drift so that it would pass between the anchored *Barrow* and the south bank. As the *Barrow*'s bulk obscured the distant power station, the divers, on a signal from the plain-clothes policeman, filed quickly out of the bar and jumped into the water. Although they were all good swimmers and covered the thirty metres to the *Barrow*'s side without difficulty, some of them were not so good at climbing scrambling nets and had to be helped aboard.

The chief petty officer divided them into teams and appointed a navy shallow-water diver to put each group through a crash training course in the use of oxygen rebreathing sets.

The *Chay Blyth* continued down river for a little way before turning in a wide circle and pushing her way back towards London to collect another party of reluctant, shanghaied day-trippers.

9

Phoenix helped Kramer and two of his NASA technicians to manhandle the crate containing the spacesuit on to the pilot's boat at Greenwich Pier, under the eyes of indifferent tourists who had grown bored with the *Cutty Sark* and were waiting for the return boat to London.

The pilot's boat pulled away from the pier at 14:10. The crate was carried below. Kramer helped Phoenix into the suit and connected it to a portable air-conditioning unit.

The afternoon was heavy with heat and humidity. Hot diesel fumes soaked through the boat's lower decks.

'You're better off than us,' said Kramer to Phoenix. 'At least you're in the cool.'

Phoenix said nothing. A fan in the air-conditioning whirred quietly as it removed the heat from his spacesuit.

10

By 13:30 the pipeline was over three thousand metres long and was within a kilometre of the power station.

'Okay,' said Jack Delmar. 'Let's get some more ballast pumped in.'

Gravel hurtled along the flexible pipes that snaked through the flooded pipeline.

Barrow was shedding her cargo at a rate of thirty tonnes a minute. The marks painted on the sides of her hull climbed slowly out of the water.

A member of her original crew finished his cigarette and flipped it over the side. He watched the butt curving down. Something caught his eye. He leaned over the rail.

'Christ,' he whispered to himself.

Jack Delmar and the *Barrow*'s captain leaned over the rail and tried to look casual.

'So what do we do now?' asked the captain bitterly.

Jack Delmar looked at the power station crouching beneath its four ghostly cooling towers and then down at the first two pipeline sections extending from the *Barrow*'s side. They were awash on the surface like an elongated drugged whale.

'Once all the gravel is in the pipeline, we can flood the fore and aft holds so we ride lower in the water.'

'Can't we do it now?' asked the captain. 'Will it matter if the gravel gets wet?'

'We can't pump wet gravel,' said Jack Delmar. 'We'll just have to take a chance that they can't see anything.'

'A hell of a chance,' said the captain grimly, and gave the order for work to resume. He looked up at one of the television cameras. 'I'd better tell them the good news.'

Weiner slipped unnoticed back into the operations room and looked at the plot table in concern: 18:00 hours was the latest time for the pipeline to be completed and pumped dry. He was about to whisper to Hendricks about his trip to Weybridge, when the Prime Minister spoke:

'This business of sending divers along the inside of the pipeline with the sections seems slow and cumbersome.'

'It prevents divers getting lost,' said a naval officer. 'And it prevents them being swept away by the current, sir. The tide's just turned, so it's going to get worse.'

The Prime Minister pursed his lips. 'Surely they won't get lost if they follow the pipeline? We could have one team pushing the pipe halves through the pipeline and two teams on the outside at the same time. Treble the speed at which we're getting the damned thing assembled.'

'Visibility is under a metre, sir,' said the naval officer, trying to keep his voice polite. 'I'm sure the men on the site would suggest the idea if it were feasible. And besides, if divers were to be swept away, it wouldn't be possible to rescue them.'

'Divers are expendable,' said the Prime Minister. 'Time is not.'

He reached for his telephone.

Between 14:30 and 15:20 the *Barrow* lost two naval divers and five members of the British Sub-Aqua Club team. The water was too turbid for anyone to have seen them disappear. The divers, struggling with the long plastic pipes in open water, soon learned to recognize the sudden increase in their burden as a sign that another of their comrades had lost his hold. They tried lifelines, but there was nothing to fasten them to – only thirty-metre lengths of plastic pipe endowed by the current with a malignant life force of their own. Three lengths were lost – swept away by the strengthening black tide with divers secured to them.

At 15:50 the *Barrow*'s captain counted the remaining halves of pipe, and calculated that the pipeline was now only three sections short of its required length. A quarter of an hour later a divemaster surfaced in the hold, spat out his mouthpiece and yelled that the last section ferried out couldn't be fitted because it fouled against the power station's steel and concrete pilings. There was a half-hearted cheer from the exhausted divers huddled in the holds.

A diver manning an electric underwater scooter was sent along the pipeline to count the reinforcing buttresses between the pipeline opening and the western extremity of the pilings. He returned with the figure fifty-one.

The pipeline opening was in the correct position.

The final task of swimming out with the twelve curved petals that comprised the dome was assigned to a team who had not dived for five hours. They had spent most of the time practising assembling the dome in the aft hold.

The heavy steel petals were lifted over the side of the *Barrow* away from the power station, and passed under her hull. Plastic floats neutralized 95 per cent of each petal's weight. One of them had a hole cut in it to accommodate the pipeline opening. This petal would be positioned first and the others bolted to it to form a dome, with the open base sealed to the riverbed by an inflatable skirt. When the water was eventually pumped out, the pressure of the Thames bearing down on the dome would be greater than the dome's buoyancy.

By the time the under water convoy had set off from the *Barrow*, with each petal assisted by four manned scooters, operation GOPHER was thirty minutes behind schedule.

258

Jack Delmar was helping to break open the crates that contained the electric golf carts for use in the pipeline after it had been pumped dry, when the pilot's boat was sighted.

11

Phoenix and the NASA technicians were welcomed aboard the *Barrow* at 17:25 by Jack Delmar. He looked curiously at the impenetrable visors and wondered why they were down.

'You might as well take your helmet off,' he told Phoenix, gesturing to the throbbing diesel pumps. 'We won't have the pipeline pumped dry for another half hour. Maybe more.'

'I prefer to keep it on,' said Phoenix. 'It's air-conditioned in here. Why the delay?'

'I couldn't even begin to tell you,' replied the American. 'As soon as we'd shifted some gravel into the pipeline, the ship began to lift. That's why we're pumping the pipeline water into the holds. Do you want to meet the captain?'

'I'd sooner see your boring machine.'

'It would be better if you'd come earlier to get the feel of the thing.'

'I was told it was simple to operate,' replied Phoenix.

The GOPHER was resting on the ramp with most of its weight supported by the outstretched arm of a derrick. It was an odd-looking machine about four metres long and just over a metre in diameter. One third of its length consisted of the spiral cutting-head.

Phoenix leaned into the open hatch. Jack Delmar joined him and pointed out the controls.

'That lever at the side controls the cutting speed and the column in the middle is for going up or down or turning.' He spoke for five minutes, with Phoenix listening attentively.

'How do I control the forward speed?' asked Phoenix, when Jack Delmar had finished.

'You don't. The cutting action of the head pulls you forward. The faster you turn the head the faster you move forward.' He pointed to a group of digital displays. 'That's your INS navigation computer. All you've got to do is keep the displays reading zero, otherwise you're off course. It's been programmed so you'll come up in the power station's Number Three inspection tunnel.'

Phoenix nodded. He had been over the maps of the galleries until he knew them by heart.

'Do you want to see the cutting-head working?' asked Jack Delmar.

'Yes, please.'

Jack Delmar had to yell above the noise from the pumps to attract his engineers. He gave them orders. They connected hydraulic hoses to the couplings at the rear of the GOPHER. A hydraulic pump started up, adding its noise to the existing racket.

'GOPHER's like a road-drill,' Jack Delmar explained. 'It has to be connected to a separate power plant by those hydrualic hoses.' He reached into the cockpit. The massive cutting-helix started turning with a loud clanking.

'Don't worry about the row.' he yelled. 'It quietens down when it's biting into something.'

He shut the machine off and waved to the men manning the hydraulic pump to do the same.

Phoenix noticed that the water level in the midships hold had dropped two metres since he had come aboard. The top of the pipeline entrance was visible above the surface.

The chief petty officer bullied a reluctant team back into their rubber wetsuits.

A third of the opening was visible by the time the first diver edged past the GOPHER, gave Phoenix a curious look and dropped into the hold. He swam into the gaping hole; the last diver was able to wade in carrying a powerful lamp.

'This is the dangerous part,' said Jack Delmar. 'There's plenty of gravel in the pipeline, but if it's not properly distributed a section could be buoyant and suddenly break loose. If that happens, we cash our life insurance and go out on the town.'

The chief petty officer allowed three more divers into the tunnel when the first diver reported that the first ten sections were holding. By the time the entire four-kilometre length of pipeline had been inspected, the bottom of the hold was covered with only a few centimetres of water. The two-metre diameter tunnel entrance in the *Barrow*'s side yawned dark and forbidding.

Alan Roberts of the British Sub-Aqua Club was fixing a portable lamp to the smooth inner surface of the pipeline when he thought he heard a faint creaking noise. He lifted the lamp off its hook and shone it on the nearest seal between two sections. It was weeping discoloured Thames water, but then so were many of the seals. The American had said some seepage was inevitable. He heard the noise again and experienced a twinge of alarm. He tried calculating the water pressure bearing against the outside of the pipeline while straining his ears. There was no more noise. Perhaps his ears were playing up after all the diving he had been doing that day.

He finished connecting the lamp and climbed onto the electric golf cart. Its tyres crunched on the gravel floor as he drove back to the *Barrow*. The strange noise was forgotten by the time the pipeline floor was sloping upwards to the daylight.

12

Maggie fell silent.

No matter how much she screamed at Mitchell, swore at him and heaped abuse on him, he remained steadfast in his determination to keep her a prisoner.

She decided on a different approach.

'Mitch? I'm sorry if I was rude.'

He smiled faintly, but still looked extremely worried. 'Forget it.'

She sat on his knee and lifted his forearm on to her shoulder. 'It's hot. How about a swim?'

'Okay. But only if you promise not to try anything.'

'I promise.'

Maggie's timing in the swimming-pool was superb. She grasped the waistband of Mitchell's trunks and heaved just as he was pushing off from the side. He turned over in the water spluttering in fury.

'Hey! Gimme my shorts!' he bellowed.

Maggie hopped out of the pool and ran towards her car, clutching Mitchell's trunks like a trophy.

Mitchell dived naked into his Mustang just as Maggie's MG disappeared out of the drive.

The Mustang was the more powerful of the two cars. He overtook Maggie on the golf club road. He gave her a safe stopping distance, then swung his car sideways, blocking the road. Maggie responded by swinging on to the golf course and accelerating down the fairway, scattering a foursome teeing up for the fourth hole. Mitchell swore and shot after her. In the four-minute chase round the golf course Maggie tried several times to turn back to the road only to be headed off by the Mustang. Mitchell eventually forced her into a bunker. He yanked the MG's door open as its back wheels spun uselessly in the soft sand.

'I'll take you after midnight, you silly bitch!' He yelled at Maggie.

'Now!'

'Midnight!'

They both stopped arguing, aware of four pairs of eyes watching them.

'You'll be hearing from the club secretary about this, Mr Mitchell,' said one of them, whose game had been interrupted. He turned to his three guests who were regarding Mitchell solemnly.

'An American,' he explained.

The three guests nodded sympathetically.

13

The dank interior of the dome, pressed against the riverbed like a giant rubber sucker, was lit by a string of battery lamps. Perforated steel plates had been placed over the mud to distribute the GOPHER's weight.

The machine was now upended – its cutting-head buried in the mud at a carefully calculated angle.

Jack Delmar was sitting in its inclined cockpit carrying out a last-minute check when the one diver who had remained with him said he could see lights approaching along the tunnel. The golf carts stopped near the dome. Kramer and a NASA technician entered, supporting Phoenix between them. Jack Delmar scrambled out of the cockpit and pulled the GOPHER's power hoses that snaked down the tunnel to one side. The two NASA men helped Phoenix into the GOPHER's cockpit. He kneeled awkwardly on the sloping floor while Kramer attached his backpack and connected the spacesuit to the spare pack Phoenix was to use during the journey under the power station's foundations. A loaded M1 rifle was placed in the cockpit. A pair of wire-cutters and a cold-light discharge tube were stowed in the spacesuit's utility packets.

'We thought we heard a noise back there,' Kramer said to Jack Delmar without stopping work. 'A sort of creaking noise.'

'You'd better take a look,' Jack Delmar said to the diver. 'Use one of the carts.'

The diver drove along the tunnel. After five minutes he too could hear the noise. He slowed down and steered the golf cart with his knees while directing a portable lamp on the sides of the pipeline. He found the broken seal immediately. It was halfway up. Water was running down the tubing and being absorbed into the gravel. The creaking was caused by fractured plastic surfaces being slowly forced inward. Even as the diver watched with mounting concern, a new fissure crept hypnotically across the concave surface. Beads of water appeared along the crack and began to swell.

Phoenix stretched out on his stomach. The GOPHER's steep angle caused him to slide forward over the controls.

'Grip the restraint-bar with your feet,' Jack Delmar advised.

Phoenix eased himself back and hooked his boots over the bar.

Jack Delmar picked a field telephone to call an engineer standing by on the *Barrow*. 'Okay. Give us power.'

The hydraulic hoses connected to the GOPHER stiffened.

'Test the rams,' said the industrialist. 'One at a time.'

Phoenix operated the burrowing machine's controls. Rectangular sections set into the GOPHER's body extended slowly.

'Okay. That's fine.'

The steering pads were withdrawn until they were once again flush with the GOPHER's skin.

Kramer made some final adjustments to the backpack and rapped affectionately on the space helmet before stepping back.

'Good luck,' said Jack Delmar, shutting the hatch. Darkness closed in on Phoenix. He twisted round, fastened the latches and looked at the luminous watch Kramer had given him.

Operation GOPHER was forty-five minutes behind schedule.

The diver picked the golf cart up by the rear and swung it round. He was about to climb back on to the seat to warn the men in the dome, when the pipe suddenly caved in with a tremendous roar and inrush of water that swept the golf cart over and threw the diver against the opposite side of the tunnel.

The men working in the dome looked anxiously down the pipeline as the sound of the imploding water echoed out of the black opening.

'What the hell was that?' asked Kramer.

Jack Delmar plugged a communication-jack into a receptacle on the GOPHER's side.

'Okay! Get going!' he barked.

The machine's cutting-head began churning down into the mud before he finished speaking. The sound of the GOPHER's hydraulic motor mixed with the thunderous noise booming out of the tunnel. It was getting louder. Kramer was about to speak when the tidal wave boiled into the dome and swept him off his feet. The wave scoured the perimeter of the dome as if seeking a way of escape.

'Full speed!' Jack Delmar screamed into the communicator. 'We've had a cave-in!'

Kramer and the technician struggled to their feet. The water was swirling round their waists. They tried to push their way to the opening against the black torrent surging into the dome. Kramer's assistant became ensnared in the thick coils of hydraulic hose and started screaming. Kramer fought his way to the opening. Jack Delmar grabbed him.

'You've got to stay and help me pay out the hoses!'

GOPHER was driving down into the riverbed.

'Christ no! We'll drown!'

'We can't drown, you fool! There'll be a pocket of air trapped at the top of the dome!' Jack Delmar gripped Kramer by the shoulder. 'You must stay and help me! Please!'

Kramer looked wildly round. Water was creeping up the tunnel opening. There was no sign of his assistant. 'You can stay!' he shouted. 'I'm getting out!'

Jack Delmar hung on to Kramer with both hands. 'Please,' he implored. 'You must stay!'

Kramer tried to pull away from the old man's clutching hands which were gripping like claws. 'For Chrissake leggo!' the water was up to his chest. He swung his fist back and hit the elderly industrialist in the face with all his strength.

Jack Delmar released his grip and sank slowly beneath the black, swirling water.

14

Louise Campion stared across the water. She reached out and touched Patterson. He was awake immediately.

'What's the matter?'

Louise glanced round the canteen and pointed across the river.

'There's a whirlpool out there. Right in the middle. About halfway between us and that ship.'

Patterson shaded his eyes against the burnished glare of the evening sun shining on the river. 'A whirlpool? Are you sure?' Then he saw it: a whirling vortex spiralling around a hole in the water.

'What do you suppose would cause that?' asked Louise.

Patterson shook his head.

'I've never heard of them on the Thames.' He turned his attention to the *Barrow* anchored on the far side of the river. 'That ship's been there all day. Do you suppose something's being hatched?'

Louise stared at the strange pattern of circling water.

'If there is, it looks as if it's just gone wrong.'

15

Hendricks was quietly telling the Prime Minister about the discovery of Simpson's body when the sudden silence in the operations room made him break off.

Everyone was staring at the television monitor that showed *Barrow*'s midships hold filling with water. The Prime Minister was about to pick up his telephone when it rang. He listened, his eyes fixed on the plot table with its miniature pipeline extending across the river from the model of the *Barrow*. He replaced the receiver and looked at the anxious faces waiting for him to speak.

'There's been a collapse in the pipeline. It's now flooding very quickly. There was a message from Jack Delmar a few minutes before the collapse, to start the pumps that power the GOPHER. The captain said the pumps are still operating, so it's possible they're still connected to the GOPHER. Whether or not it started on its journey before the collapse, we can't tell. The captain will send a diver along the pipeline when it's fully flooded to inspect the dome. We won't be certain until then.'

16

Phoenix wondered what had happened in the dome as he drove the GOPHER downward through the mud. He heard Jack Delmar's voice in his helmet yell: 'Full speed,' and then the communication link was cut.

He concentrated on keeping the inertial-navigation displays showing a zero reading.

The machine continued to burrow downward smoothly with all deviation displays showing hypnotic rows of glowing zeros. Sometimes the cutting-head slowed with a deafening noise as it chewed its way through a layer of gravel.

Suddenly the forward display flashed a positive reading. Phoenix pulled the control column yoke. The reading still glowed mockingly at him. He hauled the column back even further. He felt the machine level out and the strain on his feet relax. The digits on the forward display winked back to zero.

The GOPHER had bored successfully down until, if the miniature on-board navigation computer was correct, it was now at a greater depth than the lowest part of the power station's foundations.

The machine levelled out forged steadily through the million-year-old deposits.

The illuminated rows of zeros continued to glow out of the darkness.

Phoenix became troubled by his imagination. He found himself contemplating the tonnes of concrete above him and wondering what would happen if something went wrong with the machine. 'The only real problem is making sure your power hoses don't get tangled.' Jack Delmar had said. 'But we'll be in the dome paying them out to make certain that doesn't happen.'

Supposing something went wrong with the inertial-navigation computer? Supposing he bored right up into one of the radio-active-waste silos?

The rear display was showing a reading. Phoenix stared at it. How long had it been like that? In his confusion, he pushed the control yoke forward. More digits flashed up on the display. He slowed the cutting-head until it was barely turning so that he could unravel the sudden whirl of confused thoughts.

When the rear display showed a reading, you pulled the column back!

The rams set into the GOPHER's side pressed out, nudging the machine upward.

The digits started sliding back to zero.

He hauled the column right back against his visor until the display was once again showing a neutral reading. His weight slipped back until his lunar overshoes rested on the restraint bar.

GOPHER was now driving upwards – aiming for the metre thick concrete floor of Number Three inspection tunnel.

Phoenix looked at his watch. 21:25. Two hours thirty-five minutes before Keller's deadline, and he still had to break into the power station.

Suddenly the GOPHER gave a shuddering jerk and came to an abrupt standstill.

17

The underwater scooter purred smoothly along the flooded pipeline, towing the outstretched body of a diver. He steered the machine by gentle twists of his body. The powerful headlight on the front of the scooter was virtually useless in the opaque, polluted water. A faint trace of daylight marked the rupture where the section had collapsed. He slowed to pass the sharp edges of torn plastic, and sped on towards the dome. A white hand reached out. The fingers hooked on to the scooter's propeller guard, upsetting the steering. The corpse of the NASA technician was dragged fifty metres before the diver managed to release it. The diver pressed on – gathering together the shattered remains of his nerves.

Jack Delmar was waiting for him in the dome. The diver kept the headlight away from the dead, watching face. The body performed a slow somersault as he pushed it to one side. The diver explored the mud floor. There was no sign of the GOPHER. He found a shallow depression where the hoses disappeared into the yielding ooze. Grimacing with distaste he pushed an arm into the mud until his probing fingers encountered one of the golf carts. A hydraulic hose was wound tightly round it and had pulled the vehicle down into the riverbed. He thrust his arm deeper feeling with his fingers until they closed round the hydraulic hose below the golf cart. It felt like an iron bar so tightly had it been stretched, He pulled his arm out of the mud and returned along the pipeline with scooter's motor set at maximum speed.

'It seems,' said the Prime Minister, replacing his telephone, 'that the GOPHER managed to get away before the collapse, but one of its hoses is tangled round an electric golf cart. A team of divers is now on its way to the dome with cutting equipment.'

Hendricks looked up from his copy of the Operation GOPHER schedule. The wall clock said 22:30. 'It would also seem that we're now too late, Mr Prime Minister.'

The politician sat silently for a few minutes. The room was now crowded with cabinet minsters and service officers. The American ambassador had arrived at 22:00 hours.

'I'm going to ask Keller for a three-hour extension,' said the Prime Minister.

18

Phoenix gave up wondering what had happened and resigned himself quietly to fate.

The whole scheme had been absolutely crazy, he thought. Doomed to failure from the start. He should've told the Prime Minister what he thought of the idea when it was first put to him.

Breathing was getting difficult. He fumbled in the cramped darkness to switch his cooling and oxygen systems over to the backpack. The wave of coolness travelling down his body as the ice absorbed his body heat, and the fresh oxygen flooding in to the space helmet, cleared his head.

He had kept the cutting-head turning slowly: first in the hope that the GOPHER might free itself and suddenly and lurch forward; and then, as that hope faded, because the GOPHER would be as quiet as a tomb without the gentle vibration.

He wondered what future archaeologists would make of his body mummified in eternal Teflon. At least they would know his name: Neil A. Armstrong.

It said so on his shroud.

Phoenix started laughing.

19

'No,' said Keller's polite voice in the Prime Minister's ear. 'I'm extremely sorry, sir, but I cannot permit another extension. I take it the bill has now received the royal assent?'

'No yet,' said the Prime Minister testily. 'The palace have raised a number of queries. All I'm asking for is three hours to resolve them.'

Keller sounded concerned. 'I appreciate the difficulties, sir, but I earnestly implore you to sort them out within the next hour. Fifty-five minutes to be exact. I've got a portable television set and I'm looking forward to your appearance at midnight when you announce to the nation the terms of the new Act of Parliament based on my ultimatum. If you do not appear, then I will not hesitate to blow up the silos.'

The line went dead.

Keller replaced the radiotelephone microphone on its hook. He turned and looked thoughtfully at Louise Campion and Hugh Patterson.

'I'm afraid I'm going to have to lock you two up – just in case you have any more ideas. I'll let you out after midnight.' He paused. 'If there is an after midnight.'

He waved his Sterling towards a door at the back of the control room.

20

Phoenix had dozed off to sleep because there was nothing else to do and it conserved oxygen. He was woken by a sudden lurch – the one thing he had ceased praying for an hour earlier. He touched the sides of the cockpit. He wasn't dreaming – they were vibrating with renewed vigour. Another lurch, and the note from the cutting-head deepened.

The GOPHER had resumed boring and was now being dragged upwards by the action of the cutting-head. The displays winked. He automatically corrected course, too dazed to realize what he was doing.

The machine continued driving smoothly upwards through the compressed mud and gravel beneath the power station. Phoenix steered to one side and pulled back on to the correct course. Everything was working perfectly.

His feeling of exaltation ended when the cutting-head rammed into concrete with a terrible scream. The noise

271

frightened and confused him. He thought the gods were striving to make him mad before they destroyed him. He shut the power off and the noise stopped.

Concrete! He had reached concrete! All he had to do now was run the head very slowly until he broke through.

'It's no good driving vertically up through concrete,' Jack Delmar had told him, 'otherwise the cutting-head goes through, and you're trapped, unable to open the hatch. You've got to go through at a shallow angle – like a jet taking off.'

For fifteen minutes the massive helix bored relentlessly. Rubble and debris rattled along the side of the cutting-head and was ground to powder.

He looked at the watch 23:23. He was too late. Even if he got into the inspection tunnel within the next few minutes, there wouldn't be enough time to cut all the detonator wires.

Suddenly the GOPHER was turning about its axis. He was rolling sideways off the mattress and on to the side of the cockpit. He fought back waves of panic and tried to reason out what was happening. Another spasm shook the GOPHER. It twisted again with a sickening noise as its unprotected flanks grated against the side of the hole it was cutting. He suddenly realized that the entire machine was trying to rotate about its axis while the jammed cutting-head remained stationary.

He pressed the control yoke down as Jack Delmar had told him to do. All four steering rams extended simultaneously and arrested the turning motion. He waited until the cutting-head was turning freely again before easing the pressure off the yoke.

There was something he had to do. He slowed the cutting-head and wrestled with his memory. Cooling water! He thankfully turned the control that would pass water to the cutting-head to prevent it activating the IRIS detectors when it broke through.

He eased the GOPHER forward very slowly, centimetre by centimetre.

272

The GOPHER was through.

Phoenix cut the power, For the first time since he had climbed into the machine there was silence. Complete and utterly overwhelming silence. He twisted around, released the cockpit latches and pushed. The hatch remained firmly closed. He pushed harder. It yielded slightly, but snapped shut when he lowered his arms. He turned carefully and pressed his foot against the hatch. He tensed his thigh muscles and heaved. He placed both feet on the hatch and heaved again. The hatch opened slightly and snapped shut. Another hard push that caused something to break in the backpack and he succeeded in forcing the hatch open a few centimetres. He grasped it and jerked it from side to side, easing it forward at the same time. It suddenly fell away into the darkness with a loud clatter. He lay quietly for a few moments while the spacesuit's cooling system drained the excess heat generated by his exertions.

He climbed stiffly out of the cockpit, feeling in a utility pocket for the cold light discharge tube. He broke the seal. The clinical light from the reacting chemicals filled the inspection tunnel. Grey cartons of Cyclonite were stacked four high along one side for as far as the light could reach. An IRIS detector gleamed menacingly less than a metre away. He was about to unfold a small sketch-map to check his position, when he suddenly remembered that he was existing on the backpack. He raised his wrist to his visor and gazed at the reading in numbed disbelief.

There was less than five pounds of ice left.

The watch said 23:40. There was no time even to think about cutting the detonator wires. He snatched up the automatic rile and stumbled along the tunnel as quickly as the unwieldy suit would permit.

At 23:42 the Prime Minister sat calmly before the hastily installed television cameras. Engineers buzzed round making final adjustments to microphones and lights. The closed folder before him contained two speeches: one based on the ultimatum General Pyne had delivered, and the other based of the ultimatum imposed by Ralph Keller. The Act of Parliament which had just become law was modelled on Pyne's ultimatum. Now that Simpson was dead, only he knew that Pyne had escaped.

The red telephone was connected direct to Keller. The chances that its red light would flash with a message from Phoenix to say he had gained control now seemed extremely remote.

At 23;43 Phoenix discovered the riddled bodies of the power station staff piled on top of one another. He leaned against the side of the tunnel and tried not to be sick. It could be fatal in a spacesuit – he could drown in his own vomit. He had no choice but to climb the terrible heap to reach the lower rungs of the shaft. His lunar overshoes slipped several times on the rigid corpses. The bodies sighed as his weight forced air from their lungs.

He fastened the rifle to a clip and started to climb the fifty steel rungs set into the side of the shaft. He wondered which would run out before he reached the top – his strength, the ice or time.

At 23:51 Phoenix pushed the steel cover open at the top of the shaft and looked quickly around. There was no ice left, and no point in waiting.

He heaved himself on to the concrete and staggered to his feet. He had no way of knowing whether the IRIS system had detected his presence. The alarms would sound in the control room – not down here.

He shuffled quickly across the apron towards the main entrance.

It was unlocked.

Heat was beginning to build up in the spacesuit now that the ice was gone. He mounted the stairs. The lunar overshoes slipped on the smooth marble. He fell backwards, crashing the backpack against the railings. He picked himself up and continued up the stairs. Sweat ran down his face. Something was wrong with his breathing system. He twisted and pulled the oxygen-purge controls. A small quantity of oxygen trickled into the helmet, but not enough to sustain him as he climbed the stairs. The heat was getting worse. A film of mist began to form on the inner fixed visor. Keller wouldn't have moved IRIS detectors into the power station – they would've caused too much nuisance. He paused on the second floor to unfasten the space helmet. The restricted field of vision through the visors and a spreading film of mist prevented his seeing the detector of the wall beside him.

Ralph Keller picked up his modified cellphone cum detonator and switched it on. A portable television standing on the console was showing a late-night film. He looked at his watch.

23:55.

He stood watching the television – his fingers caressing the cellphone.

Phoenix gave up fumbling at the space helmet – the clumsy gauntlets made the task impossible, and removing them would waste valuable seconds. His aching lungs sucked painfully at the meagre oxygen supply as he raced up the stairs. The mist spreading across the inner visor was now much worse. He paused outside the control room, fighting for breath and pressing his hands together to stop them shaking.

Christ! What the hell was he to do about the helmet misting up? How long would it take to get it off?

There was a circular window in the control room. Through the fogged visors he could just make out Keller at the far end near the main console.

By now Phoenix was in despair. His hands were shaking uncontrollably – he aimed the M1 experimentally down the stairs. The foresight waved all over the place.

275

23:59.

His breath rasped out of his lungs – fogging the helmet until Keller was a blur.

Too bloody bad.

He kicked the door open, launched himself into the control room and fired.

Keller turned, his finger reaching automatically for the cellphone.

Phoenix emptied most of the M1's magazine at Keller before collapsing on to one knee, his blood pounding in his ears from lack of oxygen. He was vaguely aware of noise all round him as bullets from Keller's Sterling smashed into the steel filing cabinets near the door. A ricochet shattered the space helmet and three bullets tore into his stomach just as his lungs clawed down acrid, cordite-impregnated air. He slipped to the floor and lay face down.

At five minutes past midnight the red telephone flashed. The Prime Minister snatched it up and, remembering eyes were upon him, placed it casually to his ear.

'Yes?'

He listened.

The television director in the outside broadcast van noticed a nerve in the Prime Minister's neck that twitched.

'I see,' said the Prime Minister. He listened for a few seconds, then: 'How badly?' Another pause. 'Very well.'

He replaced the receiver slowly and looked at the faces round him.

'Phoenix has failed,' he said in a flat, unemotional voice. 'He's been shot. Keller wants me to go down to the power station alone.'

There was a deathly silence in the room.

'You can't, sir,' said the Home Secretary.

The Prime Minister stood, and gave the Home Secretary the speech based on the original ultimatum. 'I've got no choice,' he said. 'You're to do the broadcast for me.'

The Home Secretary took the document with trembling hands. 'Let me go, sir,' he begged.

The American ambassador spoke. 'You shouldn't go, Mr Prime Minister. You'd be—'

'It must be me.' said the Prime Minister, moving to the door. He called one of the armed marines into the room and told him to allow no one near the red telephone.

'I'll give you that, he's got guts,' the ambassador said quietly to Hendricks when the Prime Minister had left.

Hendricks nodded.

The lungfuls of air revived Phoenix. It was quiet in the control room. There was a terrible pain in his stomach. He picked at the smashed fragments of visor and tried to pull himself up. His legs wouldn't work. There was no sign of Keller.

He looked at the watch. Three minutes past midnight. He hauled himself across the control room floor by his elbows. There was a good deal of blood splattered over the main console and the remains of Keller's cellphone detonator on the floor. Phoenix grimaced when he saw it. Keller had been wrong that destroying it would detonate the explosives. He crawled to the radiotelephone and dragged the microphone off its hook.

'Yes?' crackled the Prime Minister's voice.

'Phoenix, sir. I've shot Keller . . .' He broke off as the pain in his stomach racked his body. 'The cellphone detonator didn't work.' There was blood rising in his throat, choking his exultation. 'But the danger's over.'

'I see,' said the Prime Minister's voice.

'Keller's gone – he's wounded, but—'

'How badly?'

The Prime Minister's voice seemed to fade as the control room spun round. 'There's a lot of blood . . . Must be badly hurt . . .' Phoenix's voice was a whisper.

'Very well,' said the Prime Minister.

Phoenix was about to speak again, but realized the line was dead. He became dimly aware of hammering on a door at the back of the control room. Patterson and Louise

Campion. Keller must have locked them up. It would be best if they remained out of the way until he had dealt with Keller.

He turned away from the radiotelephone and saw the thick trail of his own blood across the control room floor.

The Prime Minister sat silently in the darkness in the back of his chauffeur-driven car. He unwrapped a cigar and reflected that everything seemed to be turning out well.

It was the whine of the fuelling machine that attracted Phoenix. The sound of the giant machine that lowered the nuclear-fuel elements into the two reactors could be heard all over the power station.

Doomsday

1

Captain Stacy clutched his clipboard protectively.

'Miss Pyne, your friend's car is blocking the road. If you aren't gone within thirty seconds I shall have both of you arrested.'

Stacy nodded to the soldiers. They gathered closer round the Mustang that was parked in the road outside the main gate leading to the new Oil and Gas Rig Defence Force camp.

'Come on, honey,' said Mitchell, 'He's not going to let us in.'

'I'm not leaving until I've seen my father,' said Maggie firmly.

Stacy peered into the darkness and thought he could see headlights approaching. He turned angrily to the Mustang. 'For the last time, Miss Pyne, he's not here. I'm expecting an important visitor and I want this car out of the way!'

'You're lying!' snapped Maggie. 'I know he's here, and I'm staying here until you agree to let me see him!'

The headlights were now within four hundred metres. 'Take them away,' said Stacy urgently. 'And shift this car.'

Mitchell did not argue with the submachine-gun pointing at him. He opened the door and stepped out. Maggie refused to budge. A soldier opened her door and gestured with his gun.

'You'll have to drag me out,' said Maggie defiantly.

The soldier reached into the car. Maggie bit his hand when he tried to grab her.

Stacy groaned. The car was fifty metres away and slowing down.

Three soldiers dragged Maggie from the Mustang. Mitchell took a step towards her as she fought and yelled, but was pushed back by the soldiers.

'Get the car shifted!' barked Stacy. The headlights stopped a few metres behind the Mustang. Goddamit – a ministerial car. Its rear door opened and slammed before the chauffeur could move. Footsteps approached.

Maggie nearly broke away.

'What's the trouble?' asked a voice that Stacy recognized immediately from the radio and television. It was the Prime Minister.

'I just want to see my father!' Maggie yelled.

'Let her go,' said the Prime Minister.

'She's creating a disturbance, sir,' said Stacy, cursing inwardly.

'Let her go, Captain Stacy.' The voice car was quiet and authoritative.

Stacy ordered the soldiers to release Maggie.

The short, stocky figure moved forward. 'Miss Pyne, isn't it? I'm the Prime Minister. How do you do?'

'I don't care who you are,' retorted Maggie. 'All I want is–'

'To see your father. And so you shall. I'll take you to him. But first, I have some urgent business to attend to.'

The Prime Minister turned to Stacy and issued a series of orders.

Ralph Keller's right shoulder was a mass of blood and the arm hung uselessly at his side. He was standing on the catwalk watching the fuelling machine lower the deadly uranium rods into the reactor. He stared across the great vault of the power station with mad fascination as the machine completed the loading operation. The cluster of

280

mechanical claws released the rods and began lifting themselves clear. An electric motor started. The machine, suspended from overhead rails whirred towards Keller to collect the last of the rods hanging in the circular water-tank ten metres below the catwalk. The heavenly blue glow of Cerenkov radiation from the immersed rods bathed his face.

The great machine clanked nearer, its empty claws hanging down between the overhead rails like obscene ruptures.

Just these ten more rods, thought Keller. Just these ten more rods lifted out of the tank and lowered into the reactor with its cooling system switched off, and there would be an uncontrolled chain-reaction. The concrete and steel round the reactor core would hold for a few seconds, but nothing could withstand the terrible unleashed energies. The catastrophic explosion would blast radioactive particles across the face of Europe. It was a pity his clever methods of overriding the safely devices wouldn't survive; but it didn't matter – the memorial to his genius, the poisons that would fill the air and seep into the ground, would last for generations.

The machine was nearly over the tank – the cluster of claws level with Keller's eager eyes. He moved to a control board and pressed a button. The machine stopped within a few metres of the catwalk. The hum from the motors changed. The claws opened, and the whole machine began sliding gently down the four gleaming shafts that suspended it from the overhead gantry rails.

There was something wrong with the shafts. Thick red fluid was running down them and turning blue as it neared the glowing water. Keller looked up at the top of the descending machine. Phoenix was aiming a rifle at him.

'Switch it off, Keller.'

Then, for the first time. Keller saw Phoenix's eyes – staring at him past the shattered visor fragments, moving nearer, growing larger. Keller's surprised expression changed to terror. It was as if all the screaming monsters of his savage nightmares had risen as one to torment him. He backed across the catwalk, away from the terrible, approaching apparition and turned to run.

Phoenix fired. It was a difficult shot from a moving platform at a moving target.

The bullet tore into Keller's thigh. It flattened and became an anvil, smashing and tearing its way through bone and tissue. The impact spun Keller round and threw him against the safety rail. His fingers clutched at the side of the fuelling machine as he over-balanced and fell ten metres into the shining water.

Phoenix pulled himself to the edge of the machine and looked down. Keller was struggling in the flowing water, trying to climb the smooth sides of the tank.

Phoenix felt the machine stop. The twenty claws, each with three open steel fingers extended downward to the water on the ends of long shafts. Keller saw them coming and screamed. Although the tops of uranium rods were twenty feet below the surface of the water, the fingers were designed to shut when they encountered an obstruction.

They closed on Keller. They closed on his arms, his legs and his neck. The shining water seemed to burn with increasing intensity as it rose round his body. His screaming stopped abruptly as he was pushed under. The terrified face staring up at Phoenix receded into the iridescent depths until his entire body was obscured by the swirling clouds of blue smoke rising from his thigh.

The top of the fuelling machine had stopped level with the catwalk. Phoenix grasped the safety rail and hauled himself on to the narrow walkway. It took ten minutes of superhuman effort to drag himself to the control panel and push the button that stopped the fuelling machine from completing the loading cycle.

The whine from the electric motors died away.

Phoenix leaned against the railings, too weak from the loss of blood to make another move. He was cold. Numbing fingers of death were probing his body, exploring his bowels, moving through his organs.

He became aware of footsteps echoing across the open vault of the power station's central gallery.

A short stocky figure was mounting the steel steps to the catwalk. Phoenix watched the Prime Minister approaching. The polished shoes stopped near his outstretched legs. The Prime Minister knelt down.

'Well, Pyne, you seem to have managed better than I thought you would.'

The man who was Phoenix nodded weakly. 'Be able to—' His face twisted with pain. He moved a gauntleted hand over his stomach. 'Be able to pick up from where I left off.'

'No, Pyne. I don't think that's necessary now.'

Pyne tried to struggle up. 'But the bill, sir,' he whispered. 'You need me to carry on here.'

'The bill became law at midnight, Pyne.'

Pyne shook his head inside the helmet. His lustreless grey eyes stared up at the politician. 'I thought you'd scrapped it after Keller's takeover?'

The Prime Minister smiled at the dying man. 'After all that planning, Pyne? You misjudge me. Just as you misjudged Keller. That was the one mistake Simpson and I made when we planned all this – letting you choose your team. By the way, where are the other two?'

'Locked in a room off the control room. They know nothing about this. I never told them.' Pyne's words were a whisper.

'I didn't think you would,' said the Prime Minister easily. 'You're much too loyal to disobey orders.' He felt in his pocket and produced a sheaf of papers which he held out to Pyne. 'There it is, Pyne. A copy of the Special Powers Act which makes me the most powerful man in Europe. Just think, Pyne; no more forced divisions in the House; no more worrying about legislation being watered down in committee; no more worrying about which way rebel backbenchers are going to vote. There it is, Pyne. Doesn't it seem worthwhile after the worrying time we went through when you told me about the existence of the Cromwell Two Committee, and our arguments over which power station should be seized?' The Prime Minister laughed easily. 'I'm more powerful now than Cromwell ever dreamed possible.'

Pyne fell back, his body drained of strength and blood. The cold was reaching into his chest.

'What's going to happen to me, sir?'

The Prime Minister glanced at the blood on the top of the silent fuelling machine. 'Well, it looks as if you're going to die, Pyne. I'll keep you company until you do.'

Pyne looked up into the calculating eyes and began to understand. 'You're forgetting something, sir.' The 'sir' was automatic – the product of Pyne's loyalty, which even the approach of death could not entirely eradicate. 'Simpson hates your guts. He'll tell everyone.'

'Simpson is dead, Pyne. Just as you will be in a few minutes.'

Pyne shook his head disbelievingly. 'You need the threat from the power station to stay in office. You said that when you wrote the ultimatum. I remember your words . . .'

The Prime Minister smiled. 'Read the bill, Pyne. It's been drafted by the best legal brains in the country. It's one hundred per cent watertight. It sailed through the House and now it's received the royal assent. There was a clause that required the act to lapse once the threat from the power station was removed, but it was deleted. That's why I don't need you any more.'

Pyne said nothing. His eyes were closing. Air rattled noisily past his lips as his lungs laboured against the blood flooding into his throat. The Prime Minister made himself comfortable while waiting for Pyne to die.

'Oh yes, I nearly forgot. Your daughter's outside.'

Pyne's eyes opened and flickered with eagerness. 'Maggie? She's here?' He tried to pull himself up. 'May I see her, please?'

284

The Prime Minister shook his head. Pyne summoned his strength and leaned forward. The politician pushed him back. He looked at the blood on his hand with distaste and wiped it off on his handkerchief.

'You're a true bastard,' said Pyne softly, barely able to move his lips.

'At last you're beginning to understand me, Pyne. But when I walk out of here, I'll be the biggest hero in the country.'

The Prime Minister's voice was fading.

'But you, Pyne, will be remembered as a traitor. A traitor who was given the chance to redeem himself, and failed. You won't even get the credit for shooting Keller.'

Pyne only heard the words 'a traitor' before he died.

The Prime Minister leaned forward. 'Are you dead yet, Pyne?' he asked softly.

He placed his ear near the smashed visors. Pyne's lungs were silent.

The Prime Minister waited ten minutes to be certain, then stood up.

Maggie was waiting by the main entrance with Mitchell when the Prime Minister emerged. Stacy's men were holding her back.

A pretty little thing, thought the Prime Minister. Had her father's looks. If she had half his loyalty, she'd make the American a good wife.

'Is he in there?' she asked.

The Prime Minister smiled warmly at her. 'Yes, my child. you can go in and see him now. Straight down the corridor and into the main reactor room. He's at the top of an iron catwalk waiting for you.'

'May I go with her, sir?' asked Mitchell.

The Prime Minister gestured expansively. 'If you wish.'

He waited until the couple had entered the building and turned to Stacy.

'Captain Stacy, do you know what's been going on here?'

Stacy fingered his clipboard and nodded. 'I saw the Home Secretary's broadcast, sir.'

The Prime Minister unfolded a piece of paper and gave it to the officer. 'You and your men are in for a busy night, Stacy. That's a warrant for the names on the attached list. They're all members of a group calling themselves the Cromwell Two Committee. You're to round them up.'

Stacy looked at the list aghast. 'These people?' he croaked. 'But they're all–'

'Politicians, top civil servants, service officers. Pillars of society. I don't care what they are,' interrupted the Prime Minister. 'All I know is that they're traitors.'

'But one of them is the Home Secretary,' Stacy protested.

'The ringleader. You'll also find two of the terrorists in there.' The Prime Minister jerked his head at the power station. 'I've locked them in a room off the control room. A man and a woman. Arrest them too. When you've done that, send a bomb disposal team into the silos to remove the high explosive. Have you got all that?'

Stacy repeated his instructions in a trembling voice.

'Excellent, Stacy. One more thing. I've a sense of the theatrical in me tonight so haul them all off to the Tower of London.'

The Prime Minister did not wait for a reply, but turned and walked to his car. The driver jumped out and opened the rear door.

'Downing Street,' said the politician.

He paused before getting into the car and looked up at the stars. The clear sky was tinged with the first flush of dawn.

He inhaled deeply.

There was the smell of a new day in the air.

A List of James Follett Titles Available from Mandarin

While every effort is made to keep prices low, it is sometimes necessary to increase prices at short notice. Mandarin Paperbacks reserves the right to show new retail prices on covers which may differ from those previously advertised in the text or elsewhere.

The prices shown below were correct at the time of going to press.

☐	7493 0036 1	**Cage of Eagles**	£4.99
☐	7493 0496 0	**Churchill's Gold**	£4.99
☐	7493 0262 3	**Dominator**	£4.99
☐	7493 0364 6	**Doomsday Ultimatum**	£3.99
☐	7493 0110 4	**Ice**	£4.99
☐	7493 0003 5	**Mirage**	£4.99
☐	7493 1012 X	**Swift**	£4.99
☐	7493 0492 8	**Torus**	£4.99
☐	7493 0363 8	**Trojan**	£4.99
☐	7493 0035 3	**U700**	£3.50

All these books are available at your bookshop or newsagent, or can be ordered direct from the address below. Just tick the titles you want and fill in the form below.

Cash Sales Department, PO Box 5, Rushden, Northants NN10 6YX.
Fax: 0933 410321 : Phone 0933 410511.

Please send cheque, payable to 'Reed Book Services Ltd.', or postal order for purchase price quoted and allow the following for postage and packing:

£1.00 for the first book, 50p for the second; **FREE POSTAGE AND PACKING FOR THREE BOOKS OR MORE PER ORDER.**

NAME (Block letters) ....

ADDRESS...

....

☐ I enclose my remittance for ....

☐ I wish to pay by Access/Visa Card Number

Expiry Date

Signature ....

Please quote our reference: MAND